CHASED BY A BILLIONAIRE

LOVECHILDE SAGA BOOK 3

J. J. SOREL

Copy Edit & Proof - Red Adept

AUTHOR'S NOTE: This is a steamy romance with descriptive sex scenes and some violent themes that are not overly graphic.

jjsorel.com

CHAPTER 1

Savanah

WHEN I NOTICED THE line at Cirque snaking all the way up Carnaby Street, I rolled my eyes and puffed. "Why don't we go somewhere else?"

Out on the hunt, acting like hungry tigers ready to pounce, Jacinta and Sienna ogled every attractive man that strutted past.

"We're here now," Jacinta said, with Sienna nodding in agreement.

With more than its fair share of hot guys, that colorful nightclub was *the* place to be, and being a Saturday night, we were pushing our luck. A-Listers came from everywhere, and whenever Hollywood was in town, they'd jump the queue.

As I waited in line, I kept looking over my shoulder, which had become a habit. I'd messed up again, and suddenly Bram, my ex—who made Dusty look like a kitten in comparison—was stalking me.

The son of a lord, Bram had ticked all my boxes until I discovered that he was a drug addict who, when chasing his next hit, became a monster. After he'd attacked me one time too many, I escaped. Only in our exclusive scene, it wasn't easy to hide. Everyone hung out in the same places.

As we moved forward, Sienna smiled. "There, you see? The line's moving along now." Wearing a green mini and a fluffy pink jacket, she looked cute and stylish at the same time.

Jacinta reached into her purse and pulled out her party tin—an antique container with a picture of Cleopatra. She passed me a blue pill, and I shook my head.

"Really?" She tipped her head to the side and frowned.

"I'm not out for a big night. My mother's expecting me back at Merivale. I promised to help her with a function."

"You're not staying the weekend?" Jacinta turned down her mouth. "I thought we were doing lunch at my friend's new Notting Hill café."

I returned an apologetic smile. "Can't get out of it, I'm afraid."

We were now about six people away from the front entrance, and after watching so many refused entry, I didn't like our chances.

"We'll just have to bat our eyelashes at security." Jacinta smoothed down her long blond hair with her hands. Her dress was so short her knickers were almost noticeable, and the back of her dress dipped to the crack of her bum.

"I'm dressed like a nun compared to you two minxes." I chuckled.

"Blue's your color, though." Sienna touched the silky fabric of my Stella McCartney knee-length dress.

I looked ahead, and my breath hitched. "Shit. He's here."

"Who?" Jacinta looked around.

"The bouncer at the door." I slid my eyes towards Carson while he dealt with a man who was stumbling about and rather stupidly poking his finger at Carson.

My heart raced. "I want to run away."

Sienna shook her head and frowned. "Who is it?"

"Shh... He might hear us." I leaned in. "That's Carson."

Of course, she turned to stare. "Wow. He's a hottie."

"Who?" Jacinta asked.

Sienna spoke in a loud whisper. "That's the hung-like-a-horse guy."

He must have sensed all the attention because he turned, and his eyes fell on my burning face.

Although it had been three months since Carson stayed the night at Mayfair, following my being attacked and robbed, I still couldn't get him out of my head. And then I met Bram, and my life slid into chaos.

"Shit, he's smoldering. He reminds me of Channing Tatum."

Jacinta was right. Carson was the dead ringer of that burly actor.

"Now I know why you've been pining all these months. Look at those muscles. They're about to burst out of that polo." Sienna giggled.

While reminding myself to breathe, I tried pushing aside Carson's rejection, which had shaken my self-confidence. And whereas once I might have cracked the odd joke with him, now I felt awkward and tongue-tied around him.

"He's not interested anyway," I said. "Maybe my tits aren't big enough."

Jacinta rolled her eyes. "Nonsense."

"Maybe he's gay."

Sienna frowned. "Didn't you say he had a boner?"

I reflected on my failed attempt to seduce Carson and nodded.

"Gay men do not bar up over girls fondling their dicks. Trust me. I know." Sienna pulled a smirk.

She would know. Sienna kept falling for unattainable men.

When we arrived at the front of the line, I came face-to-face with Carson.

"Hey." My easy-going vibe hid a sudden rush of nerves as I locked my wobbly knees. "Didn't know you worked here."

"I've been here for about a month." His eyes remained on mine, and suddenly it felt like it was just us.

I cleared my throat. "Declan mentioned you were returning to Re-boot." That was ages ago when I'd heard that, but I needed to find something to say.

He ran his hands over his buzzcut. Carson had once told me he preferred being close to bald because his hair went curly. He had the ideal symmetrical-shaped head for it. "I'm having to stick around. My brother..."

I didn't quite catch the rest. He seemed more nervous than me.

"Anyway, in you go," he said, with that uneven smile of his that dimpled his cheek, giving him a sexy, boyish look, despite him being a man.

A mature, sexy man.

Stop drooling.

Sienna and Jacinta both screeched with excitement as we entered the massive darkly-lit room.

"How good are you?" Sienna placed her slim arm around me, her charm bracelet jiggling on my shoulder.

With its red walls, velvet chairs, and changing lights resembling colored stars, that nightspot teased one's senses. In each corner, there were sword swallowers, fire eaters, burlesque dancers, and contortionists. One act was more astounding than the next as the latest dance tunes vibrated through our bodies.

Sweat and perfume thickened the air as everyone yelled and screamed. The venue seemed to shake from exuberance, which was typical of the club scene. It normally worked for me. I preferred sweating it out on a dance floor to thumping it out at a gym.

After battling through the crowded bar, we got our drinks and found a spare bit of wall to lean against to check out the talent, something we always did. Tonight I was tired. All the drama with Bram had kept me awake at night.

Although I should have reported Bram to the police, I couldn't involve my family, who were already on my back about my crappy boyfriend choices.

This time for a good reason.

"Carson likes you." Jacinta gave me the lift I needed with that heart-warming observation.

"Do you think?" I studied her. "He never answered my calls."

"How often did you call him?" she yelled over the music.

"Three times. He's just not interested."

"Bullshit. He looked shy."

"I'd say probably embarrassed. I pulled him off, you know."

"Did he come?"

I shook my head. "He stopped me. He could be gay, for all I know."

She laughed. "No way. He can't be gay. You just took him by surprise."

I recalled Declan telling me how Carson, despite being a bit of a player, was also super sensitive, which at the time struck me as a contradiction.

After tossing back two shots of vodka, I loosened up. I tilted my head towards some actors I recognized from movies.

Jacinta noticed too. "Say, isn't that Colin Farrell?"

It looked like the dark-haired Irishman. He was drinking with a couple of actors, whose names escaped me.

"I love it here." Jacinta kissed me on the cheek.

At least Carson had made their night. Mine, too, because seeing him had reminded me of the type of man I wanted in my life: good, honest, sexy, and down-to-earth. The absolute opposite of the types I'd been dating up to now. One bad boy too many and here I was, sleepless and constantly watching over my shoulder.

We hit the dance floor, and some boys joined us. In her short, tight number, Sienna, as always, attracted a lot of attention. Having had her breasts enlarged, she'd become a testosterone magnet.

We were all twenty-nine going on sixteen. Only in my case, I'd become tired of the party scene. Something had changed in me. Maybe I'd grown up at last.

An hour later, after having downed a few more shots and worked up a sweat dancing, I settled back against the wall, while Jacinta and Sienna got chatting with a couple of boys who looked to be in their early twenties. All I could think of was Carson and having had a few drinks, I plucked up the courage to ask why he hadn't returned my calls. I also wasn't much in the mood for a big night, so I decided to leave, giving me a good excuse to chat with him on my way out.

I went to the powder room and sent Jacinta and Sienna a text. They'd hooked up with their young guys, so they wouldn't miss me. That was what we did; we stuck together until one of us met someone and slid off for a bit of fun.

As I stepped into the night, I saw Carson with his arms crossed and wearing a "don't mess with me" expression.

Taking a deep breath, I stood next to him, when his colleague, who saw me first, tapped Carson on the arm.

He shot me that cheek-dimpling half-smile, and I went to putty again. "You off, then?"

"I thought I might. Not much in the mood. I'm tired, and I have to return to Merivale tomorrow to work on some interior designs for the new casino."

"I've heard something about that. Declan mentioned it."

"Are you thinking of applying? They're going to need security." I preferred the idea of him at Bridesmere, where at least we could chat freely.

Just as I spoke, I saw Bram at the end of the line. "Oh fuck."

"What?" Carson's brow creased.

"A stalking ex just turned up."

"Another one?" His bewildered frown made me almost laugh.

Yep. I'm crap at picking boyfriends.

"This one's really bad." A shaky breath left my lips.

"Really?" His head moved back. "Dusty didn't strike me as someone who'd give up his seat for the elderly."

"He's a lamb compared to Bram." I tucked myself behind Carson to hide.

"I'll make sure he doesn't get in. But if he's got an invitation, I have to let him in. Those are the rules."

"I can't leave now because he'll see me." My eardrums pulsed from fear as I relived Bram's hands around my throat.

Carson cocked his head towards a door by the cloakroom. "Go in there. That's where we sit for our break. When he's inside, I'll let you know so you can leave. Okay?"

My palms had gone all sweaty and my mouth had turned dry, such was the Bram effect.

I released a tight breath. Carson had come to my rescue again. He may not have taken to me as a woman, but he was watching my back. And right then, I needed protection more than hot sex.

CHAPTER 2

Carson

As I gestured for him to enter, Bram, sporting a neck full of tats, shuffled past, wearing "wanker" all over his doped-up face.

I couldn't understand how a gorgeous and sophisticated woman like Savanah could fall for such a self-entitled jerk. But then she wasn't alone. Since working at that exclusive club, I'd noticed that girls fell for dickheads like him all the time.

"Hey, Steve, I'm going for a quick break. Back in five," I said.

On entering our private space, I found Savanah staring down at her phone.

She was one of the reasons I hadn't taken Declan's offer to run Reboot. Just smelling her musky perfume roused memories of her sexy body rubbing against mine. Something told me that once I had a taste, I wouldn't be able to stop. So I kept my distance instead because when I thought of Savanah, the word "complicated" came to mind.

"He's inside. The coast is clear." I rolled my lips as tension took hold of my senses, which had nothing to do with her drugged-out ex.

"Thanks so much." She returned an uneasy smile, mirroring mine.

In that elegant blue dress that hinted at what lay beneath, Savanah's beauty, as always, captivated me.

Those wide hypnotic blue eyes made me lose my tongue again, and I couldn't string a coherent line around her.

As she held my stare, waiting for me to speak, I splayed my palms. "Is there something else?"

"You didn't return my calls. Any reason?" Slanting her pretty face, she became that rich girl who clicked her fingers and got what she wanted.

"Sorry." I scratched my prickly jaw. "I've had a lot on lately."

She looked down at her feet. "I thought it could have been because of what happened." Her arched eyebrow raised.

Is she referring to the way she pressed her soft hand against my swollen cock?

"I'm not sure what you mean." Never good at bullshitting, I shifted on the spot.

"Oh, come on, Carson. Don't go all coy on me." She teased me with a smile, which sent a bolt of heat to my dick.

"I've got to get back." I turned to leave.

"Am I just not your type?"

She'd gone deadpan and unreadable, although I think I caught a hint of insecurity in her eyes.

I exhaled while searching for the right response. "You're beautiful, Savanah. Never doubt that."

She kept scrutinizing me as though trying to read more into my words. "Are you gay?"

I had to laugh. "Nope. One hundred percent into women." I scratched my neck. I had this sudden urge to fuck her against the wall and show her just how much I liked pussy. "Okay then. Bye." I turned away. "By the way, if he's as bad as you say, you need to get a restraining order."

She looked lost, and I felt like a prick for abandoning her. "I'm meant to be working."

"I'll follow you out and make a dash for it. And hey..." She paused and then tranced me out with her mesmerizing eyes. "Thanks. I owe you one." She flicked me a flirty smile.

Does she mean a drink or something else?

As she walked off, some men in line whistled at her.

"She's a stunner," Steve said, stating the bleeding obvious.

I nodded. "I know."

"I think she likes you." He grinned.

"She's too rich for me."

He pulled a shocked look. "You need your head examined. I'd love to meet a rich chick."

"Call me old-fashioned, but I want to be the one that brings in the money."

"That's so fucking nineteenth century, man. My missus works in admin. Without two wages, we wouldn't be able to survive."

"I get that. And that would be fine. But she's a fucking billionaire."

And my best friend's sister.

His eyes stretched wide like I'd told him she sold weapons for a living. "Holy shit. That's even better still. Imagine that. A big house. A swimming pool. Trips around the world. Sign me up."

I laughed. Steve was a dreamer. Unlike me. The army knocked my dreams out of me. As a thirty-two-year-old realist, I was aware of my limitations, and a sophisticated woman like Savanah would get bored with someone who preferred fishing to partying.

Although I couldn't quite figure out Savanah's fascination for rough-looking guys, I knew that we came from completely different worlds.

Having experienced my share of lust, I'd never hung around long enough to see where things could go.

My mother broke my heart when she died. Alone in the world at sixteen, I'd convinced myself better to remain unattached than undergo that kind of crippling separation again.

Although I was physically tougher than most, I had work to do emotionally because one didn't experience things I'd seen and not be affected. But for now, I decided to keep life simple, and Savanah was the opposite of simple.

About ten minutes after Savanah left, Bram strutted out with a cigarette dangling from his smirk.

On my approach, he tilted his chin up at me, as though I was standing in the wrong place. He wore ripped jeans and a jacket with holes, designed that way I could only imagine, since he was part of the rich classes despite dressing like someone sleeping rough.

"I'm allowed to smoke here." As though to make a point, he puffed smoke into my face, and my fists clenched.

I took a deep breath and counted to three, an anger management technique I'd learned from the army. "Smoke all you like. But listen, if I hear that you've been stalking Savanah Lovechilde, and as much as lay a finger on her, you'll have me to deal with."

His eyes narrowed as he sized me up and down. "Who the fuck are you?" I grabbed him by the arm and squeezed his puny biceps. "Hey, man, you're fucking hurting me."

Releasing my grip, I walked off.

"I can have you up for assault," he yelled.

I turned. "You don't want to mess with me."

After I resumed my position at the door, Steve asked, "What was that about?"

"He's been knocking Savanah about, and now he's stalking her. She's terrified of him."

"He looks like a fucking dick. But hey, careful. He used a lord's pass. His father's someone. And they've got skilled lawyers."

I shrugged it off. I wasn't in the mood to talk about lawyers. Angus had already done enough damage when he jumped bail. I didn't know where he was, and my role as the protective brother was over. I tried and lost everything so that now I had to start again.

I clocked off, collected my cash, and headed back to my empty flat.

As I drove home, I thought of Declan's offer. The pay was excellent, and I had a deep fondness for the sea.

Time was slower in Bridesmere. I even got to read again. While serving for the SAS, I fell for the Jack Reacher books. I related to that character because there were days when I felt like dropping everything and taking a long walk away from my past.

Wasn't my moving to Bridesmere just that?

What about Savanah?

Could I fend her off?

And why would I want to?

CHAPTER 3

Savanah

"It's being named Salon Soir?" I did a turn of the circular room with mahogany accents.

My mother nodded as she pointed down at a mosaic of Bacchus feasting on wine while naked nymphs pranced about. "That's nicely done."

"Given its classical themes and décor, I envision the room will attract an older crowd, I suppose. I can organize an event if you like." My enthusiasm went up a notch. The casino would need security.

Mm... I wonder who I could ask?

A sparkling chandelier illuminated an oval table with a roulette wheel—the centerpiece of a room filled with gaming tables.

"No slot machines." I ran my hands over the dark-green felt.

"This isn't the suburbs, sweetheart. Crisp is vying for an exclusive crowd."

"It's very Casino Royale." I pointed at an arched entrance with red velvet curtains. "Where does this lead?"

She shrugged. "Vague on detail. Reynard mentioned something about a private club."

I studied her. "Like a girly bar or something?"

My mother's brow pinched before smoothing over. "This is Reynard's world. His business."

We stepped outside and walked to the resort, which shared the same parking bay as the new casino.

"I'm surprised you allowed it."

"I had little choice. Rey owns this land."

I stopped walking. "I didn't know that. I thought it belonged to the family. How'd that come about?"

"It's a long story." She fluttered her hand for me to keep moving. "I've got an appointment at the Pond. As you have, I believe."

That evasive response came as no surprise. Whenever Crisp was mentioned, the subject quickly changed.

I climbed into her black BMW. "You realize we could just walk there from here?"

My mother pointed at her high spiked heels. I'd never seen her in flats before.

As we drove into Pond's parking bay, I asked, "What time are guests arriving for Ethan's birthday?"

"Seven." She lowered the shade and peered into the mirror and touched her face.

"Is Orson coming?"

"Probably."

That curt answer made me frown. "Is it serious between you two?"

She waited until we'd stepped out of the car before speaking. "No. We have little in common."

As the frosted glass doors parted, I noticed Clarice at the front desk, so I held back the questions despite being intrigued by my mum's involvement with Mirabel's manager.

Her private life had always been a mystery. And now with Will locked away and Bethany having absconded, as a family, we were giving my mother space to heal.

I couldn't tell whether she'd gotten over Will or not. I'd never seen her show emotion until she opened up about her painful upbringing. As someone who wore her heart on her sleeve, I could have done with a dose of her stoicism.

The foyer radiated a calming aroma of lavender and citrusy smells, while in the background, nature's ambient sounds floated in the air.

"Welcome," said Clarice, the spa director.

"Is Manon here?" my mother asked.

Clarice's face changed from warm to cool in an instant as she nodded. Mm... Manon weaving her charms again.

On cue, my niece tottered over in her skyscrapers, nightclub wear, and a fluffy cardigan I'd been searching for in my wardrobe. Now I knew who had it. And this wasn't the first time. Many of my things had gone missing since Manon moved to Merivale.

I tapped on the sleeve of the hot-pink McQueen cardigan I'd picked up at a vintage store in Carnaby Street. "This looks familiar."

She stroked it fondly. "I only just got it."

I tilted my head. "From where exactly, since it's an '80s vintage?"

"Can't recall." She turned her back on me and spoke to my mother. "Your normal treatment?"

My mother nodded and followed her down the hall.

Refusing to allow Manon to get to me, I headed into the changing room to prepare for my massage.

A few minutes later, Jason, the masseur, greeted me with a toothy smile. "It's been a few weeks."

"I've sure missed this." I sighed. "I've been in London helping Ethan with the hotel." That was partly true, despite me hanging out with my girlfriends and finding ways to escape Bram, whom I suspected had my phone tracked.

As Jason rubbed his hands, I lay with my face poking through the cushiony hole. He applied some divinely fragrant oil and, massaging firmly onto my back, started to untangle knots.

"Last time we spoke, you were seeing a new boy." He ran his hands smoothly over me, and my skin sighed with pleasure.

"Not so good anymore, I'm afraid. I had to hide when I saw Bram at Cirque."

"It's turned nasty?" He rubbed my neck.

"Yep." I exhaled loudly. "He's turned into a psycho."

"I hope he's not hurting you. Your shoulders seem tight."

"That doesn't surprise me. I'm pretty tense all over." I chuckled darkly. "I just have to stop falling for bad boys."

"Tell me about it. My last boyfriend was ex-military and boy did he like it rough." He sniffed.

I remembered Bram's mouth on my neck, his hands holding my arms up against the wall, which I'd confused for passion. It soon turned scary when he pinned me there. I struggled, but he squeezed harder, and fear coursed through me.

"At first, it was kinda hot." He kneaded into my lower back. "But then he revealed an aggressive streak. Josh couldn't come to terms with being gay. He was trying to date women which messed up his head." He worked down my leg. "Is that okay?"

"Yes. It feels good." I breathed in as he applied pressure to my foot. I always felt great after one of his massages. "That sounds screwy."

"I've started seeing a gorgeous man. He's a gym junkie and seriously hot, but also sweet and sensitive."

"I'm so happy for you."

I could still feel Carson's arm around my shoulder as he helped me to his car the night I was mugged. His solid presence was so comforting. I never wanted him to leave. And despite his rejection, this unrelenting crush that started from the moment Declan introduced us, had deepened.

"I got a weird vibe coming from Clarice at the mention of Manon," I said.

"Manon bosses Clarice around. I think she'd love to sack her."

"She has my sympathy. Manon seems to have my mother around her finger."

"I guess she's her grandmother. Between you and me, I think Manon wants Clarice's job."

"I'll have a word with Ethan," I said.

"She's in thick with Andrew."

I frowned. "You've seen her with him?"

"We had drinks here the other night to celebrate Pond's first year, and she got pretty chummy."

"He's married, isn't he?" I asked after my brother's spa partner, whom I'd only met once.

"He is."

"She's only nineteen."

"The daddy thing's pretty popular these days. And he's rich," he said.

"She loves flaunting it, that's for sure."

"Oh, she's a minx all right." He giggled while massaging my toes.

"But we're stuck with her. That's why I've been staying in London more than usual."

"It is lovely here. I love Bridesmere."

"So do I." I sighed. At least Bram had an aversion to being outside of London and his dealers.

With that heavy thought swirling, my spirit sagged.

CHAPTER 4

Carson

WHILE DRAKE DEMONSTRATED A push-up, his new client watched on, wearing the same hopeful expression I'd seen on men wishing to bulk up to attract women.

Starting from an early age, I had to muscle up to survive the tough gangs at our council estate, which had very little to do with pussy. Although beefing up had that nice payoff, too, I soon discovered.

On seeing me, Drake held up his finger to his client and then came over and hugged me. "Hey there, big man."

I laughed. He wasn't exactly puny. In fact, Drake had bulked up considerably since the last time we met. For a twenty-two-year-old, the former troubled teenager had matured not just physically but mentally. In his early days at Reboot, he didn't hug and seemed uncomfortable with any form of friendly contact.

That's why Reboot had been so important. Apart from giving them work and focus, the boot camp had also brought the boys a family of friends and a reliable support network. I witnessed firsthand boys turning their lives around in the few months I worked there.

As a teenager, I was one punch-up away from prison when I joined the army. Only in this case, it wasn't the army but Reboot that had helped kids like Drake, who'd gone from a brawling street kid to someone with a purpose.

"You're back, I hear," he said.

"Sure am."

"The security firm didn't happen?"

Exhaling a breath, I hated this conversation. "I had to sell up after a big debt fell over me. Back to square one."

His blue eyes filled with sympathy. "I'm sorry to hear that."

"You better get back to him." His student was about to pick up some hefty weights. "You don't want him getting a hernia."

He patted me on the shoulder and returned to his older client.

Declan walked in and, seeing me, his face lit up. That's why I loved being there because like the lads, I also felt part of a family. Angus, the last remaining member of my biological family, was only ever after money.

My mother, bless her soul, would have done anything for us. She loved and cared for us even when burdened by chronic pain, showering us with affection. Maybe if she hadn't passed away when Angus was young, he might not have turned bad. Something I reminded myself of when faced with my brother's fall from grace.

"Let's go for a walk, hey?" Declan opened the door, and we stepped out onto the grounds. "I trust you settled in well?"

I nodded. "Thanks for the work. I missed this place."

Declan held my stare. I think he got that my life hadn't been a bed of roses back in the city. Not that he judged me. He understood the bad hand I'd been dealt. He was the only person who knew about Angus skipping bail, and how my heart snapped in two for failing to protect my brother from himself.

"Perhaps we can find time to do some fishing." He tossed a twig.

"I would love nothing more." I chuckled.

For some, it was Ibiza or a sun-drenched beach holiday, whereas for me, it was fishing. I'd only fished once with my father. I was fourteen at the time, and he hired a boat. We paddled up the Thames, tossed a line in, and spent the afternoon drifting along. It was the only positive experience we'd ever shared, and after he left, three days later, I returned to the hard streets before joining the army.

Wearing a blue Ralph Lauren polo, designer jeans, and smelling of fancy cologne, Declan didn't exactly look like someone who fished. But then, this was the same man who'd worn combat gear and risked his life around a crazed bomber threatening to blow up a classroom of children.

While serving in the SAS, he'd lived rough, like all of us, and as an equal, Declan never complained when confronted by the uglier side of humanity.

"Reboot has changed. We're only taking ten boys at a time for a three-month stint."

"How's it been going?" Leaves crunched under my feet as we traipsed through the forest—a favorite relaxing walking spot for me and another reminder of how much I loved being there.

"Great. They seem to enjoy growing things. There've been a couple of troublemakers, as there always are." He sniffed. "But overall, I'm pleased."

"And you've become an organic farmer, I hear."

"Yep. I love it. Me and the boys have set up a weekend farmers' market, which has become so popular profits are covering their wages."

"Why only ten boys?"

"That's all the space we have after expanding the gym, which has become a hub of activity. You should see it in the evenings."

"I bet. It's a great space. Drake keeps growing."

Declan smiled. "He's practically running the gym. Do you think you could do some personal training for a generous fee? We've got so many on the waiting list. Mainly women." He raised an eyebrow, and I chuckled.

"That sounds like fun. Why not? I'm just happy to be back. How's the wife and baby?"

"My beautiful wife and Julian are great, thanks."

"How old's he now? I've lost track. Was the christening only six months ago?"

"He's now one." Declan wore a tight smile. "Sounds like you've been through a bit."

"Nothing too traumatic." I exhaled. "I just have to stop worrying about Angus."

"You did your best. If there's anything I can do to help..."

I shook my head. "It's all good. Being here is a godsend. The pay's too generous. I'll be back on my feet in no time."

"So, we'll see you later today for the party at Merivale."

Savanah sprang to mind, and confusion swept through me again.

If only she weren't Declan's sister.

"You did get my invitation, didn't you?"

I nodded. "Sorry, I haven't had time to respond. But sure. Why not? Merivale's always a pleasure to visit."

"Ethan will be happy to see you."

"I guess I should hire a suit or something." I stared down at my watch.

"No need. Come the way you are. It's a party. All kinds of people are coming, including local farmers and friends of Mirabel's."

"That sounds colorful."

"Never a dull crowd or moment at Merivale."

I chuckled at his dry tone. "Can't wait."

We hugged and headed off in opposite directions.

SINCE MERIVALE WAS ONLY a mile or so away from the village, being a nice evening, I chose to walk to the party. As I travelled down the vibrant green leafy lane, I breathed in a lungful of cool sea air, feeling energized.

The walk gave me a chance to switch to social mode. I thought about the superrich with their clipped and well-rounded words and how they sounded like stage actors. I had to watch myself in case I swore. For most of the part, I just nodded, smiled, and opened doors for the ladies.

Savanah made me nervous though, which, in a way, made me laugh. Since when did I run from a beautiful woman?

Damaged or heavily intoxicated women were the only females I avoided. And although Savanah didn't strike me as damaged, I suspected she suffered from emotional malnourishment. An army counsellor once described me as suffering from that, by suggesting—despite my grumbling to the contrary—that I lacked the emotional strength to trust in my heart. Pretty general stuff, I thought at the time.

I entered through the iron gates into that Disneyland world where the bushes looked more like sculptures than the usual messy random-ness of nature. Everything was in its right place, manicured to perfec-tion, and one could have played snooker on the grass.

Dressed in standard black, Drake, along with another guy, stood cross-armed at the entrance. Soon as he saw me, Drake's rigid stance eased, and his hardened, security-guard expression turned friendly.

"Hey, they've got you working around the clock."

"The pay's good. I've just put down a deposit on an apartment." He brimmed with justified pride.

Was this the same boy who'd arrived at Reboot two years ago, freshly out of jail, with enough attitude to get himself locked up again?

"I'm really pleased for you. Well done." I patted his shoulder. "Sav-ing's not easy these days. Too many temptations."

"I don't smoke. I hardly drink. I don't like to gamble." He smiled shyly, as though admitting to wearing girls' underwear.

An earsplitting giggle caught my attention, and when I turned, I saw a girl of about eighteen with long dark hair, a short skirt, and serious high heels, sashaying towards us. Not that I was looking, but her boobs were hard to miss as they ballooned out of a low-cut top.

Reynard Crisp joined her, which had me wondering if they were a couple, despite him looking more like her grandfather. But in that rich scene, it wasn't unusual to see older men courting young, beautiful women.

"Here we go," Drake uttered under his breath.

"You know her?" I frowned.

"That's Manon. I tried to save her from that old dickhead, but it looks like she fucking likes him after all."

I studied him. "You sound pissed off. Have you been there?"

"Nope. I wish." He sighed. "I mean, look at her. She's fucking gor-geous. But trouble. We had a drink at the Thirsty Mariner, and she wanted to come back to mine, but I got scared." He rolled his eyes. "I need my head examined."

"You probably did the right thing."

"Once wouldn't be enough with her. That's for sure."

I smiled. This conversation had an element of déjà vu about it. Namely one princess who inhabited that fairy-tale mansion I was about to enter.

One taste of Savanah and I would have gotten hooked. I still couldn't forget the way her body felt against my back. And if she fucked the way she swayed those hips, I would have, for certain, been a fucking goner. For sanity's sake, I stayed away, despite it taking the strength of The Rock to not slide into her.

Crisp lit a cigar, while Manon, who kept eyeing off Drake, smoked and chatted to the tall, skinny man with icy eyes.

"She's Mrs. Lovechilde's long-lost granddaughter, I'm told."

"That explains it."

He looked at me with interest. "What?"

"The fact she looks like she's come out of a council estate."

He sniffed. "Yeah. She's one of us, all right. She's just trying to pretend she's something else."

I nodded slowly. "You know a lot about her."

His mouth tugged at one end. "You could say that. I mean, she's fucking beautiful, who happens to be a prick teaser."

"From where I'm standing, it looks like she's pretty tight with him."

"He's a fucking sleaze. Declan and Ethan hate him. I can't blame them."

I tapped him on the arm. "I better get in there for a drink, I suppose." Just as I spoke, a horde of women dressed up to the nines with guys just as well-presented walked up the path, talking loudly and ready for a night of expensive champagne, good food, and coupling.

I looked forward to two of those things.

CHAPTER 5

Savanah

AS THEY WALKED THROUGH the grounds of Merivale, Mirabel held onto her son's little hand, with Freddie trotting close behind. Our former Jack Russell seemed to tag along everywhere they went.

"Did I miss something about tonight being fancy dress?" I asked, bending down to kiss my cute nephew. Dressed in a wizard's outfit, he looked more like Ethan every day.

In a green floral maxi with a purple headband, Mirabel could have been at a hippie-themed party herself.

"Cian's got this thing for wizards. And when we passed a costume shop with an outfit in the window, close to tossing a tantrum, he just had to have it." She rolled her eyes. She often complained about how Ethan spoilt Cian by giving him everything his little heart desired.

My tiny nephew, meanwhile, chased Freddie, waving his magic wand in the air, like he was casting a spell on the poor creature, who didn't seem too keen to be part of Cian's experiment.

"I think he wants to make Freddie fly. We watched a toddler's show about wizards, and now he's got this thing about waving his little wand around."

I laughed. The children had brought a welcomed playful atmosphere to Merivale, especially after the drama of the past two years.

We made our way through to the back and entered the yellow room that faced the pool area.

Ethan strolled in just as we arrived.

"Hey, birthday boy." I kissed him on the cheek. "I've got your present upstairs."

"You needn't have." He picked up his son and swirled him in the air, making the cape flap, just as Declan and Theadora stepped through the French doors.

My mother had cordoned off the pool area after the last party when some heavily inebriated soul fell into the water and had to be given CPR. However, she couldn't bear to cover it over. At night, the pool turned into a rippling kaleidoscopic light show thanks to a lit-up cascade running down the rock wall.

I kissed little Dylan's soft, puffy cheek, and when he smiled, I went all warm and fuzzy. Before my two nephews, I'd never thought of myself as clucky, but I'd suddenly developed a maternal pang.

I wouldn't be ditching my contraceptive pill anytime soon, however, especially after the losers I'd attracted so far. I couldn't trust myself to get it right, and being a single mother would never work for me.

Declan cradled fourteen-month Julian, who when unleashed turned into a destroyer on chubby little legs. They called it curiosity. I called it chaos. While standing close and looking gorgeous as always, Theadora wore a red gown which, with her milky complexion and dark hair, suited her. Apart from some lip gloss and light mascara, she had very little makeup.

Unlike me. If I could dip my head in a jar of foundation, I would. I had the best makeup artist in Clarice at the Pond. I hadn't stopped thanking Ethan for setting up that spa. No one applied makeup like Clarice, who, as a former model, had interesting stories to tell about the pre-social-media nineties when one could fuck up and somehow slip under the radar. Not like now, where regrettable sex tapes that, in moments of complete madness thanks to party drugs, came to mind. Although I'd deleted them, I wondered if one would come to haunt me one day.

"So are we ready for a night of frivolities?" Declan asked.

I couldn't tell if Declan was being cynical or not. He used to hate these big parties, often hiding in a corner with one of the older guests, chatting about airplanes or vintage cars. But since marrying, he seemed happy to go along with whatever functions my mother organized, including those held at Elysium.

I got the feeling that Theadora enjoyed dressing up.

What woman didn't?

For me, parties were a good excuse to shop for a new outfit. And the possibility of meeting a hot guy who promised more than a few nights of fun also added to the buzz.

"Are you performing?" I asked Mirabel.

"Theadora and I are doing a couple of songs." The pair shared a smile.

"Like that excellent Carmen piece at Mum's soiree?" I asked.

"No. Just a couple of new songs." Mirabel and Ethan exchanged a loving smile, yet another reminder of the love that filled the room whenever both my brothers and their wives were around. Despite a tinge of envy, I felt happy for them all. They'd gotten it so right.

"I haven't heard the songs yet," Ethan said, clicking his fingers for Freddie, who leapt up in the air, mesmerizing Cian. "But I'm sure it's going to be sensational." He blew Mirabel a kiss, and Declan drew Theadora close and kissed her hair.

"Please spare me the PDA." Everyone laughed as I stuck my fingers in my mouth and pretended to chuck up.

"Is Orson coming?" I asked Mirabel. "Mum's tight-lipped as always."

"Last I heard he is. Only nothing is going on between them. Orson would like to, but from what I gather, your mother's not so keen."

"They are very different." I bent down to take the ball from Freddie's mouth before Cian lunged for the canine.

"Opposites can attract." Mirabel's eyes slid over to Ethan, who wore a pale-blue-and-green-check blazer over blue fitted slacks. I'd noticed his choice of clothing had turned more colorful since partnering with Mirabel.

"What do you think about Orson and Mum, Declan?"

He shrugged. "It's none of our business."

"I agree," Ethan said.

I regarded Theadora and Mirabel and rolled my eyes. "They just don't like our mother dating."

"That's not true," Ethan protested, tossing a ball at Freddie, with Cian unsuccessfully racing the dog for it. "There are bigger questions to ask."

Declan rubbed his neck. "Yeah, like where's Bethany?"

"I asked Mum yesterday, and she's not interested in finding her or the mysterious two billion dollars that obviously our dear half-sister pilfered. I think Mother's happy to be rid of her."

Ethan nodded slowly. "Can't say I miss her."

"We've just got the next best thing: Manon." I didn't hide my resentment.

Theadora sat opposite me on a pink chaise lounge, looking like a painting in her draping gown and hair in a top bun. "You don't like her?"

"She keeps stealing my clothes, for one."

Mirabel grimaced. "Oh, I'd hate that."

"And Mother refuses to believe me."

Ethan shrugged. "Best keep out of that, I think. Mother's too busy trying to protect Manon from Crisp's greasy hands."

Steering the subject away from my pesky niece, I turned to Declan. "What happened with Will's appeal?"

"It was thrown out. His five-year prison sentence has been upheld. As far as I'm concerned, it's too light a sentence."

"Too right." Ethan matched Declan's venomous tone.

"Oh well. Enough of that. I'm going out there to hang out with whoever." I smiled. My heart beat a little faster than usual with anticipation after learning that Carson had accepted an invitation to the party.

I walked up the hallway and headed for the private bathroom hidden behind the library.

Leaning into the mirror, I fixed my lipstick and brushed down my hair, which had grown to my shoulder blades. The brown shade made my eyes stand out. I'd been blond for a while, but I preferred my natural shade. The fact Carson mentioned he preferred brunettes might have had something to do with it.

I ran my hands down my dress and lifted my boobs in my push-up bra. Turning around, I checked my butt, which was probably my best feature along with my legs. All those ballet lessons as a girl had paid off.

My Prussian-blue fitted Alexander McQueen dress accented my eyes and was just above my knees, making my legs look longer. I ran my hands over my bare legs down to my six-inch chunky heels.

As I moved down the hall, I dodged staff racing around with trays of canapes and champagne and grabbed a glass along the way.

I ran into a few of my mother's friends, who all looked the same. Although we'd held so many parties, which meant I'd been seeing these same faces all my life, I still couldn't remember half their names.

Only those who'd caused some scandal stood out. The well-behaved ones, who huddled together like library books in their designated categories, were a blur to me. I was always nice, of course, fake-smiling my head off.

I stepped into the front red room, where guests always convened at the beginning of all our functions.

Carson stood out. Not only for his casual gear of black jeans and loose checked shirt, which made him look like he'd just stepped out of an Irish pub, but because he was so tall and muscular and had my hormones pinging. Or was that my pulse racing?

Men didn't normally affect me like that.

If I liked a guy, I'd flirt and turn it into a game. But with Carson, from the moment I laid eyes on him, my body responded differently. I'd forget to breathe and became rather brainless in the conversation department.

Women kept checking him out too. As always, there were plenty of pretty girls in skimpy designer clothes in our scene. Wealth attracted good-looking people. Maybe that's why I preferred rugged men. I found well-spoken men in bespoke jackets as arousing as nerdy guys discussing the latest app.

Orson had cornered my mother, and I even caught her blushing, but then, it could have been a man I spotted standing close. He was handsome in that older male, George Clooney way, and my mother seemed to be stealing glances.

Go, Mother. After what happened with Will, I wanted her to find true love, and it couldn't have been fun being with a gay husband. Despite my deep love for my father, I still felt sad for my mother.

Back to her evasive best, my mother refused to talk about her long-lost daughter, my evil stepsister, Bethany, or discuss Will's incarceration.

"There you are," I heard over my shoulder. I turned and Sienna smiled back at me.

She leaned in and kissed me. "This is nice." She touched my dress.

"'90s Alexander McQueen."

"It's gorgeous. And that's a yummy shade of blue. It's so your color." Her eyes, painted in a sparkly turquoise shadow, did a sweep of the room. She cocked her head towards a guy in a burgundy velvet jacket. "He's kinda cute."

"That's Gareth. He's gay."

She sighed. "Again? What happened to my gaydar? It's so out whack lately."

"That's because the alpha gays are harder to spot."

"Say, your security guy's here, I noticed," she whispered.

"He can't hear. He's way over there." I grabbed another glass of champagne from a passing server.

I passed her a glass as she kept sizing up the guests.

That's what we did: gawk, gossip, and giggle. "Carson seems to have Clarinda and Justine all over him."

"I've noticed." I stole a look at the man who'd stolen my heart, and our eyes collided, causing my legs to wobble. I had to look away just to find my balance, which had little to do with champagne.

Sienna's attention went to our new waiter. "Oh my god, he's gorgeous."

"That's Aziz. He's recently arrived from Morocco."

"Don't tell me he's gay too," she whined. Her eyes were wide and expectant.

I shook my head. "I don't think so. The female staff have taken a shine. He's studying law and works here during breaks. He's staying in the servants' quarters."

"Oh, really." Her face brightened. "You might have to introduce us."

"Just hang around the side of the hall. That's where they all mill around between shifts."

I touched her arm. "I've got to talk to my mum."

"She's looking gorgeous."

"Can't go wrong in Chanel. And green is her color."

I left Sienna and joined my mother, who had Orson hanging on her every word.

Wearing an apologetic smile, I asked Mirabel's manager, "Do you mind if I steal my mother for a moment?"

"But of course. I was just boring her with all the ins and outs of the music industry."

She inclined her head. Her way of being nice, despite me reading relief on her face that I'd rescued her from listening to someone babble on about their work.

"He talks so rapidly. It's hard to keep up. I'm exhausted," she whispered.

"That's cocaine."

"I thought as much." She studied me. "You're not still using, are you?"

"I only tried it a few times. I'm already jumpy enough."

She scrutinized me. My inability to finish projects had always concerned her. At least my new role as advisor on acquisitions for Elysium and Salon Soir had captured my interest. I liked art and might have just found something I enjoyed, enabling me to maintain focus. There was that arts degree I needed to complete too. I was going fine until Bram messed with my head.

My mother followed me into the ballroom where the band was setting up.

"There are so many people here," I said.

"Yes. It's a good turnout." She looked around the room. "Do you think the lighting's dim?"

I shook my head. "It's nice and moody. Better for dancing. A bit like a club."

We walked to the other side of the room and stood by the bay windows that looked out to the ocean. Night had only just arrived, and the silvery sea rippled serenely. "I whisked you away because you looked a little bored."

Her mouth curled into a slow smile. "Orson's a little too keen, and I don't think he's getting the hint."

"Just tell him you're not interested."

"That's not me, darling. I generally give them the cold shoulder, and that seems to work, but not in his case, it seems. I could be out of practice." Her mouth curved to one side.

"There's not much to it. If you like them, you make conversation and smile at everything they say."

"Thanks for the lesson on the etiquette of flirting." She slanted her head.

I giggled at her dry tone. "You're looking great, by the way."

"Thanks, sweetheart." Her warm smile had me questioning again who was this woman I called Mother.

I wish she'd told us earlier about her life growing up. Maybe she wouldn't have carried such a weight on her shoulders all those years. I did, however, understand her shame given our snobby and brutally judgmental rich scene. My father was never like that. He was so inclusive and always maintained that good and bad existed in everyone, regardless of money or race.

"So who's that dashing George Clooney lookalike I noticed hovering close and giving you the eye?"

Her face reddened, which was rare for my mother. She wasn't the blushing kind.

"He wasn't giving me the eye." Her lips twitched into a smile. "He's a friend of the Lazenby's. Sebastian met Carrington at Eton. He's been living in Italy. On Lake Como. He's a writer."

"Oh? He's gorgeous."

She studied me for a moment. "Are you interested?"

I shook my head. "Well-groomed older men in tweed jackets are not my thing."

Give me a buff, ex-military man in ass-clinging Levis any day.

"I hardly know him." She touched the wave of hair framing her face.

"It's so nice to see your hair like that."

"I tried a new hairstylist, and he suggested waves for a change."

Her thick and glossy dark hair, normally tied back or in a bun, suited her worn loose.

"But you like him?" I smiled.

"He's attractive, yes. And intelligent."

"Sounds like a perfect match to me."

"He's an impoverished writer who has just come out of a divorce. Which is probably why you've noticed him staring at me." She pulled a mock smile. "There are plenty of men like Carrington looking for a rich home."

I laughed. "You make him sound like a stray dog."

She rolled her eyes and chuckled.

"Oh, Mummy"—I took her hand—"it's not just your wealth. You're stunning. At every function you've got men dripping off you."

Her head pushed back. "Hardly. I'm the host. And sure, Orson's rather fresh."

"I thought you might have, you know..." I raised an eyebrow.

"I haven't slept with him, and while he's attractive, we have little in common."

"Then give Carrington a go. He's more your type, and he's an academic. What does he write?"

"Historical fiction. He's working on a novel about Charles the Second."

My jaw dropped. "Oh my god. Didn't you do your master's on him?"

"I'm surprised you remember that." Her eyes looked over my shoulder, and I turned to see Crisp.

My mouth turned down. I refused to even strain a fake smile. Instead, I scowled at him, to which he returned a saccharine smile. I think he enjoyed being hated.

"A seasoned voluptuary whose sole ambition was to match Louis the Great's incomparable artistic contributions. Charles the second's greatest achievement, however, was siring an impressive number of children to an equally impressive number of women, he said.

"You sound like you knew him personally," I said.

"He's one of the more colorful monarchs and rather too fascinating to overlook." Reynard gave my mother a knowing smile.

I left them alone and stepped outside the ballroom. I wasn't looking at where I was going when I ran into a solid form and uttered, "Oh."

A pair of large hands landed on my arms.

I looked up, and Carson's hazel eyes met mine.

"Sorry. I was lost in thought."

He smiled. "Isn't that best left for staring at the sea or sitting somewhere alone?"

"I guess so." I looked up at him and had the sudden desire to drag him off and have him fondle me. Okay, maybe more than fondling, like ravage me perhaps. "So where are you off to? Chasing some pretty staff member?"

His head jerked back like I'd accused him of exposing himself. "No. Of course not. I'm just off to powder my nose."

I laughed. That was the last thing one would expect from someone as butch as him.

"Your nose looks a little shiny." I opened my Louis Vuitton clutch. "Here. I can lend you some face powder."

He touched my hand and sparks rushed up my arm. "No need."

We shared a smile, and his eyes held mine again, making me forget to breathe.

"See you back in there. Maybe we can chat. Have a drink?" I tilted my head.

He smiled back. "Looking forward to it."

A sigh exited my lips as I watched him walk off with that easy stride. I'd done nothing but fantasize about him after my embarrassing failed attempt at seduction. Feeling a little swollen between the legs, I headed back to the party to corner someone for some small talk.

CHAPTER 6

Carson

MIRABEL HAD THE SWEETEST voice I'd ever heard. She strummed her guitar and sang a heartfelt song about her love for Ethan, who looked very moved, biting his lower lip as she sang. If the woman of my dreams sang a song with such loving lyrics, I imagined getting a little misty-eyed myself.

After Mirabel finished her song, Theadora took to the stage and performed a classical piece on the piano. Her fingers moved with such freedom and skill that I might have been watching her perform at a concert hall, especially in that decorative ballroom.

The pair then joined forces and performed a song about a moonbeam kissing the sea, and I made a mental note to ask Mirabel where I could download the song. She sang about trusting one's heart and closing one's ears to harmful whispers. "Love comes in all forms," she boomed. "Take it with two hands, hold it, caress it, soothe it, and make love to it."

Savanah, whose attention was on the stage, must have sensed me staring because she turned, and her tantalizing blue eyes trapped mine. With that dark hair slinking down the nape of her long neck and over her slender shoulders, Savanah made sensuality look effortless.

I hadn't been able to get her out of my mind, despite determined efforts to stay away. But then, Mirabel's lyrics about embracing love with two hands by throwing away doubt kept repeating in my mind. Life was too short to deny myself pleasure. Something I knew too well because as a soldier, surrounded by bombs exploding in every direction, I was constantly reminded of the fragility of life.

Savanah was one woman I could imagine losing myself to. I'd already done that in a sense just from that night of breathing her in, while her curves pressed against me.

After capturing the audience's imagination, including mine, the women bowed to rapturous applause, and from there the party kicked off with everyone singing "Happy Birthday" to Ethan.

A three-tiered cake was wheeled out, and after a few blows, Ethan extinguished the candles.

"Speech," came from among the crowd.

Ethan was dragged up to the stage and stood before a microphone. He hugged and kissed his wife and whispered something that made her smile. He then shifted a bit on the spot, something I found odd since he'd always come across as comfortable in his own skin.

"I'm told that if I don't give a speech, I'll be strung up and quartered." He chuckled with a grimace. He turned to Mirabel and asked, "How old am I again?"

Someone yelled, "Fifty going onto five."

He laughed.

"Two years younger than Jesus," another guest yelled.

"Oh, I'm thirty-one. That's right. And no, I'm not losing my mind. It's been a whirlwind year. Mirabel had to remind me last week that it was my birthday." He chuckled. "Anyway, it's great to see you all. Old faces and new, and ones that were once old."

He waited for the laughs to die down and added, "I'd like to give a big heartfelt thanks to my beautiful wife, my mother, Declan, Savanah, and—last but not least—Theadora for organizing this night. I've had the best year of my life, and it can only get better. I've never been happier, healthier, or more driven thanks to my beautiful wife and my delightful precocious son, Cian, who bring me much joy and laughter every day."

He turned to Mirabel, and she nodded with an encouraging smile.

"Um... I'd also like to announce that we're expecting another child."

Whistles and cheers echoed off the grand ballroom's walls.

"I only heard about it this morning. The best birthday present ever."

Draping his arm over Mirabel, he kissed her on the cheek and then held up his glass of champagne. "Here's to a great night. I'm told the band is fab. Have a dance, a few drinks, and a jolly good old time on me."

More cheers, and down he stepped to meet his brother and family for hugs.

I trundled over to the barrel of beer on ice, grabbed a bottle, unscrewed the top, and took a thirsty sip before embarking on small talk with some of the guests.

When the band came on, I perched myself against the wall, tapping my foot.

Declan came over and joined me. "Hey."

I nodded. "It's a great night. This is some room."

"Can you believe we used to play cricket in here?" He chuckled. "Sometimes even football when my mother wasn't around."

"You couldn't have played outside? There's no shortage of land."

"On those wet, miserably cold days. And at nights."

I shook my head. "I can't believe your world. But then you became one of us. I can't quite figure that out."

He sniffed. "My mother couldn't either. But hey, I would do it all again. And I got to fly. I love my planes. You know that."

Declan was a hero in the true sense of the word, and one of us. The only time he showed off his wealth was when we hit the bars during breaks. He insisted on buying all the rounds and made sure we had the best steak.

A man in a green suit bounced around in jerky moves like he'd stood on hot coals as he flirted with two women in gowns with slits up their thighs.

"He's out there," I said.

"That's Orson. He thinks he's living in the seventies."

"I can tell."

Theadora joined us and kissed me on the cheek. "Lovely to see you." She looked over at Savanah for some reason. "You're not dancing? There are lots of single girls here."

"Maybe after a drink or two, I might pluck up the courage," I said.

"That doesn't sound like you, Carson," Declan said.

"I've gotten bashful in my old age."

Theadora giggled at me and then took Declan's hand. "Come on, let's dance."

Declan saluted me and joined the scrum of dancers.

"Start Me Up" by the Stones came on, and I rocked my body ever so slightly.

Savanah, who struck me as tipsy, sashayed over. "You're not dancing?"

"I don't dance." I returned a tight smile.

Her head jerked back as though I'd admitted to being a fruitarian.

"But just then, you were grooving on the spot, I noticed."

"I love the Stones."

Back to her sassy best, she placed down her glass and removed the bottle from my hand. I rather liked a bossy woman on the odd occasion, especially in bed. Even her soft hand on my arm raised my temperature.

We hit the dance floor, where she swayed her hips and waved her arms up in the air, while I moved my shoulders and hips ever so slightly. I wasn't what you called an exuberant dancer. There was only one kind of dancing I liked and that involved being naked in bed with a willing partner.

But it was worth making a fool of myself just to see Savanah move. I particularly liked it when she spun around, revealing stockings clipped onto a garter.

Did someone turn on the heating?

"Nights in White Satin" came on next, giving me goose bumps. That song always touched my soul, or were Savanah's beautiful eyes making me tingle?

She was about to walk from the dance floor when I grabbed her hand. "Where are you going?"

CHAPTER 7

Savanah

DESPITE SIX-INCH HEELS, I only reached Carson's shoulder. He held my hand, and butterflies fluttered through me, and his steady gaze stole my breath. I read experience, strength, and dependability. He struck me as deep, unlike the immature men in my scene with their baboonish grins. But then, they were boys whereas Carson was a man.

"I thought you didn't know how to dance," I said, as he wrapped his arm around my waist and pressed his strong, firm body against mine.

"I didn't say I couldn't dance. I just said I didn't dance." His mouth curled at one end.

He smelled of bath soap, pine, and like a man who could make me come with just one touch.

Taking the lead, he moved like liquid. My feet seemed airborne as we slid together as one.

His firm hold made me feel secure. I would have even jumped out of a plane with him holding onto me, harnessed in a parachute. For someone who hated heights, that was huge.

Drooling attraction aside, I had to keep reminding myself that he'd already rejected me.

If I'm not his type, then what's that growing against my stomach?

I might have even melted on the spot if he wasn't holding me up.

"You're great at this," I said.

"Thanks. Those ballroom dancing classes weren't a complete waste."

I looked up at him and frowned. "You're pulling my leg."

He shook his head slowly. "I took a few classes."

"Why?"

His shapely, alluring mouth curled into a slow smile. "Let's just say I was trying to impress a girl."

"Then she would have been impressed. I'm just letting you lead me."

"That's the way it should be."

I raised my face to meet his. "Are we talking about dancing here? Or something else?"

His mouth tugged up at one end. "That's what I meant. What did you have in mind?"

Words escaped me. The way he slanted his head, wearing a sexy smile, rattled me.

As we glided together, it felt like we were in our own universe. The other dancers went all blurry like a ballroom scene painted in water-colors, and my feet seemed airborne.

After dancing to three ballads, the band paused for a break. Wanting more, I snapped out of an erotic dream and had to bite my tongue to stymy a groan.

Nevertheless, determined to keep Carson close, I hung around, if only to keep those pretty, ogling women from pouncing on him. Rich girls liked to fuck men like Carson before marrying wealthy fops to please their families.

That wasn't me. When I turned thirty, which was only a year away, I had one billion pounds coming to me, thanks to my generous grand-parents. Not that I wanted to marry Carson. I just wanted to fuck him. Badly.

From the moment I saw him in that worker's pub with my brother, my body went into overdrive. Just looking at him sent a need blazing through me.

"Have you seen the garden?" I asked, just as he was about to walk off.

His eyes had a twinkle in them, as though he'd read me as saying, "Let's step outside so you can touch me, and I can suck you off."

Or is that just my dirty mind?

He wore a lazy smile. "You go first."

"You just want to perve on my arse."

Fuck all these formalities and niceties.

He leaned in, and his breath sent a fiery blast through me. "Guilty."

My cheeks flushed. "Yours isn't too bad, from memory."

We held each other's stare, and I'd forgotten where I was again. I was swollen and hot and needed a wall to lean against.

I led him to the pool area, knowing it would be quieter there.

When I noticed that the kaleidoscopic color wheel was turned off, I climbed up the ladder to switch it on.

"Hey, what are you doing?" he asked, holding the steps for me.

"Just switching on the pool lights." I pushed down the lever. "How's that?"

"Um... Hot." He sounded like he was having trouble talking.

"You mean the pool lights?" I asked.

"I'm not looking at those."

A whoosh of wind raised the skirt of my dress, and I suddenly realized he could see everything since I'd gone commando.

Under the dim lights, his eyes grew heavy with lust as I stepped down.

I couldn't even have recited the alphabet if I tried. My brain had turned to sludge, and it was like crackling electrodes had connected the air between us.

His tongue swept over his lips, and he puffed as though frustrated by something.

As he gazed deep into my eyes, he pulled me in and held me tight, as if his life depended on it. My chest squashed against his solid six-pack.

His hot, moist lips pressed against mine, and I left my body.

Clutching my waist, he kept pressing our bodies together to keep me there.

As if I'd run? Not with those burning, full lips caressing my mouth like it was something X-rated. Especially as his hands explored my body.

I felt his dick lengthen against my stomach. Such was our tight embrace his throbbing bulge matched the aching pulse between my thighs.

As I shivered in his arms, his tongue penetrated through my parted lips and danced with my tongue for a hot, hungry kiss.

Heavy breathing filled the space between us like we were already fucking.

That kiss lasted forever, as we explored each other's lips like every little kink and curve revealed something new. His fingers walked over my hips and clutched my ass, squeezing at it.

"You forgot to dress, I see." His steamy breath massaged my neck.

"I rarely wear panties," I said.

He grunted. "I wish you hadn't done that."

I studied him with a smile. "Done what?"

"Shown me your ass."

"Why? Did it offend you?" I teased.

"Quite the opposite."

I wanted him to admit to being driven wild with lust. Not that I climbed the ladder to provoke him or anything. I didn't expect him to be standing underneath. If anything, I felt a little embarrassed.

And a tinge hot. Okay, maybe blazing hot from how his eyes seemed to burn for me.

"What are you going to do to me?" I ran my tongue over my lips.

"What I'd like to do to you needs a bed."

"We've got a lot of those here."

He pulled me in tightly and kissed me, or I should say gorged on my lips as though starving for them.

He fondled my breasts. "Gorgeous tits."

"They're on the small side."

He lurched his head back and frowned. "Are you kidding? They're fucking perfect." He ran his hands over the fabric, and my nipples puckered, screaming for his mouth. "They're big enough. I don't like big tits."

I frowned. "All men like big tits."

"That's crap. I'm a man, and I talk with my mates."

"You talk about women's tits?"

"I was in the army, remember? That's all we talked about."

"Women's breasts?" I laughed.

"Well, among other things." He looked shy and boyish, and I wanted us naked.

"Pussies too?" I cocked my head with a grin.

"I'm more a dog man myself."

I slapped him, and he crossed his arms to defend himself when we heard a girl's voice.

It was Manon, and my heart sank. Talk about crashing down to earth. I was about to drag Carson off to continue our steam fest when I heard Reynard Crisp's voice.

They couldn't see us there, and curiosity won the day as I remained put.

"You feel nice," Crisp said.

"Not here," she said.

"When?"

"Soon. In London. Away from here."

"You must remove that image from that site."

"That photo is bringing in some good money."

"You're about to become a millionaire. When?"

There was a pause.

"I promise soon," she said. "You know my price."

"As long as you're intact, you'll get that. But it's for an entire week. Yes?"

Feeling sick from what I'd heard, I shook my head and gestured for Carson to follow me back inside.

"That sounded seedy," he said.

"We figured he'd try to fuck her in return for cash."

Carson looked as horrified as I felt. "And that makes it right?"

As we stepped into the yellow room, I said, "Can we not talk about what we just heard?"

"But she's young and impressionable."

I forced a smile. "Manon's nineteen going on thirty. She's been playing with him for a while. I imagine he's going to set her up. It's all the rage."

His forehead remained creased. "Are you all like this?"

"Hey, don't compare me to Manon. I'm not like her at all. She's taking advantage of the fact he's got a thing for young virgins. And I'm sure he's offering her a ton of money."

"Shouldn't you talk to her? Give her some sisterly advice."

My brow pinched. "Sisterly advice? Have you met her?"

He shook his head. "Not properly. She strikes me as a bit of a flirt, and she's all over Drake."

"That's not so surprising. He's hot." I smiled tightly. "As someone who prefers men my age or a little older, I'm personally not into him. Drake's also too nice for her, and he's not rich enough. Manon has made no secret of her ambition to live the high life."

"And that makes what we just heard right?"

Why the fuck didn't I move away sooner?

We could have been rolling on my bed naked by now. Instead, Carson had gone dark on me, as though I'd been the one luring rich old sleaze-bags.

"Hey, don't judge me. I'm not the one that brought them together. It's her choice."

"But she's so young. And an entire week with a man like that. You don't know what he might do to her."

"She might like it." I shrugged.

"You speak like you've had experience with this sort of thing."

I studied him, searching for his earlier playfulness, but was met with a steely, earnest gaze.

"I have never needed to sell my virginity. I've just made some bad choices. As I'm sure you must have. So don't you dare judge me."

He scratched his strong jawline. "I need a beer." And off he went. Just like that.

I released a frustrated breath.

What just happened?

Should I chase him and apologize?

What for?

I just spoke the truth. So why did it feel like I was being punished?

Talk about crashing big time. In a matter of minutes, I'd gone from the heights of steamy arousal to the lows of being unfairly judged. A heavy sigh deflated my chest as I headed back into the party.

My mother appeared lost in a deep and meaningful with her new Prince Charming. With his eyes glued to her face, he seemed to hang off her every word.

I approached them and greeted her new friend with a smile.

"This is my daughter, Savanah." My mother gestured. "And this is Carrington."

"Cary, please." He leaned in and kissed my cheek. "Nice to meet you."

I looked from him to my mother. "I'm sorry to interrupt, but can I steal my mother for a minute?"

"I'll get a refill, I think." He pointed at the empty glass in her hand. "Can I take that from you?"

She nodded, with a dreamy look in her eyes. I imagined that was me staring at Carson's handsome face before Manon's cancerous scene.

He casually strode off with my mother watching him.

"My god." I waved the air as though shooing flies. Only this was more like fairy dust. "Feel those sparks in the air."

She smiled at me as though I was talking nonsense. "He's an interesting man."

"Oh, Mummy, please. He's gorgeous, and he's into you."

Her cheeks reddened. "Anyway, what did you want to tell me?"

Since we were within earshot of some guests, I pointed towards the yellow room. "Why don't we go in there?"

Once we were alone, I told her about Manon and Crisp.

Looking dismayed, she opened her palms. "I know. It's disgusting. But I'm powerless in this situation."

"Shouldn't you at least talk to her? I mean, she might live to regret it. And he could hurt her."

"Why this sudden interest? I thought you disliked Manon," she said.

"I do. But still, he's creepy."

She sighed. "I'll have another word with Reynard. I've already tried talking to Manon. Plenty of times." Her mouth formed a tight line. "The thought of it makes me ill. At least they could have kept it private. I would have preferred not to know."

"Then tell Reynard to step away. You're close to him. Surely this unsinkable relationship you share wins you some influence."

She released an audible breath.

"What's he got over you, Mother?"

"I can't say."

Only after telling us about her hidden pregnancy, did my mother reveal vulnerability, and now, for a fleeting moment, I read defeat in her eyes.

I softened my tone. "Has he got something over you? Is that what it is? You can tell me."

She switched back to deadpan. "I'll talk to Manon again."

There she went again, steering the subject away from Crisp, motivating me to press her, nevertheless. "From what I heard, there's already been some kind of intimacy between them."

Her eyebrows collided. "You heard that?"

As I relayed that Manon had him begging, and how she was flaunting herself online, my mother went pale.

"It may not be as salacious as you think. Maybe she's shown him pictures of herself in bikinis."

I laughed at how old-fashioned that sounded. "Mum, girls like Manon are posting pictures of their vaginas."

Looking horrified, my mother might have just seen a rotting corpse. "Please tell me you haven't done that." Her eyes narrowed. "Have you?"

Not deliberately.

She wasn't the only one with secrets. I planned to keep to myself that heart-shattering sex tape Bram sent me, threatening to destroy and humiliate me unless I met up with him.

"No, of course not. But there's OnlyFans and all kinds of seedy websites where girls like Manon can post pornographic images of themselves for money."

"But she doesn't need the money." A note of anxiety crept into her voice, and guilt sliced through me for upsetting her. "I've set up a trust fund for her that she's aware of. I've even told her that if she stops playing with Reynard, I'll give her what he offers, plus more. But only when she turns twenty-one. In the meantime, I allow her shopping sprees with a generous limit, and she's earning a good wage at the Pond."

I opened my palms. "Then maybe she likes Crisp. She wouldn't be the first nineteen-year-old to marry a man who could be her grandfather."

"He's not the marrying kind. He'll do his deed, give her what she demands, and then move on to the next. That's Reynard."

I studied my mother, who looked shaken. After all, it was her grand-daughter. "He's horrible. I don't get it."

"Best to stay out of it, darling. Please. Don't concern yourself."

"Set her up in her own place away from here. That way, I can forget she exists. She keeps stealing my clothes, for one, and I just don't trust her. She's just like her mother."

A line grew between her brows. "She's my granddaughter, and she's an asset at the Pond."

"They don't like her. She's stealing products there too."

"Let's not talk about this anymore. Especially not tonight. I'll talk to her."

I followed her back to the party where I saw a girl I hadn't met before all over Carson.

Although I wanted to crash that flirty interaction, I noticed Manon chatting to a younger man, almost pinning herself against him.

Stepping in between them, I turned to Manon. "Can I have a word?"

"I'm kinda busy." She pulled her smarmy "fuck you" look.

"Now." Pissed off, I eyeballed her.

She'd messed up my night. Okay, not deliberately. Even so, by now, Carson and I could have been lying naked on my bed, getting sweaty.

She rolled her eyes and then followed me into the bathroom.

"So, am I wearing something of yours again?" Her whiny little voice made me want to slap her.

"I heard you talking to Crisp out there."

"You shouldn't have been eavesdropping." She leaned into the mirror and touched up her eye makeup with her finger.

"He's known to be rough."

"Mm... that sounds like you've been there. Are you jealous?"

Out of frustration, I puffed. "Look, Manon, I'm this close to reporting you. Clarice knows that you're stealing products. Ethan's turning a blind eye because of Mother."

"So what? He can afford it." She ran her fingers down her long, dark, waist-length hair.

There was no doubt that Manon was a stunner with that slender body and large chest. Her almond eyes went from doe-eyed and seductive when on the hunt to cold and hard, just like her mother's, whenever confronted.

"I'm just trying to warn you about Crisp."

She pulled a dark smile. "I don't mind men treating me rough. My father used to hit me all the time. I kind of liked it. It meant he cared."

I shook my head in horror. She was seriously damaged.

Father? Or did she mean stepfather? There was a lot about this girl we had to learn, it seemed.

"Then you're in for a hard life. There are men out there that don't just stop at hitting."

She pushed me out of her way. "Thanks for the boring aunty talk. But I can look after myself. I wasn't born with a crapload of money and he's promised me two million pounds. My mother tried to sell me last year, but I didn't like the guy. He stank. So I ran away."

I left it there. I washed my hands of Manon. She was as twisted and jaded as her mother. And that absent father of hers sounded like a violent pig.

I stepped outside and looked for Carson.

That steamy scene by the pool, and how he'd pressed his enormous bulge against me, dry-fucking me while crushing my lips with his hot, hungry mouth, proved he felt something for me.

CHAPTER 8

Carson

COLLETTE LEANED CLOSE, DROWNING me in heavy perfume. "Why don't we have a dance? I like this song."

Even my third beer couldn't help wipe Savanah and that kiss from my mind and dick. If I could wind back the clock, I would take it back to that hot smooch.

I kept eyeing her off as she chatted with some guy with ruffled hair, wearing a green jacket and reeking of wealth. Although I tried not to make this sudden obsession obvious, her eyes kept finding mine. Like she was waiting for me to look.

All I wanted was Savanah, especially after feeling her sexy body pressing against mine. But somehow a bouncy, flirty blonde attached herself to me.

It had been a while since I felt a woman's body. Only Collette wasn't the woman I craved.

After seeing Savanah up that ladder, my cock refused to go limp. I had to hang my shirt over my jeans. To make matters worse, I saw more than just her curvy ass. I also glimpsed at her hair-free pussy, and now all I could think of was having a taste. Or more like a fucking banquet. She'd made my dick restless. Starved for pussy. Only I wanted her pussy, not some stranger's.

"Come on, then." Collette pulled on my hand.

I snapped out of the sexual fantasy playing havoc with my libido and followed Collette to the dance floor. I turned, and Savanah's eyes met mine with a question.

It was a party. People danced. I didn't normally. But I needed something to take my mind off the fantasy rolling on in my head of Savanah, naked, and sliding over my cock. I just hoped Collette wouldn't grind against me. She'd get the wrong impression since my dick demanded attention.

A DJ had taken over from the band. I'd been told that normally the parties went into the early hours, and being midnight, the ballroom had converted into a nightclub. At least I wasn't working the door, turning away packs of prowling males.

I liked James Brown, so I found it easy to groove along to the beat. Collette shimmied her shoulders, her tits close to spilling out of that low-cut dress.

I preferred mystery myself.

Collette turned her back to me and practically rubbed her butt on my groin. I took a step back just as Savanah joined the dance floor with her good-looking rich boy. She swayed and twirled teasingly to the thumping beat.

If only I could have swapped partners, but reluctant to offend Collette, I kept some distance from her gyrating body. Instead, I ogled Savanah, whose smooth, undulating moves won her the first prize for dancing.

Having had enough to drink, I dropped the modesty act and made my move, dancing up close to Savanah. Her dance mate gave me a strange look, as did Collette, especially when I took Savanah's hand.

She gave me a puzzled smirk as I led her away to the other side of the room.

"Hey, that was cheeky," she yelled over the music.

"I didn't like the way he looked at you."

She stopped dancing, and her eyes widened. No more shocked than me. Acting like a tomcat was not my style. But Savanah was not like any woman I'd ever known. And by that, I didn't mean her wealth. If anything, I found that aspect a big turnoff.

I stood so close that our noses nearly touched. With those provocative, serpentine moves, she had me imagining her gyrating and bouncing naked all over me.

Taking her soft hand, I led her out of the ballroom.

By this stage of the night, everyone was drunk, lost in deep conversation in some corner of that enormous mansion, or outside doing weed and chasing each other around like children.

Savanah giggled. "Where are you taking me?" Her hand in mine triggered electrical sparks through me. Now, that was a new sensation. Never had that before from just holding a girl's hand.

"Somewhere dark and away from sleazy old men and young girls."

She stopped walking. "Then this isn't the right path. Because there will be a few of those lurking in those wee bushes."

Her Irish accent made me laugh.

"Let's go around the back of the hall, and I will show you the rest of the house if you like."

"That sounds good." I smiled.

We walked in silence along the pathway and past a table of drinking and smoking staff. Savanah waved to them. "Have one on me. It's been a big night."

They all cheered.

I liked how that family treated their workers. They paid well, and I hadn't noticed that snooty attitude often associated with the wealthy and their subordinates.

"Are you always this generous with your staff?"

"Why not? They work their butts off. We're a demanding lot."

I stopped walking and drew her against me. "I've noticed." As my lips hovered over her mouth, her warm breath tickled my cheek, and my pulse pumped.

Our mouths crushed and then whistles came our way. I pulled out of her arms and saw a pair sharing a spliff.

"There seem to be more people outside."

She giggled. "Our parties are famous for lasting till the morning. Sometimes all weekend."

"Your mother doesn't mind? Aren't there fights with drunks and whatnot?"

"There's always security around, and Declan normally hangs in here too."

"I thought he'd go home and sleep."

"They stay here."

"And the noise doesn't keep everyone awake?"

"The upstairs sleeping quarters are cordoned off. The rooms all lock, and the walls are so thick you can't hear from one room to another."

Her eyes danced flirtatiously.

"That's good to know because I want you screaming my name before night's end."

"You better not make a promise you can't keep." Although it was dark, under the dim lanterns that lit the cobbled path, I noticed her eyes turn mysterious. I couldn't tell if she was being serious or playing with me.

"Call me old-fashioned, but I like to initiate."

She paused, and her full lips curled up at one end while she scrutinized me. "Then you won't like it when I do this." Her hand touched my cock, and it thickened immediately, engorged and ready to pounce, especially after that glimpse of her naked pussy earlier.

"Mm... My god, Carson."

I grimaced. "That ladder episode has stayed with me."

"Tell me, what did you see?" She tilted her pretty face, and her rosebud lips twisted into a teasing grin.

"Your pretty pussy. All fucking naked."

"Mm... Did it make you hot?" She rubbed my dick again, causing it to throb.

"What do you think?" I grabbed her wrist and moved her hand. "Not yet. Not here."

We entered through a side door and climbed some stairs.

"This is the servants' access." She stopped walking and looked up at me. "Knowing how private you are."

"Although I am private, I imagine you'd want to keep this between us."

She shrugged. "I don't mind who knows."

"You don't mind people knowing that I'm going to fuck your brains out?"

"Better not make promises you can't keep." She ran her tongue over her lips, and I pushed her gently against the wall.

As I slid my hands up her toned legs, I went to kiss her when I stopped.

Frowning, she watched me pull out a hanky. "What are you doing?"

I wiped her lips, rubbed my thumb over them, and kissed her. "Mm... That's better."

We leaned against the stairs and again I fell into a sexy dream. Her soft, moist lips met mine, and our tongues tangled.

On hearing a voice in the distance, we separated.

"You don't like makeup?" she asked as we continued down a long hallway filled with old-fashioned portraits.

"It looks great on you. Anything would, really." I bathed in her smile. "But I prefer the taste of naked lips and skin."

"At least I don't believe in fake tan products, so you're safe there."

I hissed. "Not a fan."

"You sound very experienced."

"No more than you, from what I've observed."

"Hey. What are you implying?" She placed her hands on her hips, and I pulled her into my arms before she could say another word.

My body pressed firmly against hers as she melted into my arms. I took her face in both hands and tilted her head back, and I lost myself in her soft, succulent lips.

Her hips and tits pressed against me, and my heart sped in anticipation of her twisting and moaning, naked and sweaty, against me.

Sensing someone in the distance, I had to drag myself away from her again.

"Let's get to that bedroom, shall we?" Impatient to see her naked, I led her by the hand. "They're a cheery bunch." I pointed at the somber faces on the wall.

"They're the Lovechildes going back a few hundred years. They're not a cheerful bunch at all." She chuckled.

"Is there a painting of you?" If not, she needed one. With that smudging eyeliner making her eyes all sultry and deep, her rosy pout and milky skin, Savanah made the perfect art subject.

She grabbed a key out of a vase and opened her door. "There's a portrait somewhere. I hated it so much I had it relegated to one of the rarely visited sitting rooms."

Turning on the light, she signaled for me to enter the salmon-pink walled room that smelt of roses.

"I can't imagine a painting of you being anything but beautiful." I stared into her stunning blue eyes that normally wore a teasing gleam, only now they shone with a hint of vulnerability, just like the night I found her cut on a London pavement. That lost girl's expression made sense in line with her ordeal, but not here in the safety of her comfortable life.

"Is anything the matter?"

She looked up at me, wide-eyed and reminding me more of a girl than a woman. Shaking her head, she bit her lip.

Enough talk. I took her into my arms, and our kiss went from tender to devouring in a matter of seconds.

Although I'd always loved women's lips and how they felt on my mouth and cock, Savanah's sexy mouth, a combination of raw sex and silky sensuality, was from another universe entirely.

Unzipping her dress, I slid it off her curves, leaving her in a clingy petticoat.

I had to step away so that I could look at her. "You're beautiful." I dipped my finger between the line of her cleavage, and her nipples spiked through the smooth fabric.

She looked up at me. Her cheeks flushed and her eyes shone with a hint of suggestion. "I took off my suspenders, I'm afraid. They were digging into me. Next time." Her eyebrow raised. "I mean..." She bit her lip and again revealed insecurity. Where was that super confident, swing-through-life girl?

I brushed a loose tendril away from her cheek. "You're not the kind of woman I can only taste once."

I pushed her onto the bed and ran my hands over her breasts, which fit perfectly in my hand. Her nipples pricked my palms and made me salivate.

I slipped down the thin strap of her tiny lace bra and palmed her breasts before sucking on her nipple. She moaned sweetly, and I grew rock-hard.

She unzipped my jeans and freed my aching dick, ran her finger over the throbbing veins one by one, tormenting me. Moving her hand, I had to stop her. I was on fire.

Just as I went to remove her petticoat, Savanah sprang up. "Wait. I need to turn the light off."

Before I could protest, since I wanted to feast on all of her, the room went dark.

"There's no need to be bashful, Savanah. You've got a fucking hot body."

She turned on a cute ballerina lamp which made me smile.

At least the dim light enabled me to see her womanly form with those long, slender legs that I dreamed of wrapping around my neck.

I helped her wiggle out of her petticoat and trailed kisses along her soft thighs, licking all the way until I landed on her clit.

She flinched, but I held onto that soft, toned ass and ran my tongue over her bud.

I wrapped her legs around my shoulders and gorged on her like a man starved of pussy for way too long. Maintaining a soft lapping motion, I sucked and teased. Her breathy moans told me I'd found the right pressure.

Her flavor turned my cock blue. As I sucked and lapped her up like a creamy treat, her legs trembled against my shoulders.

"Oh my god," she groaned and dug her nails into my arms, making for nice pain.

Arching her pelvis, she nearly swallowed my tongue and squirted her orgasm to the back of my throat. Talk about hot.

My heart raced at how her tight, slick pussy squeezed onto my finger. "I need to be inside you. We'll just have to take this slowly. I don't want to hurt you."

"Please..." she whimpered. "Hurt me."

Although that response raised my eyebrows, my dick was about to erupt. I'd never wanted to come that badly from eating pussy before, especially after I ran my tongue over my lips and tasted her cum.

I jumped off the bed.

"Where are you going?"

I soaked in the erotic vision before me. Savanah lay on the bed, legs still apart, her inner thighs glistening with juice and her lips parted. Scratching my jaw, I could barely speak. "To get a condom."

"I'm on the pill. No need."

I rubbed my head. "Um... Aren't you fucking around?" I hated this kind of discussion, especially in the heat of the moment.

"I had recent tests."

"I'm clean too. I haven't fucked for a few months and..."

Pulling me down onto the bed, she took my cock into her hand and ran her tongue over her lips. Before I could stop her, she had that sexy pout wrapped around my cock.

"Mm..." came out of her, like she was eating something delicious.

All the blood in my body raced down to my shaft as a burning need to blow beckoned.

I removed my dick from her mouth with great reluctance. She didn't just kiss like a fucking goddess; her lips knew exactly what I liked.

"I want that tight little pussy creaming all over my cock."

I parted her thighs and then entered her slowly, her pussy gripping onto the head of my cock like a vise.

In an agonizing, slow circular motion, my dick battled through constricted muscles, opening her up little by little and setting off a fierce ache so pleasurable it was close to unbearable.

Grinding slowly, I had to think of anything but how insanely hot she felt to avoid exploding.

A desire to thrust hard swept through me, but unwilling to bruise her, I took a deep breath instead. I rocked my hips against hers, stretching her pussy open, almost feeling like it would rip open. The deeper I inched into her, the more I wanted to blow.

We moved in and out like we were driven by some primitive sexual hunger, and her moans grew louder, more desperate.

"Am I hurting you?" I had to ask because she sounded in pain.

"Yes. Divinely so. You're really fucking big. Oh my god."

I paused for a moment.

"Don't stop." She clutched onto my arse and pushed me into her deeply.

She spread her legs so wide, I would have paid a fortune for that image. "You're very flexible."

"I did ballet for fifteen years."

"That explains these beautiful legs." As I continued to pump into her, I squeezed her curvy butt. "I want you to cream all over my cock. I need you to come. Like now."

My breathing turned ragged as we built up a rhythm. The intensity of friction seemed to ignite sparks. Our pelvises rubbed together as she clutched onto me, our slick bodies pressed tightly together.

I'd never experienced this kind of heat.

I looked into her eyes and then tasted her lips as her pussy clung to my cock.

She groaned into my mouth, and my deepening thrusts intensified to make her go all the way. "I need you to come," I repeated.

Unable to hold back, I let go. My head exploded. And a galaxy of stars along with it.

She screamed, writhing in my arms as we drowned in our orgasms.

I'd experienced no one like her, and I'd fucked a lot in my life.

This was something else. Savanah was something else.

CHAPTER 9

Savanah

IT FELT LIKE HEAVEN in his arms as he kissed every inch of my body. His mounded chest tasted like salt as he caressed the contours of my hips and stroked my hair.

I'd never experienced this kind of passion before. The way he devoured me all over. When he thrust into me, his eyes held mine, taking me somewhere deep. He seemed to fuck with his entire soul. It was raw and primal between us, but also tender and caring.

As he kept stroking me, I could have just stayed in his arms forever. His warm, strong body made me feel safe. Every time I closed my eyes, I found myself under the sun in a field of flowers, dancing like an innocent child.

Although I was anything but that. Carson had removed my armor and stripped me naked, leaving me giddy and overwhelmed and all the emotions in between.

I think I might have just fallen in love.

A few tears slid down my cheek after I came and, hoping he didn't notice, I nestled into his neck. I seemed to be drowning in emotion. The last thing I wanted was to frighten him by acting all weepy. Of course, not helped by Bram being on my trail, which had turned me into a nervous wreck.

"That was insane," I said at last.

"For me too." His deep voice penetrated my ear, which rested on his chest. "You came? I felt you. Yes?"

Is that need in his voice?

A smile the size of the sun grew on my face.

He kept stroking me. His feathery touches made me want to lie there forever.

"How is it you haven't fucked for so long?" I asked. "You have a reputation for being a player, I'd heard, and Collette was virtually fucking you on the dance floor."

"I've grown up. Sex is no longer a sport."

"You weren't exactly showing that much interest in me."

"That kiss by the pool?" He lifted his head from the pillow to see me properly.

"It was nice. It was hot. I felt you." An ache returned in my sex. "I guess I'm referring to the fact that you stormed off."

"Let's forget about that, will we?"

Happy to. Didn't need Manon in this conversation. It was bad enough that she'd crashed my moment of passion.

"Seeing you up that ladder was pretty hot. I almost visited a bathroom to finish myself off."

I giggled. "What stopped you?"

"It didn't seem right. I was a guest."

I laughed. "I'm sure you wouldn't have been the first."

I rolled onto him, and his lips ate away at mine.

Burning need swept through me again, thinking of that gorgeous fat cock growing in my mouth.

I slithered down the bed, and he was already semi-erect. "All this talk about seeing my naked butt has made you hard again."

"Oh, Savanah." He sighed as my mouth moved up and down his veiny shaft.

It didn't take long for him to grow rock-hard and for my jaw to ache. I'd never had such a big dick in my mouth before.

He stroked my throbbing clit as I sucked and licked his cock, loving how hard and velvety it felt in my widened, salivary mouth.

He pulled his dick out, and I frowned. "You didn't like that?"

"Quite the opposite. I want to blow inside of you, not in your mouth."

My breasts felt heavy, and my nipples tightened with arousal, dragging against his chest as he slid slowly back into me.

I wrapped my legs around him and clawed at his arms as he drove himself into me, and before I could say "Fuck me," I rode him on top, taking every inch and filled to bursting. My legs closed around his waist, and my hands roamed over his chest and muscular arms, clinging to his body.

I MIGHT HAVE GOTTEN an hour of sleep when I woke to his cock growing hard against my ass, and his arms wrapped around me.

Stretching me to the limit, he filled me so deeply my dry throat, raw from fucking all night, rasped for air. His penis throbbed inside me, nearly splitting me open. I writhed and bucked, clutching him tightly with my pulsating muscles.

We moved as one, with his dick sliding in and out, creating that divine friction. Being half-asleep, it felt like a sexy dream. The deeper his girth inched into me, the more addictive he became.

Building and building to that big bang moment, he angled his cock in ways that sent me flying. My neck was damp from his heavy breathing, while nerve endings fired off until the sparks turned into a blaze, and a thunderous climax sent me flying. Hovering on the edge of consciousness, we fucked until my head swam with euphoria and cum gushed out of me.

After I finally found sanity, I rolled over and laughed. "Well, I think that's a record for me."

His handsome face scrunched. "How so?"

"I've never fucked that often in one night, nor come as much."

His sleepy eyes melted into mine as a smile grew on his handsome face. "We share that. I haven't fucked this much either. You're just impossible to leave alone. You're sexy and feminine and fragile..."

"Fragile?" I had to ask.

"I'm not sure where that came from." He rubbed his head and gave me an awkward, bordering-on-shy smile.

Mm... Am I that transparent?

Given my fear of Bram and the sex tape that had arrived the morning of the party, angst must have been written all over me.

I held his gaze, hunting for more detail, but Carson reverted to his man-of-few-words role.

Okay, I could do that. It was morning and maybe a little too soon for dissecting that loaded comment.

I removed myself from his arms and rose.

Parched, I was desperate for water.

After I grabbed a bottle of water from a small fridge in an adjoining chamber, I walked to the bed naked, and his eyes darkened with lust again.

What a sight he made with his legs slightly apart and his cock thickening.

Again?

"Did someone slip you some Viagra?" I asked, pointing at his enormous erection.

"Yeah." His sexy half-smile grew.

My brow pinched. "Really?"

"You're pure fucking Viagra, Savanah."

As I passed him a bottle of water, he took hold of my hand and studied my arm.

"What the hell?" His going from playful to intense jarred.

I'd forgotten about the bruises I'd been so careful to hide. Carson had helped me forget Bram knocking me around. At least he didn't hit me in the face. Bram wasn't so silly to give me a black eye.

I pulled my arm away and tucked it behind my back. As if that would change anything. He'd now seen me exposed.

I'd kept his attack to myself. Bram would have come after me, and that sex tape would destroy me.

"Who did that to you?" he asked.

"Umm... I just knocked it."

"That's bullshit. Tell me," he demanded.

"Look, Carson, please. Don't get involved."

"Is it that guy who you were hiding from at Cirque?"

I nodded slowly. "He's promised to stay away." My voice cracked. The sex, or the lovemaking as Carson called it, had opened me up.

He took me into his arms and rocked me, and then the tears just sprang out of me like a burst faucet.

"You do realize I'm going to have to fix him, don't you?" he said.

CHAPTER 10

Carson

As the door opened, piano music floated through the air, and I was greeted by a woman I'd never met. "Hi, I'm Carson, here to see Declan. He's expecting me."

She directed me inside where Theadora, on seeing me, stopped playing and welcomed me with a smile. "Carson, how are you?"

Partitioned by screens, the stylish room reminded me of a movie set with its tasteful combination of antiques and modern art.

"That sounded nice," I said.

"I'm learning a new piece." She smiled. "Can I offer tea or something? Declan's upstairs."

"I'm good." I noticed a winding iron staircase. "You've had a floor added."

"It was that or move. We like it here too much. And now we've got a superb view of the sea. I'll take you up."

"I can just go up. Don't stop playing on my account."

"I need a break. And I want to make sure Declan isn't letting Julian stare at a screen." She rolled her eyes. "He's too much of a softy with our son."

I smiled. "Dylan's pretty cute. Difficult to resist, I imagine."

She nodded slowly with a chuckle. "Oh yeah. Some days he runs the show, and he's only fourteen months."

Ascending the stairs, I entered an enormous open space with surrounding windows where an all-encompassing view of endless sky and white cliffs being pounded by the ocean dominated. I would never have gotten off the leather recliner had I lived there.

"It's spectacular." I stood by the wall of windows. "Who needs to watch a television when you've got all of this?" I pointed at the blue sky where a V-shape of seabirds glided past.

"I know that's me some days. I love to sit and daydream," Theadora said.

"Sounds healthy." I remained transfixed by the ocean's turbulence.

"And lazy."

"For someone who plays the piano so effortlessly, I wouldn't exactly think of you as slack."

She smiled sweetly. "That's nice of you."

Declan entered, carrying his son. "Carson."

"Hey." I touched the warm, puffy cheek of that stunning, blue-eyed toddler. Sucking on his thumb, he returned an adorable shy smile.

Whenever I visited Declan and his family, my heart always grew.

I'd never really given fatherhood much thought, but Declan's bliss was contagious. After a session with my former army comrade, I always left optimistic about life.

I used to fall into a dark hole when thrown into the company of cheery families. I'd since moved on from that negativity. On a deeper level, I'd just resigned myself to never marrying or having kids. Declan and Theadora, however, made having a fulfilling marriage look easy. Appealing even. Which made my goal of becoming that solitary man who just rolled with life look rather sad and gutless.

Savanah crept into my thoughts.

Where did that come from?

One night. That's all it had been.

So why can't I stop thinking about her?

"Julian's looking more like you every day," I said to Declan.

He lowered his son, who, like one of those motorized toys, waddled about, moving in all different directions.

"He's energetic," I said.

"He's that and more." Declan chuckled.

Theadora took Julian by his tiny hand. "Come on, Jules. We'll go down and make some fairy bread."

He wrapped his little arms around his mother's legs, and I couldn't stop smiling. If ever I needed a poster for domestic harmony, I'd found that in Declan and Theadora's home.

After mother and child left, I settled onto a leather sofa, crossed my legs, and stretched out my arms. One could take up lots of space in that room.

"Your mother has asked me to head security for the casino. I thought I'd run it by you."

"That doesn't surprise me." He raked his fingers through his hair.

"You sound pissed off."

He sighed and walked over to the window. "Ethan and I are pretty pissed off about it." He shook his head. "A fucking casino. Can you imagine?"

I shrugged. "A classy place that facilitates money laundering. But hey, I'm sure it will attract a decent clientele."

"Not with Crisp behind it."

I revisited that ugly and intrusive moment with him and a girl young enough to be his granddaughter. Manon wasn't exactly playing the role of a shrinking violet, either.

"About Reboot," he said. "I was hoping you might consider the role of CEO again."

"That sounds like a big role. I mean, I was fine with the lads, but with the commercial side of things, I wouldn't know where to start."

"I have nothing but faith in you. I just need you to make sure the operation runs smoothly by appointing the right staff and overseeing the budget. You're the captain of the ship, so to speak. Name your price, and the gig's yours."

"I'd be taking over from you, then?"

He nodded. "I'd like to focus on the organic farm and market, and I'm also about to volunteer for Air rescue. Love the idea of flying and helping where I can." He pulled a tight smile.

"Theadora okay with that?"

"She wasn't exactly jumping for joy when I told her."

"You'd risk all of this? And you've got a family. Those light aircraft can be rather dangerous."

"I've volunteered my plane, which is well maintained, and I'll avoid electrical storms, and only if they're down on pilots."

That new role would help me save for an apartment, I thought. "Sure. I can do it. Thanks for thinking of me."

"You were there from the start. You were always going to be my first choice." He fiddled with a telescope.

"That's a pretty big lens," I said.

"You can see the rings of Saturn on a clear night."

I smiled. Declan was a big kid at heart. That's why I liked him. One always forgot he was a billionaire except for when he was dishing out the cash.

"I guess that means no moonlighting as head of security for the casino, then?"

He wiped the telescope lens. "It's a night gig. If you're up to it, I won't stop you." He looked at me. "Do you need the extra work?"

"I could use the dough, for sure. I'd like to get into my own place and clear a few bills."

"You know that I'm always here if you need money," he said.

"Thanks, mate. I'm right." I smiled tightly. Declan's generosity had always blown me away. "I'll offer my services to your mother for the next month or two and see how things travel. Perhaps I can teach Drake the ropes, and he can become my assistant."

Declan nodded. "I think he'll like that. He's focused on getting ahead. Have a chat with him."

I rose. "Off to see your mother." I paused. "What do you know of Bram, Savanah's ex?"

"He's fucking trouble." He shook his head, looking like a worried brother.

"Have you met him?" A knot formed in my chest. I wanted that thug's head on a platter. Not just because of this burning need to make

Savanah safe, but because men who beat women needed their balls chopped off. At the very least.

"We went out for Savvie's birthday to catch his band in London. I'm told he also writes poetry." He rolled his eyes. "He's nothing but a junkie. When I met him, he was off his face."

"What's he play?"

"He's a singer. The music's hard to define. According to Theadora, he sang unbearably out of tune. I agreed with that." He chuckled dryly. "She also described him as a Peter Doherty wannabe."

"Who's he?"

"Oh, some guy who dated supermodels and made taking drugs a fashion statement." He sniffed.

"I saw bruises on your sister's arms. I also helped her hide from him at a club I was working at."

He frowned. "Did she show you?"

I shuffled on the spot. "Um. I noticed it. She was trying to hide it."

"Why didn't she come to us, I wonder?" Declan muttered, looking like the worried brother. "Ethan's having him investigated, and we've got someone on his trail in the hope of catching him buying drugs. That way we can get the prick locked away."

"That's a plan, I guess. But for now, he's stalking her."

His brow creased. "She told you?"

I squirmed. The look of surprise on Declan's face wasn't lost on me.

Should I tell him now that I'm smitten with his sister?

I held back on that. Mainly because I wasn't sure what Savanah wanted. I couldn't tell whether our night of passionate sex was just her venting her vixen act on me or something deeper.

Her head on my chest, with her body all curled up against mine, kept invading my thoughts, however. I'd also been walking around with a hard-on, thinking about how she felt, and I was smiling more often.

It wasn't just fucking, though. Having someone to hold and touch felt just as nice.

"She's told me something but hasn't gone into detail."

"I'll have to convince her to lay charges then." Declan rubbed the back of his head.

"She doesn't want to. I've already suggested that." I recalled the frightened look on Savanah's face. Bram obviously had something over her.

"What about his father, the lord?" I asked. "He wouldn't want his son harming the family's reputation."

He laughed. "It's de rigueur in this scene. Drugged-out kids of the gentry are as common as drunken louts at a Man U. game."

"So how did you get it so right?"

"I went off-course for a while. No drugs, though. Ethan faired worst. He had his cocaine and sex addiction. I was more into fast cars, planes, and unwinnable wars."

I nodded slowly. "You've never flaunted your wealth. You were always one of us."

"That means a lot." He smiled. "It wasn't until I fell in love with my beautiful wife that everything fell into place. Same for Ethan. We're both happy and in love. I would give all this away in a blink if I had to choose between Theadora and the comforts of wealth."

Did I want that?

Maybe.

I needed it to be simple, but could my dick do simple?

Savanah and her moaning in my mouth as I entered her filled my thoughts. That was pure, unadulterated lust. Nothing more. And we were like chalk and cheese.

As we headed back downstairs, I said, "I like what you've done to this place."

Little Julian scampered over. "Dadda. Dadda." He held a model plane and was about to throw it when Declan removed it from his hand.

"How did you get ahold of that?" he asked.

The maid came running out. "I'm so sorry, Declan. I was cleaning it."

Theadora brought out a pot of tea. "He loves that plane."

"I made that in grade six." Declan removed the wooden plane from his little son's hands.

Declan shook his head and smiled. "He wants what he can't have."

"Welcome to being human." I chuckled. "On that philosophical note, I bid you all farewell."

"Are you going to Salon Soir's opening?" Theadora asked as they walked me to the door with Julian following along making cute gurgling sounds.

"The casino's having an opening tomorrow," Declan added.

I nodded. "Your mother asked me to work as security."

"You can't. You should just enjoy the night," Theadora said. "There'll be lots of pretty girls." She virtually winked at Declan.

My head jerked back. "Am I giving off some kind of lonely vibe here?"

She chuckled. "No. But a girlfriend wouldn't hurt."

"In that scene? My bank account's not exactly up for brunch at Harrods."

Declan patted my back. "Theadora wants everyone loved up. She enjoys wearing pretty gowns and having any excuse for a wedding or a party. Right?" He drew her in tight and placed a lingering kiss on her cheek.

"Talking of looking pretty, I'll have to hire a suit then, I guess," I said.

Theadora giggled. "You're far from pretty, Carson."

Smiling, I kissed her cheek and waved goodbye.

Protecting Savanah from Bram, and how I'd like her naked, gyrating over me again, entered my thoughts as I walked back to Reboot.

THE SCENT OF PERFUME and cologne wafted thick through the air. There was no shortage of exposed skin on show, while the men mainly wore tuxedos. Some were clad in waistcoats, and others wore white dinner jackets. All in all, suitably swanky as they poured through the doors into the new casino.

My jacket felt strapped on. I'd allowed the girl to talk me into a snug fit. According to her, women liked their men in suits that showed off their muscles. Not that I was on a mission to pick up. Too complicated in that wealthy scene. Besides, there was only one woman I had the hots for, and that presented all kinds of issues.

Working as security, Drake stood at the door, but instead of a cross-armed stance and stony face, he was all smiles because of Manon. Wearing a tiny dress that left nothing to the imagination, it seemed she had him eating out of her palm. His eyes filled with stars while she giggled and flirted.

I needed to remind him that security work meant looking tough the whole time and not dropping your guard. Even if a pretty girl offered to show her tits or blow you.

Spoken from experience. In my early days out of the army, I'd done just that and lost a few jobs, thanks to a raging libido.

"Hey, big man." Drake smiled.

"Hey." I nodded at him and then Manon, who looked me up and down with a smirk.

"It's quite a place." I pointed at the rock-walled façade lit by a changing color light show. The design blended so well with Elysium to appear as though both establishments were connected. I couldn't have imagined Caroline Lovechilde approving of that. One of a few mysteries surrounding that family. I just couldn't understand her affiliating with someone like Crisp. I'd met a few snakes in my life, and he would have been right at home among those slippery characters.

"So, look, um..." I turned to Manon. "Can you give us a minute?"

She shrugged like a teenager being told not to smoke and then sashayed off.

"Fuck, she does my head in," he admitted.

"She's seriously out there." I referred to her skimpy gear, which was composed of fabric barely covering her nipples and arse.

"Tell me about it." The twenty-year-old sounded tortured.

I sniffed at his grimace. "Are you sleeping with her?"

"I wish. She just offered to go down on me the other night. Then that old, red-headed dickhead dragged her away."

"Best not get involved there. He's your boss."

"Mrs. Lovechilde employed me." His mouth lifted at one end. "I mean, you employed me too."

"About that." I took a breath. It wasn't much fun giving orders.

I was about to speak when, in the distance, Savanah tottered along in super high heels, while, close behind, wearing a bright-blue velvet suit with messed-up hair, Bram strutted along, looking half-asleep.

I noticed Savanah's hand behind her back holding onto his, as though trying to hide him.

What the fuck.

A knot curled in my stomach. We'd only met yesterday for some hard, raunchy sex.

Maybe that's all it was for her. She wanted my body. My dick. She couldn't take it out of her mouth or stop touching it.

"You were saying?" Drake snapped me out of that sexy thought.

"You need to stay on guard. No flirting. Pull on the tough-guy look. Think of what you might do to some arsehole if he were to hurt your mum. That kind of attitude."

He sniffed. "I'd fucking kill him."

"Maybe that's going far. But in this job, you're playing Mr. Tough Guy. You can't go all goo-ga over a chick. Even if she offers to blow you. Yeah?"

He nodded. "I'll work harder at ignoring Manon and her flirty chit-chat."

"Good idea. In any case, she's trouble." I stared straight into Savanah's heavily painted blue eyes as I spoke, and instead of grinning back, she looked stressed out.

Why is she holding that dick's hand?

She's meant to hate him.

Bram hooked his arm around her shoulders and leaned into her, making her lose her balance. I had to help steady her by taking her arm.

"Thanks, Carson." Her mouth trembled into a smile.

Is she also drugged?

"Hey." I looked from her to her date.

"This is Bram."

He grunted and pulled a cheesy grin. Sarcastic arsehole. I don't think he remembered my threatening him at Cirque.

He leaned and kissed her as though to claim her, while her panicked, wide eyes remained glued to my face.

After a tense pause, I said, "Oh well, should be fun. See you in there."

I needed a drink badly.

CHAPTER 11

Savanah

WITH ITS RED EMBOSSED wallpaper, black furnishings, and pink chandeliers, Salon Soir, reminiscent of a 19th-century bordello, was a little gauche for my tastes.

My chest tightened as I unclutched Bram's clammy hand, hoping he wouldn't notice.

Just when life had smiled on me, thanks to Carson and a couple of nights of unimaginable pleasure, Bram shattered my bliss, and *boom*, I came crashing down.

My reckless past had finally caught up with me. That sex tape sitting on my laptop came with an ultimatum—I was to parade as Bram's girlfriend and fuck him when he demanded.

Bram liked to hurt me whenever we fucked. As a virgin to tenderness, and thanks to Carson, I'd discovered the joys of fucking in all its shades of spice combined with endless soft caresses and deep kisses.

I couldn't stop staring at him in that tuxedo that clung to his manly body like I would if we were alone and naked. But it was more than just his hot body and our off-the-charts chemistry. He'd also inspired me to take a deeper look at myself.

Identifying as shallow, I was that girl who always ran a mile from self-reflection. Even just admitting that filled me with self-loathing, especially now that Bram had enslaved me.

What the fuck had I seen in him?

At least Bram didn't expect us to be exclusive. A small mercy. However, I sensed Carson wouldn't be one to share. I know I'd hate to share him.

"As a committed libertine, I don't believe in being shackled by monogamy," Bram announced, as though making that mission statement qualified him for a fucking badge of honor. Dick.

"This is the deal: we fuck when I'm in the mood and hang out together at family affairs, boring as they are. The best drugs come from our scene." He chuckled.

He might have been discussing travel arrangements or our dinner menu.

"But why?" I asked.

"Because I need to show my dear papa that I'm hanging out with the right girl."

Knowing I was fucked whichever way, I raided my mother's medicine cabinet for her stash of Xanax.

"Mm... all your regular bores." Bram looked around the circular room filled with green-felt tables and a dimly lit bar in the corner. "Let's have a spin of roulette, shall we?"

I could barely speak, especially with Carson and his questioning gaze burning into me from across the room. Being apart hurt. I wanted to be by his side, flirting, talking nonsense, getting tipsy, then going back to Merivale for more screechy sex.

The problem was that if Carson heard about my being blackmailed, he'd get involved, and Bram's father, known for heavy-handed tactics, might even have Carson killed.

All these crazed thoughts of doom and gloom ran through me as I stood among that noisy crowd. For now, I had to remain tight-lipped and paint a happy face.

How the fuck did I get myself into this predicament?

"Are you coming?" Bram asked, his dark eyes dilated and heavy-lidded.

"No, you go ahead. I'm not into roulette."

He yanked my arm, making me wobble, and as I looked over at Carson, he pulled a what-the-fuck frown. I returned a shaky smile, assuming he might intervene. My heart wanted so much for Carson to save me from this monster, but with that sex tape blocking my chance of happiness, I plastered on a fake smile instead.

"You're with me. All loved up. Cheering me on when I wipe their entitled little arses."

"Like yours, you mean?" I replied coldly.

His eyes narrowed, and then he burst out laughing. "You make me fucking hard when you give me cheek, bitch."

I rolled my eyes, sucked back a breath, and let him drag me over to the gaming table.

Crisp, Bram's father, and other guests sat around the table, stacking their chips.

"Evening, Daddy." Bram stood by his father. They even had the same beady eyes.

Meanwhile, I looked over at Carson, slid my eyes and tipped my head ever so slightly towards the powder room. I needed to speak to him, badly. At least to give him some kind of watered-down version of this latest drama.

Ethan swung by with his arm linked to Mirabel's. Wearing a green-and-white-polka-dot ruffled dress, she looked Spanish with a flower in her long, lustrous red hair.

"Are you performing?" I pecked her cheek.

"No. But I saw this at a vintage market and couldn't resist."

"You look gorgeous as always," I said.

Ethan had grown a beard, and every time I saw him, I couldn't help but giggle. "Hey, hipster brother."

He laughed. "My barber's missing me."

"I bet he is."

"Mother hates it, of course."

I chuckled. It was the lightest I'd felt all night. "Speaking of which, she's arrived with Carrington on her arm. They've become serious."

He nodded. "She's got stars in her eyes, all right."

"What do you know about him? Other than he's a writer?"

Ethan nodded a greeting at Kelvin, who stood out in a purple sparkly jacket.

"Kelvin's looking like a Christmas decoration again," he muttered, making Mirabel laugh.

"Mum's happy. That's the main thing," Ethan said. "Cary seems like a nice guy."

"Will was a nice guy, and look what happened there," I said.

Bram yelled out something, drawing everyone's attention over to the roulette. Always the performer, he downed a shot and clicked his fingers for the roaming server.

Humiliated, I wanted to hide under a rock.

"You're still seeing that dickhead?" Ethan asked.

I sighed. "It's a long, shitty story. I could use your help."

He was about to respond when Declan arrived with Theadora. She looked like a goddess, as always, in a red silk gown with a short train.

Carson met my gaze again. From the moment I arrived, we hadn't stopped stealing glances, which only intensified this pressing urge to talk to him.

A couple of babes joined Carson, giving him that, "Can we see what's inside those fitted slacks?" look.

I wanted to scream, "Stay away. He's mine." A painful sigh made my spirit deflate as I dug my nails into my palm.

I turned to my brothers. "I need to talk to both of you outside."

Declan looked concerned. He had good cause to be. This time, I'd made a mess of things.

"What's happened?" he asked.

"Just give me five minutes. I'll meet you both outside by the fountain." My mouth trembled slightly. I hated to have to tell them about the tape. Shame turned me to stone.

However, I don't know where I would have been without my brothers. Despite their critical attitudes towards my choice of boyfriends, they always supported me when things went bad.

As I headed to the powder room, Bram stumbled over. Already drunk, it seemed. "Where are you going? You should be with me, by my side, cheering me on. I'm fucking winning."

"I can hear you."

He laughed at my cool response. "Encouraging as always."

"I've got to go to the powder room, and Declan needs to see me about a family issue. Don't worry. I won't take off without telling you. Since I'm now chained to you."

"Ooh." He pulled a wicked smile. "I like the idea of that. We have the cellar at Benson Hall. A former dungeon, I'm told. That idea gives me a hard-on."

I wanted to puke. He'd become even more repulsive with those drugged, menacing eyes. And imprisoning me in a dungeon would be his kind of thing. Bram loved the macabre. He'd even spoken of an interest in Satanism. That's when I should have run. Instead, I found him refreshingly eccentric, and being the son of a lord helped. My mother would be happy for a change, given my predilection for darkish characters. If only she knew... Bram made my other, so-called commoner boyfriends look like teenagers who smuggled the odd bit of booze and smoked cigarettes.

I purposely took a long way around so that I could talk to Carson. He deserved some explanation. He'd even texted me last night. We'd been together for two nights in a row. Unable to stop touching each other. My sheets smelled of him. And then Bram sent me that sex tape along with an ultimatum, and I couldn't bring myself to answer Carson's text about meeting up after the party.

I would have given anything to fall into his arms and be just us together alone.

I didn't recognize the pair of blondes who were close to rubbing themselves all over him. Knowing how much he hated overly made-up girls gave me some hope.

But would he stray?

Just because we'd been inseparable for two nights didn't exactly make us a couple.

I thought of him gloriously naked in bed, his arms bulging with muscle. And his legs a little apart, making room for his enormous cock.

I leaned in to take him in my mouth when he asked me to remove my lipstick. I couldn't believe it. Normally, I would have given whoever did that the middle finger, but I was putty around him. He could have asked me to bungee jump off London Bridge, and I would have, which was major for someone who hated heights.

After I'd cleaned my face, upon his request, I felt so exposed I hid my face with my hands.

He moved my hands and stared into my eyes. "You're naturally beautiful, Savvie. Don't fucking forget it. You don't need that shit on your face. Now suck my dick."

I'd saluted the former soldier, got down on my knees, and ravaged him. Just as he then devoured me, turning me into a writhing, orgasmic wreck. It was like we were starving for each other.

The pleasant memory faded, and harsh reality came crashing back down as I crept over to him. My legs felt like wood.

On my approach, his attention moved away from the girl whispering in his ear, and his eyes burned into mine again.

"Hey, Carson." I grimaced and smiled meekly at the same time.

"I see you've brought your boyfriend." He cocked his head towards Bram, who banged on the table like a petulant brat. He yelled something and his father grabbed him by the arm and then looked over at me.

Shit. Lord Pike expects me to babysit his out-of-control son too?

"It's complicated. Can I see you later?" I bit my lip.

He cocked his head towards the gaming table. "But you're with him."

I released a deep sigh. I hoped Bram would flake out somewhere in a corner so that I could sneak off. Embarrassing as that would be. My mother was already giving me strange looks. Bram made my ex, Dusty, look like a volunteer for old people's homes.

This was bad.

I wanted to cry.

"It's not how it looks." Tears pricked my eyes and, before he could respond, I fled off to the powder room.

I found Theadora leaning into the mirror, painting her lips.

Unable to hold back the flood of tears, I fell onto the armchair and buried my head.

Theadora kneeled at my feet. "Hey, what's happened?"

Tears spewed out uncontrollably.

"I've got myself into a fucking predicament."

Her brow pinched, and she pulled up a chair and took hold of my hand. "What's happened?"

"I've just asked Ethan and Declan to meet me outside, only I'm ashamed to tell them what's happened to me." My voice trembled as I stifled a sob.

"If it would make things better, you can tell me. It won't leave this room."

Her understanding and gentle tone helped me calm down. Theadora had become a role model. That sister I'd never had. And someone I'd grown to love and respect.

"There's this sex tape." I knitted my fingers to stop them from shaking.

"Are you being blackmailed?"

I nodded. "It's what's on the tape that's freaking me out. It's so humiliating."

"Why don't you just pay him off?" She rose. "Come on, let's fix your face. And look, I'm sure Declan and Ethan won't force you to share all the details, but they will know what to do."

I sighed heavily and nodded. "I just hope they don't ask what's on the tape."

I had to tell someone, or I'd burst.

"Does it show footage of you having sex?" she asked delicately.

I tissued the mascara off my cheeks and fixed my eye makeup with my finger.

"I was at a party that had descended into an orgy of sorts. We'd all taken E's." I swallowed tightly. "I ended up in a bedroom with Bram, who seemed to take delight in watching me…" I stammered. Theadora was family and not Jacinta or Sienna, who loved talking about sex in all its shades of wantonness.

"So, with more than one man?"

Her delicate tone encouraged me. "Two men and a woman. She went down on me, while I blew one guy, and the other jerked off." I released the breath trapped in my chest. "No fucking detail spared."

Theadora looked justifiably shocked. "Who shot it?"

"Bram."

Her jaw dropped. "Ew."

I nodded. "He's pretty fucking sick."

"There's absolutely nothing that Declan can't solve," she said, leading me out by the hand.

"He's the family hero, all right. Ethan's pretty good too." I gulped back another lump.

We stepped out into the crowded room to find Bram yelling at the croupier. His father had to drag him outside.

"Oh, shit," I muttered.

Theadora returned a sad smile. "Hey, why don't we go through the back? That way, you don't have to interact with him."

"I'm so glad you're here, Thea." A smile quivered on my lips.

I followed her through the back, where a security guard opened the door for us to pass.

When I removed my shoes because of the hill before us, Theadora followed suit. I raised her train so that it wouldn't soil, and she grasped onto it.

Just my luck, as we arrived outside the front, we found Lord Pike tongue-lashing Bram, like he was berating an unruly child. Although cold comfort, I wasn't the only one his crazed son had embarrassed that night.

"Wait here," Theadora said, as we stood behind a tree.

I could see Bram turning around looking for someone. Probably me.

He lit a cigarette and perched himself against the fountain with a newly erected statue of Venus posing on a shell filled with coins. I'd thought that sculpture tacky, as did my mother. A friend of Crisp's designed it, which came as no surprise—taste took talent, not wealth.

I sent Theadora off to get my brothers so I could remain in hiding.

Crossing my arms, I leaned against the tree, wishing I could rewrite the past year. Keep Carson and get rid of everything else, including Manon taking up residence at Merivale.

They joined me, and Theadora held my hand.

"I can see your boyfriend's off his face and causing trouble. Drake's not sure whether or not to toss him out. I would've by now," Declan said.

"He's blackmailing me. I'm in trouble." I looked at Theadora for courage, and she squeezed my hand. "There's a sex tape."

Declan frowned. "If he wants money, that's easy enough."

I shook my head. "Not money. I'm to parade as his girlfriend."

"And be exclusive?" Ethan asked.

"Nope. He's into guys too. Maybe more so, I think." My face crumpled in dismay. With each word, the ugliness of the situation grew like a deadly tumor. "He's parading me as his girlfriend for his dad. Lord Pike wants Bram to marry money." I rolled my eyes. "You know our scene, the same predictable rubbish."

In the distance, Bram staggered about with a cigarette dangling from his mouth, accosting people with babble, and making a general nuisance of himself.

"So his father, who knows our family well, is lumping that piece of shit on you. On us?" Ethan asked with a hint of anger.

"Yep. That's about it."

"Lord Pike's known for gambling debts and womanizing. He's not exactly Mr. Nice Guy," Declan said.

"Runs in the family." I sighed.

"And you'll be a billionaire in your own right when you turn thirty, Savvie," Ethan said.

I sighed. "His dad wants my money, for sure. And Bram needs to keep up his stipend. His father's threatened to cut him off if he doesn't settle down. With me, it seems."

"That's not going to happen." Declan crossed his arms in defiance.

Knowing I wasn't alone in this struggle helped lift my spirit.

But I also needed Carson more than ever.

CHAPTER 12

Carson

BRAM ACTED LIKE A first-class dickhead. What was Savanah doing with him? Holding his hand, showing the world they were together.

But why did she keep looking like the sky was falling? Every fibre in my body screamed to rescue her from that idiot, but I couldn't. We were meant to be a secret.

Does she need saving? Or is it just some twisted game?

I couldn't believe she'd even turned up with him, especially after telling me how much she detested him, something I could relate to because Bram behaved like the drunken clowns I used to toss out of clubs.

Drake kept glancing over at me. I could see he wasn't sure whether to step in and do just that. When Bram first started acting up, Drake headed over to have a word with him, but then an older man, who I gathered was Bram's old man, stepped in, said something to Drake, and then dragged his son outside himself. Ten minutes later, Bram returned and again caused a stir.

I stepped out for some air and spied Savanah with her brothers and Theadora. They looked lost in conversation. Not in that playful, joking manner, either. Savanah gesticulated and shook her head over something. She had every reason to look worried. Her boyfriend was a fucking troublemaker.

Drake had returned to the entrance, and I went over to join him. "You're first big encounter."

He shook his head. "Nope. A while back, I had a run-in with Reynard Crisp at Merivale. I knocked him to the ground and am amazed he didn't get me blacklisted, since this is his place, I'm told."

"That was on my recommendation. And Crisp strikes me as thick-skinned. I'd say he's suffered a few blows. You can't get around with that kind of arrogance and expect to make lots of friends."

"I feel like roughing him up every time I see him sleazing onto Manon. She's too fucking young for him."

"Don't let her get to you." I glanced over at Savanah, who was waving her hands about while lost in discussion. "Anyway, I'm off." I tapped Drake's arm.

There were only so many champagnes I could knock back, not to mention pretty girls offering a night of fun. I just wasn't in the mood.

There was only one woman I wanted, and she'd arrived with the worst guy possible.

My phone beeped, and the message read: "I need to talk to you. I'm not really with Bram. Can we catch up?"

I responded: "I'm leaving. When? Where?"

The three balls bounced and then a response: "At mine, in say one hour?"

While reflecting on her request, I scratched my prickly jaw. How could I be alone with her and just talk?

One look at Savanah and I wouldn't be able to resist pressing that soft, supple body against mine. Taking a deep breath, I tapped: "Sure."

Too keyed up to go home, I headed over to the Mariner for a beer. The pub suited me better. All those rich, well-spoken people got on my nerves. Not one real person amongst them, other than the Lovechildes, who treated me as an equal.

AN HOUR LATER, I headed back to Merivale and entered through the back, where Savanah waited for me by the lit-up swimming pool, smoking and rocking her body.

"Hey." I joined her. "I thought you'd kicked the habit."

She puffed out smoke from the side of her mouth to avoid my face. "I did. But then drama kicked in."

I positioned myself in front of a raging fire in a rusty iron pit.

"Can I get you a drink?"

I stared at her tumbler and shook my head.

"I'm having a G and T." Her hand trembled slightly.

"Where's Pete Doherty's ugly younger brother?"

She giggled and then turned glum within a breath. "He's somewhere, I guess." She looked down and then lifted her eyes slowly to meet mine.

"Look, Savanah, I don't share."

"No." She puffed her cigarette in silence while fiddling with her glass. "I have to keep seeing him."

"Okay. So why am I here?" I warmed my hands over the fire. Although the night had a bite, it wasn't just the air turning me chilly.

She frowned. "Why are you being like this?"

"Like what?" I shrugged.

"You're not even going to fight for me?" Savanah raised her hands, and her bruised wrists caught my eye.

I took her hand. "What are these? I don't recall seeing those on you last night."

She pulled her hands away. "It's nothing."

"Bullshit." I sat down again. "Is he hurting you again?"

She bit her lip and refused to answer me.

"Tell me," I pressed.

"It's complicated." She sighed. "But hey, can't you stay with me tonight?" A flirty smile touched her lips.

Any other time, that breathy invitation would have seen our clothes in a heap on the ground and me ravaging her delicious pussy before she could say, "Come to bed."

Savanah was turning me inside out. I wanted her badly, but not like this. Not with her dating that fuckwit and not telling me why.

"I don't share, Savanah." I pointed at the dark marks on her wrist. "Tell me, did he do that?"

The glass quivering in her hand answered that question.

I puffed out a breath and rose again. "If you won't let me in, then there's no point in my being here."

"I'm only trying to protect you, Carson. Please believe me."

Her voice trembled, and my heart snapped. Overwhelmed by the need to hold her tight and kiss that pain away, I summoned military stoicism. Savanah would turn me into a cowering wimp if I didn't remain strong.

"I can look after myself, thank you very much. It looks like you're the one that needs protecting."

Seeing her looking so lost made it impossible to move. I couldn't leave when she was in that state.

I sat down again. "I'm not sure what I can do unless you let me in. Tell me what the fuck is happening. Why are you with him?"

"It's complicated. For now, I've got to be with him."

"Are you fucking him?"

She shook her head. "Not since I've been with you."

"Then why are you with him?"

Savanah lit another cigarette. "I can't tell you. Please don't ask again. I just want you here with me."

She touched my crotch, and my dick lengthened at the hint of her soft hand.

"It looks like you want to be here too." She gave me a teasing smile.

Looking into her eyes, I maintained a straight face. "I want you, yes. To fuck you over and over, but I don't share."

"We're not even in a relationship, Carson. And you looked pretty cosy with those supermodels earlier on."

"As you already know, I prefer my women down-to-earth." I shook my head in frustration. We were going around in circles, getting nowhere. While Savanah might have enjoyed playing games, I hated them.

"You're the one that turned up with a fucking date. And now this bullshit story of yours has me questioning whether you're with me for my dick while dating that waste of space for his title."

Her jaw dropped, and a huff escaped her parted lips. "Oh my god. That's so not true. I like you for more than your dick."

I opened out my palms. "Then why the hell are you putting yourself through this?" I pointed at her wrists. "He needs to be reported."

"It's a sticky situation that I'm trying to get out of. I hate him."

I had to move if only to place distance between us. Her rose perfume triggered memories of her moaning my name while coming into my mouth.

"I'm not the queasy kind. Not much shocks me. My instincts are to help, not judge. In saying that, I don't do complications either."

CHAPTER 13

Savanah

WHAT A CRAPPY NIGHT. I'd hardly slept, and then Bram called to demand we meet for lunch.

I never wanted to see him again.

I'd cried all night. I couldn't believe Carson walking away like that. But yet I also sympathised with him. I wouldn't want to share either.

On a deeper level, my heart warmed knowing that he cared. Cold comfort maybe, because if he didn't, he would have held me all night.

In reality, this deepening attachment to Carson had become so overpowering I'd become a shadow. My heart barely pumped, and I almost couldn't breathe without him.

While Bram demanded that we hang out in London, I needed to come up with some excuse to remain at Merivale, close to Carson.

Squirming at the thought of talking to Bram, I took a deep breath and made that call. "Um... I'm not well. Got a migraine."

"Take some drugs. I can shoot you up." He didn't even sound like he was joking.

"No. I don't want that. You're just stressing me out."

"You'll be more stressed out when I upload that footage to social media."

"How much?"

"You know my price, Savvie."

"I can double what your father pays you."

"As tempting as that sounds, I like having you around. You make me look good."

"Will your daddy whip you if you're not with someone like me?" I already knew that answer. Lord Pike was known for his heavy-handed tactics. The man was a brute.

"We blue bloods must stick together." He chuckled lazily.

"I've got to go," I said.

"Tomorrow. In London. Meet me at our regular. Yeah?"

I exhaled. "Okay."

Someone wake me out of this fucking nightmare.

In need of some advice, I headed over to Declan's house to speak to Theadora, since she knew of that disgusting sex tape in all its sordidness.

"I thought you'd be in London." Declan kissed my cheek.

"Not in the mood." I smiled tightly. "Just dropping in for a cup of tea with your darling wife and to cuddle Julian."

Just as I spoke, my nephew raced out and wrapped his little arms around Declan's leg. He was so cute that the angst I'd arrived with faded instantly, and I giggled for the first time in a while.

"Actually, there's something I need to tell you." Declan looked serious, and my mood reverted to its earlier gloom.

"Oh?" I followed him into the living room with the astounding leadlight windows.

"Mother's seeing that writer, I've just discovered."

My breath returned to normal. I was expecting something more dramatic, going on his darkish tone.

Theadora joined us and hugged me.

"Oh, is that all?" I sniffed. "They were just having breakfast by the pool when I left."

"He stayed the night?" Declan frowned.

I pulled a face. "They've been together since Ethan's birthday."

"Shit." He puffed.

I opened out my hands. "What's the issue? Mum's a grown-up. I'm sure she knows what she's doing."

"We just don't know this guy. And can you imagine a Lovelace with a Lovechilde? Just the surnames alone make me question this alliance."

I laughed. "You make it sound political. I think it's cute. Anyway, Mother's smiling. That's all that counts. And who says they're going to marry?"

"Our mother's a stickler for tradition."

"Whatever." I shrugged. "I like him."

Theadora popped Julian down in his little chair and positioned a laptop in front of him. She wore an apologetic smile. "It's his first time today."

Declan smiled lovingly at his wife before explaining, "When visitors come, we let him stare at screens. Otherwise, he runs wild."

"Oh, the joys of parenthood." I chuckled.

Declan stared down at his watch. "I've got to go."

He leaned in and kissed Theadora and then Julian, lost to the screen, peering at a flying pig.

After Declan left us, I turned to Theadora. "What am I going to do about the tape?"

"I'd involve the police."

"But then he'll show it around and I'll be ruined." I knitted my fingers. "I'd hate Carson to see it."

"If anyone will understand, it's Carson. He's the most nonjudgmental person I know. You shouldn't deny yourself a relationship that makes you happy."

I sighed. "I know. Only he'll see me differently." My voice cracked, and tears soaked my cheeks. I loved hearing Carson describe me as a goddess. Would he still see me like that on learning of that tape's content?

Theadora wore a sympathetic smile. "He's a good man. And he's besotted, by the sounds of it. I'm sure you can get through this."

"He doesn't want to be with me while I'm hanging out with Bram. Which is understandable, I guess."

"Then you must tell him. You don't want to lose him, do you?"

I shook my head emphatically.

I can't lose the best thing that's happened to me in a long time. If ever.

A<small>FTER LEAVING</small> T<small>HEADORA</small>, I walked back to Merivale, trying to figure out a way to tell Carson about the sex tape.

A car parked outside the gates of Merivale piqued my curiosity. When I got closer, I recognized Cary talking to a woman who looked upset. Unable to walk away, I snuck behind a tree and then caught them hugging.

My heart sank. This was not what I wanted for my mother. She'd been so cheery since meeting Cary. I'd even heard her singing, and my serious mother didn't normally even hum.

He kissed her on the cheek and then jumped out of the car. He even looked around before heading back to the hall.

I leaned against the tree, my heart racing.

Not another drama.

Not for my poor mother. I couldn't stand it. She'd been through so much. And while she might have jumped into this relationship a little hastily, as a passionate woman who'd fallen hard, I got it.

Instead of going inside to avoid running into Cary, who might then know he'd been spotted, I headed for the duck pond.

I sat on a wooden bench and sighed at a pair of stunning black swans. The pretty sight gave me a chance to pause for a moment and marvel at nature. As the elegant creatures slid effortlessly over the shimmering pond, I forgot about sex tapes and cheating partners.

Snapping back to reality, I pulled out my phone and called Ethan.

"Hey, Sav, what's up?"

"Are you at Merivale or London?"

"I'm about to fly to Paris. Lovechildes is about to launch. You will come to the party? You got the details?"

"I did."

"Don't sound so enthusiastic. Are you shitty about the designer?"

"How can I be? Pierre Justine is only the most sought-after in the industry. I'm not that silly. I'm on the board, after all."

He chuckled. "So what's up?"

"I just saw Cary in a car outside Merivale, cosying up to a woman."

"Right? He was there at the house?"

"He's been here since your birthday. He hasn't left."

"You're fucking kidding me. And you were going to tell me when?"

"You were at Salon's opening. Mum was there with him, looking all loved up. You couldn't have missed that."

"I didn't know they'd shacked up, though."

I exhaled. "So do I tell Mum? She has a right to know."

"Too right, she should know."

"I'm shit at this. I need someone to hold my hand. She's been through so much, and now this guy—who's made her happier than I've ever seen her—has got a fucking secret."

"They've all got secrets, Sav. Just how bad, is the question."

"True." I paused. "Maybe I'll wait until Declan's here. I'm off to London tomorrow and then Paris for the opening."

"Don't bring Bram, please."

"What can I do? He'll want to come. How can I get out of that?"

"Bring Carson. Employ him as your bodyguard. And in the meantime, let Declan deal with Lord Pike and see if he can get his son to remove the tape. Yep?"

That was the best plan I'd heard all day. Especially the bit about Carson as my bodyguard.

"That sounds good. I'll try to keep Paris a secret. Bram's the last person I want tagging along."

"We'll do some digging on Carrington. What's his surname again?"

"Lovelace." I tossed a pebble into the pond and watched the rippling circles grow.

"Shit. That's his surname? Like Linda?"

"Who's Linda?"

"Star of Deep Throat." He chuckled.

"That sounds salacious."

"It's a famous '70s porno. I'm sure they're unrelated."

On that crazy note, I bid him farewell and closed the call.

An image of me, wide-mouthed, taking Carson's big dick to the back of my throat, followed me back to the hall.

CHAPTER 14

Carson

SOMETHING TOLD ME THAT Caroline Lovechilde guarded her privacy as she might a guilty secret. Eye contact didn't seem to come easily to her, but when she did, one felt the full force of her intent. Most of the time, she'd steal the odd glance before returning her focus downwards. I'd seen that same cautious flicker in my mother's eyes. She'd also suffered at the hands of a monster.

Feeling edgy, I wondered if she knew about me and her daughter, whom I'd now reluctantly pushed away. I was already missing having Savanah's warm body wrapped around mine.

Caroline pointed at the chair facing the green leather-topped desk. "Take a seat, if you will."

Twirling a gold fountain pen, she looked down at her sharp red fingernails before raising her eyes to meet mine.

"I called you here for a couple of reasons. I need you to go to Salon Soir over the next couple of nights."

I nodded. "You want me to spy?"

"Yes." Her unblinking stare pierced. "It's come to my attention that there may be some nefarious activities at the back of the casino."

"Care to elaborate?" That cordoned-off room I'd seen at the opening came to mind. Ethan had joked at the time it was probably for sex parties.

Eyes down, she kept twirling her pen. "Drake relayed to me how he'd witnessed young girls entering through a door at the back."

I frowned. "You mean like a strip club or something?"

She swiveled her seat and stared out the window. I could see this wasn't a straightforward conversation. The same for me. It felt strange talking about anything of that smutty nature with Caroline Lovechilde, who, with that dignified manner, came across as straight-laced.

"What exactly did he tell you? I'm surprised he said nothing to me. I only just left him then, at Reboot."

"That's because I asked that it remain confidential." She turned to face me again. "He kept his word, which is a good sign. I need to know I can trust those I employ."

"Agreed." I took a breath. "So, what exactly did he tell you?"

"He heard a girl scream, and when he went to investigate, he spied a very young girl crying in Manon's arms, who then coaxed the distressed girl back inside."

"By back inside, you mean through the back entrance to the private room?"

She nodded.

"Did Drake report it to Reynard Crisp?"

"He didn't." A straight line formed on her mouth. "He came straight to me the next morning."

"And you haven't spoken to Crisp or Manon about this?"

She shook her head.

"If there's an illegal activity, the police should be informed."

"No," shot out of her mouth like a missile, making me flinch. "I need to know what Manon is involved in. That's why I'm asking you to treat this delicately. It's between us only. Not even my family. Not Declan. No one. Can I rely on you? I'll pay whatever you ask."

I scratched my bearded jaw. "It's not a question of money, Mrs. Lovechilde."

"Call me Caroline, please." Her mouth curled slightly. "I believe that you're also accompanying my daughter to Paris on the weekend as her bodyguard."

I'd gotten that call before arriving for this meeting and had agreed to the job. The money was excellent. But how I'd deal with Savanah after hours was the tricky part. Especially for my highly reactive dick. That woman had me under her fucking spell.

"Yes. I'll be escorting her."

"Good. She's gotten herself mixed up with a troubled man." She rolled her eyes. "Only this time, he's got something on her. No one will tell me. Do you know what it is?"

Her eyes penetrated mine.

Does she know I've been with Savanah?

"I take it this is the second matter you wished to discuss?"

She nodded.

"Although your daughter"—I chose my words carefully—"struck me as jumpy, she wouldn't exactly elaborate." I couldn't spill on the little Savanah had told me in strict confidence. "Being a drug addict, Bram's extremely volatile. That much I know. I wouldn't trust him."

"No." She sighed. "I've witnessed his boorish behavior." She shook her head, looking more like that worried mother by the minute. She even reminded me of my mother, who, with that same concerned frown, jumped every time a knock came at the door.

"Getting back to our earlier discussion, I'd like you to case the back of the casino. You were in the army with my son. I'm sure you're good at this kind of thing." She smiled tightly.

Faraway places, with strangers threatening to blow us up, I am.

"Consider it done. I'll report back to you. I'll do a recon now. Good excuse to jump on Drake's new trail bike." I sniffed.

The frown remained on her face. "Recon?"

"Reconnaissance. I'll ride through the forest and find a vantage point for later when it's dark."

"That's a sound plan." Her face softened. "Declan always spoke highly of you. You helped him while he was on those dastard missions. I'll never forget that. Or this." Her eyes met mine, and from that moment, our relationship deepened. Or so it felt like to me.

Did that mean I couldn't fuck her daughter?

That wasn't happening anyway while she dated that fuckwit.

I rose. "Okay. I'll report back on Friday."

She held out her hand, and I took it. Her eyes met mine again. I read a lot in that look. Like she needed me to protect her family from some hidden evil.

THE FOREST AT NIGHT had this kind of peaceful magic about it, despite all the scurrying and rustling coming from night creatures, which made me pause and clutch my Beretta. I carried that gun as one would a good luck charm. It was also a habit, after a decade in the military. Despite my hatred of automatics, I was fond of the vintage Italian gun passed down to me by my grandfather.

A torch was out of the question as I couldn't blow my cover, so I adjusted my night vision in the forest. Helped by the moon, I found the path to the back of Salon Soir with ease.

My phone beeped, and I looked to see it was Savanah. She'd called earlier about the Paris trip, sounding like it was some exciting romantic getaway.

If only.

I'd never been to Paris and, being human, an element of anticipation buzzed through me. Having watched enough Bond movies, I appreciated heritage architecture and extraordinary art, but I was there to protect Savanah. Which wasn't really a job. I would have done it for free.

I could no more look away from Savanah than I could from my family.

Pausing against a tree, I took the call. I'd given myself plenty of time to navigate the terrain, having already pinpointed a good vantage site behind a large elm, a few steps outside of the wood.

"Hey," I said.

"I just wanted to speak to you again. I'm in London."

"With that dickhead?"

"Yep." She sighed. "I told him about Paris and that it was a family affair. He insists on coming. I just don't know what to do. I hate him."

"Savanah, I can't help you if you don't let me know what he's got over you."

"It's a sex tape." Her voice cracked.

"Oh, is that all? I've had a few of those in my time. They're kinda cute."

"This is not one of those, trust me." Her words slurred.

"Have you been drinking?"

"I'm drunk. Otherwise, I wouldn't have told you about that fucking horrid tape."

Gripped by sudden frustration, I feared for her in that state. She was ripe for abuse.

A memory of her wounded on the pavement flashed before me, making my temperature rise. "Are you home, at least?"

"I am. He's gone off to score a deal. I hate him." She sobbed.

I took a deep, steadying breath. Protective instincts had me itching to see her.

"I miss you." She sounded like a fragile child. All I wanted to do was rock her in my arms and stroke her silky hair. Not sexually, but as a loving friend.

Did I love her? It was way too soon for that. But I couldn't get her out of my mind or even my heart.

Savanah made me feel needed. I liked that feeling. Too much for my own good, it seemed.

"But you'll be sleeping with him, won't you?"

"He's always too out of it for sex. That's one small blessing. I can't stand him anywhere close." Her tortured giggle made my body tense. "He probably won't even come home till morning. He likes to knock around with his druggie friends. We're only together as a show, you realize."

"He sounds fucking awful."

"He is. You've got to save me."

"Look, Savanah, I'm working right now. I'll see you on Saturday. We'll talk about this sex tape and how to get you out of this predicament. And please, do me a favour: try to stay lucid. Drinking won't help."

"I will. And Carson..."

"Yes."

"I love you."

She cut out, and my heart raced. I felt dizzy.

Those words terrified me yet injected some kind of emotional steroid through me, filling my veins with energy of the kind I hadn't exactly felt before.

Did I love her?

My body did.

With that thought swirling around, I turned off my phone.

Just as I snuck out of the wood, something darted out of the scrub. I reached for my gun but then noticed a fluffy tail disappear in the scrub.

Dressed in black, I'd even streaked my face. I was that soldier again. I'd never stopped because I aimed to protect. And I wanted to deliver for Caroline Lovechilde because loyalty was paramount to me.

Although my bank account looked healthy, thanks to the Lovechildes' generosity, I also liked them as people. They'd accepted me for who I was and didn't lay on the airs and graces.

I positioned myself behind an elm that I'd discovered earlier while riding Drake's new trail bike. I'd turned into that boy again, racing through the wood, getting off on the adrenaline. I even promised myself a new motorbike.

Fifteen minutes later, a van arrived. The driver stepped out along with Manon. He opened the side door, and six girls spilled out. I couldn't exactly see what they looked like, but they struck me as young. Manon seemed to give them a pep talk.

She knocked on the door at the back of the casino, and when it opened, the girls, dressed in short skirts and high heels, filed in.

One girl refused to go in. I didn't need to be a clairvoyant to guess what that meant. They were being asked to either perform naked or have sex. It had that look about it.

I would report back to Caroline and suggest an anonymous tip-off to the cops.

But what was Manon's part in this?

CHAPTER 15

Manon

THE HOTEL BOASTED A postcard view of the Eiffel Tower and Champs-Élysées. Positioned close to the Louvre, the location couldn't have been more fitting for a luxury destination.

"How did you swing this?" I stroked a silk embroidered scarf covering a white grand piano. "I must have missed that board meeting."

Ethan smiled at my guilty smirk. "When it came up for sale, I jumped at it. You got the minutes?"

"I did. But you know me. I can't get past the first addendum."

Ethan flashed me a sympathetic smile instead of criticizing my somewhat slack attitude toward family business matters.

Cian came scampering along the marble floor with Mirabel close behind and showed me his model of the Eiffel Tower.

"Oh, that's nice." I bent down, kissed his little cheek, then smiled at Mirabel and hugged her.

"I can't get it out of his hand." She splayed her palms. "He's besotted by that little structure."

"An architect in the family could be good." I grinned.

"More like a train driver or an astronaut." Mirabel's comment made Ethan laugh as he gave her a lingering peck on the cheek.

Mm... Loved up as always.

Six months pregnant, Mirabel, looking all boho chic, was the picture of health in her green floral dress and lace-up ankle boots.

I pointed at the carved ceilings with shimmering crystal chandeliers. "It's almost a replica of London." Even the mahogany carpet, red velvet curtains, and an intimate bar decked in Art Deco reminded me of our hotel.

"That's our brand, so to speak." Ethan grinned, looking justifiably proud. He'd done a stellar job with that grand hotel.

"Each room has its distinct flavor. Some are modern, others classic. To suit all kinds of tastes. You got the photos?" he asked.

"I did." I smiled apologetically. "I'm just all over the place."

"Declan spoke to Lord Pike, who promised he'd have a word with Bram."

"It didn't work because he's here." A heavy sigh deflated my chest.

Ethan shook his head. "You've got Carson looking over you, at least."

"That's something, I guess." I sighed while playing it cool. Ethan didn't need to know how much I pined for my security guard.

My mother stepped through the revolving doors, with her arm linked in Carrington's for all the world to see.

"Has anyone spoken to our mother about that woman in the car?" I asked.

Ethan shrugged. "Declan was meant to."

A server circled with a tray of champagne, and I almost leapt at him.

It had been a harrowing time with Bram tagging along. He even jumped on my flight and acted like a first-class arsehole by demanding endless drinks. When I spotted him at a bar close to the hotel, I hurried past before he dragged me in. Bram couldn't speak French, and he would have pinned me down.

Carson stepped through the revolving door at the same time as Declan, and then he stopped to say something to my brother. Wearing a tux, my bodyguard looked good enough to ravage.

He let his gaze wander over and trap mine, then his eyes turned into fingers, doing things to my body that screamed X-rated. My knees liquefied, and a pang of desire rushed through me. Was that electricity fizzing through the air?

Everything about Carson reminded me of sex. Hot. Screechy. Deep, hard sex that left me legless and beat any drug I'd ever tried. Only now he'd become my addiction.

How painful not being able to sleep with him these past few nights. If only he'd let me in again. I didn't mean to tell him about the sex tape. I'd been drinking. But at least he now knew. I just had to hide the sordid details from him.

We moved into the function room, which, going on the embellished ceiling, was a former ballroom. Through arched windows, Paris shone like a priceless diamond, especially with the Seine and Eiffel Tower splashed in golden light.

Playing his role of security guard to perfection, Carson kept his distance, so I joined Declan instead.

At his feet, Cian propped up his model of the Eiffel Tower, and Julian sent his little car rolling along, voicing engine sounds while knocking the structure over. It was all very cute, and for a minute there I forgot I was at the opening of our family's five-star hotel.

Standing close, my mother chatted in fluent French with some local celebrities and dignitaries.

Theadora came over and kissed me. She raised the layer of my ruffled silk dress. "This is gorgeous."

"Thanks. I picked it up at this sweet boutique around the corner from the hotel."

I regarded her in a red sheath with a rose-sculptured neckline. "You're looking stunning, as always."

"It's something I picked up here as well. The boutiques are to die for."

I smiled. I had to agree there. Paris was a favorite shopping destination.

Declan was laughing with Carson when I joined them. If only to get a whiff of my security guard, I breathed him in deeply for that hint of bath soap, cologne, and male scent. I would have smothered myself in that smell if I could.

"Did you have a word with Mother?" I asked Declan.

He puffed. "Why is it always me? Why can't you? I've only just finished talking to that dick, Lord Pike, who couldn't care less about his son blackmailing you, by the way. Even my mention of lawyers and police didn't seem to worry him."

Frustrated and defeated, I shook my head.

"Get Carson involved. He'll sort it out," Declan said just as the man who'd stolen my heart walked away.

"I don't want him seeing the tape." My voice trembled. "I'm a fucking nervous wreck."

Declan draped his arm over my shoulder for support when a noisy laugh rang through the room. People stopped and stared at Bram, making his grand entrance and wearing an "I'm here, look at me" satisfied smirk. Stirring the crowd, he seemed to dance as he walked.

That nonconforming, poke-tongue at convention was what had attracted me in the beginning because there was a little of me in there. I'd always had a dislike for the stiff conventions of our lot. Even as a girl, I preferred to play outside with the farmers' kids than hang around in my pretty dresses and smile sweetly at the guests.

But with that dark heart of his, Bram now terrified me. He'd imprisoned me and had stomped all over my soul.

Bram's father entered with Reynard Crisp, just in time to see his son making a dick of himself. He'd seen it often enough. Like most rotten people, he was probably too thick-skinned to care.

"So the mortician's been invited, I see." I tipped my head towards Crisp.

"Ethan wouldn't have done that. But you know Mother. She can't go anywhere without him in tow," Declan said, sounding as disgusted as I felt. For good reason.

"It still amazes me you can stand being in the same room as him, and it must freak Theadora out."

He sighed and nodded. "We just turn away. You know this scene. There are plenty of mutual haters—enemies who continue to rub shoulders because of some fifteenth-century convention."

"With Bram's slippery father as a close mate, they're like a pair of snakes."

Declan nodded. "They probably muscled an invitation. Have you discussed the tape with Carson? I'm sure he doesn't need to know all the details. He'll be able to deal with this."

"How?" I asked. "He's not a tech whiz. We need someone to hack into Bram's computer and delete it."

"Has anyone seen it other than you?"

"No idea. He just keeps threatening to post it everywhere."

"Carson's good at solving these types of problems."

"So are you. Why aren't you helping me?" I hated how shrill my voice had become.

My nephew was running between people's legs, and Theadora came over to Declan, looking defeated. "Your turn. You're the one that gave him those sweets. Now look at him. He's running amok."

I had to chuckle. Both my nephews were wild.

Our mother joined us. "You should take the children to the day center."

Ethan swung by, holding Cian's hand. "Just taking him there now. I'll take Julian if you like. There are other children there."

Declan nodded. "Good idea." He kissed his son's cute cheek, and off they scampered.

I remained by my mother's side. Despite being introduced to Carrington or Cary, as he was now known, we hadn't really spoken a lot. That normally happened after a few functions. Especially dinner parties. That's where the people revealed their natures. Nothing too deep. Our cohort was a shallow bunch. The only deep ones were the quiet ones that often smoked outside or hung out with the original editions at Merivale's library.

Dressed in a tweed jacket, his greying hair combed back with a hint of product, Cary looked very much the writer. He spoke with a deep voice, and my mother became so absorbed in his every word, I could have threatened to run naked, and she would have said, "That's nice, darling."

Recognizing her starry-eyed look, I imagined that was me around Carson.

I tried to hide from Bram behind her and Cary. At least, he'd found a way to occupy himself by rambling to a pair of women in their twenties, who seemed fascinated by his drugged rock star act. If only they knew. They could have him.

"How's your room?" I asked, looking from my mother to Carrington. I knew they were sharing. He practically lived at Merivale and largely kept to himself. Janet mentioned he spent his days writing in one of the less-frequented sitting rooms.

"Our room radiates a certain eclectic charm. Lots of color. I imagine you'll approve." My mother smiled.

I was still getting used to her smiles. She was always so serious when our father was alive.

"I do like my room. Ethan's done a smashing job. I love that he's collected local contemporary art. Some pieces are fun and eccentric. There's one with just a tiny eye in the middle of a large white canvas." I chuckled. "With such stunning views, minimal art makes good design sense, I suppose."

I turned to Cary. "Do you think that a busy interior conflicts with a spectacular view?"

"I think you can have both. I'm not a fan of minimalism. Give me as much visual stimulation as possible." He smiled and looked over at my mother as though seeking her validation. "There's so much creativity in the world. Nature and art can coexist in a harmonious marriage."

As he uttered 'marriage' his eyes found my mother's.

Mm... Interesting.

I liked him, though. At least he was chattier than Will. On those odd occasions of running into Cary at Merivale, he'd comment on the sky or a bird or talk about a piece of art that had captured his imagination.

"Do you come to Paris often?" I asked him.

"When I can. It's an inspiring city, boasting some of the finest literature in history."

"Cary's more Montmartre," my mother said.

"Oh? You stay there?" I asked. "All those steps."

"I'm a big fan of Simone de Beauvoir." He cast his eyes on my mother, and of course, she looked impressed. But he could have admitted to liking the outer suburbs of London with their ugly high-rises, and she would have still sparkled with admiration.

Bram laughed loudly, and my mother's attention slid his way. "I see you've dragged that buffoon along."

"I'm trying to get rid of him. You know that."

"He's an embarrassment." She rolled her eyes, and Cary returned a sympathetic smile.

"He's that and more... He's my epiphany."

Did I just say that?

Cary's eyebrow raised. As a writer, he couldn't ignore that comment, I could only guess. "Your last bad choice?"

"Yep. Got it in one." I played with my fingers. "I fell for his rebellious rock star act. He's in a band, you see."

"He's creative then?"

"He's more a poseur than anything else. He loves being the centre of attention."

He grimaced. "Oh, he's vain. How tedious. And by the looks of it, drugged." He watched on as Bram smirked and swaggered through the crowd. "One needs a modicum of talent to play the enfant terrible, and decadence is only praiseworthy when executed with flair."

"Of which he lacks," my mother responded dryly.

At least, Cary's illuminating comments offered some healthy distraction, as I somewhat reluctantly—mainly because of Bram looking at me—clambered out of this intellectual rabbit hole and returned to the cruel reality of rotten choices.

Bram got talking to someone else, and I breathed again.

"You look pale, sweetheart." My mother frowned.

She sensed something more than just my embarrassment in this latest shitshow. I'd kept Bram's tendency to be violent to myself. That would have distressed her and involved the police, resulting in Bram sharing that soul-crushing sex tape.

He'd cornered a couple of supermodels, who looked amused by his antics. Watching Bram was like witnessing an awful actor having to improvise after forgetting his lines.

Meanwhile, looking amused, Cary seemed fascinated by Bram, as a writer might be, considering how flawed characters always drew the greatest interest. "As Bertrand Russell so aptly put it, 'The trouble with the world is that the stupid are cocksure while the intelligent are full of doubt.' I often think of that when looking at people like him."

"Sad but true," my mum added, wearing that concerned mother look, the same worried expression she wore before having my wisdom tooth removed. If only I could extricate Bram with a visit to the dentist.

To quell my nerves, I just kept drinking champagne to forget Bram's threat of exposing me with a cock in my mouth to the world.

Oh... the fucking horror.

Bram finally joined us, and after he held out his bloodless, bony hand to Cary and kissed my mother's very unwilling cheek, he clutched my arm. Not in a gentle way, either.

His dark, stoned eyes promised malice or something just as unpalatable, like me having to suck him off while he watched porn. I wanted to scream. To cry. To engage a hit man.

Stop it.

Things had gotten so bad I'd considered going to such murderous extremes. Anything to get him off my back and me onto that path that would see me finishing my art degree and convincing Carson that we could make us work.

"Hey, come out for a minute. I need to tell you something." He scratched his arm. He'd obviously hit up. I wanted to chuck up.

Why the fuck isn't his father doing something?

I puffed loudly, not hiding my unwillingness, and excused myself. The expression of concern etched on my mother's brow remained as she watched us move away.

I looked over at Carson, whose eyes were all over us. That was his job to watch. I just wanted those eyes all over me naked, and not with this fucking tosser.

We stood in the hallway with black-and-white images of famous Hollywood scenes shot in Paris. One of which was Audrey Hepburn, standing in front of the Eiffel Tower with open arms welcoming the world. Without Bram, that would be me—dancing down the Champs-Élysées while pointing at all the pretty sights with Carson by my side.

Oh, give me back my life.

"I've got some sniff. I thought we could share a line and make a night of it. What do you say?" A wicked smile brushed Bram's mouth.

"I'm off everything. Only drinks. That's it. I'm even cutting the ciggies."

"You're becoming a fucking bore."

"I don't want to be with you. I want this to end. Find yourself another rich girl to hang off. My family aren't idiots. They don't want you around." I took a breath. "My mother won't give me a penny if I keep seeing you."

His face darkened. "Fuck you, telling me what to do." I went to walk off when he grabbed my arm. "Where are you going?"

"To talk to your father."

He laughed. "He doesn't give a shit. He wants this. He thinks the video's a great idea." He grabbed me by the wrist.

"Let me go. You're hurting me," I said.

"Let's have this out in privacy, shall we?"

"Step away," a deep, familiar voice commanded.

Carson stood so close, I could smell him, and suddenly I felt safe.

"Fuck off gym junkie."

"I said step away." He stood over Bram. A giant against a shrivelled, horrible excuse for a man.

"Fuck off. This is between us."

Carson's eyes met mine. I know I wouldn't want to have crossed him. Not that Carson would ever hurt me. Quite the opposite.

But Bram was playing with fire. A complete idiot. I thought of Cary's earlier comment about the delusional stupid being overconfident. That was Bram all right.

Carson stood close, dwarfing Bram.

Tall, solid, and dependable meets scrawny, useless, and dangerous.

Bram stupidly pushed on Carson's chest as though that would knock him away.

Good try. Not in a million years.

I stepped away. My voice was trapped in my throat with a scream trying to get out.

He kept trying to push him like he might be a megalith. Carson exhaled and did what any self-respecting human would do. He picked Bram up by his ripped designer jacket.

While Bram thrashed about, he yelled at me, "Do you want the world to see how much you loved Killian's cock in your mouth?"

I scrunched into a ball and buried my face in my hands.

People raced out to watch the show. They must have heard that last comment. How could they not? And then, my mother arrived with Cary. Her alarmed expression told me she'd heard.

Theadora helped me up and, taking me gently by the hand, said, "Come on, let's go to the powder room."

Bram yelled, "You'll be hearing from my fucking lawyer."

My mother, Declan, and Ethan looked at me in horror.

"You need to settle this now." Declan followed us along the hall to the restroom.

"What's he talking about?" my mother asked, accompanying him. "What was he saying? Is there footage of you?"

Tears pooled in my eyes. "Why did you invite him?" I pointed at Bram's ugly father, who'd caught up with us.

"Why has that thug got my son in a hold?" he asked.

"Because he's making a nuisance of himself, like he did at the opening of Salon Soir." I eyeballed Crisp, who returned a haughty grin. Drama seemed to entertain that vampirish creep.

"Why are you with that brute?" my mother continued, ignoring Crisp.

"My son is a little troubled," Pike interjected. "He just needs a tender hand. It's your daughter that's stirring the trouble."

"From what I'm seeing, he's the one with the drug issue," she responded with a blast of ice. "This is a personal matter. Leave." Her wide angry eyes shifted from Pike to Crisp.

He returned a grunt and walked off with his ugly conspirator by his side.

My mother turned to me. "What's this about a tape?"

Carson returned and stood close by. He gave me a subtle nod.

Tears streamed down my cheeks as I turned to her. "I can't talk right now. I need some space."

CHAPTER 16

Carson

ETHAN JOINED US IN the hallway. "What the hell's happening? Can't we have one function without drama?"

Caroline Lovechilde responded with a sigh. "It's your sister and that horrible boyfriend. I had to tell Lord Pike to leave. He put up a fuss after Carson rightfully removed his lunatic son. And now Lord Pike's threatening Savanah." She turned to Crisp. "Why did you bring him?"

He opened out his large, skinny hands. "He got the invite. As did I."

Her brow furrowed as she turned to Ethan.

"I'll make sure I get his name scrubbed off the VIP list in future."

"Promise me. I don't want that man around."

Declan returned and said, "The cops are dealing with him." He looked at me. "He says you hit him."

"I pushed him off Savanah. And then I had to drag him outside when he refused to budge. He tried to punch me, and I blocked it. That's all. If I had hit him, you'd know."

Declan nodded slowly. "I wouldn't have blamed you if you had. I've been pretty close to whacking him a few times."

It took the control of someone fasting at a cake fair for me to stop myself from knocking Bram's yellowing teeth out.

I kept that to myself.

"Where's Savanah?" Declan asked.

"She went to her room," Caroline said. She looked at me again. "What was he saying about Savanah and some lewd act?"

Everyone's eyes were on me, suddenly. What a difficult fucking conversation. No one wanted to hear that there was a pornographic tape of someone close.

I didn't.

Hearing that had made my fucking veins stiffen, and now I understood why Savanah panicked.

"Has she said anything?" Caroline asked Declan.

"Not with that much detail." Declan rubbed his neck.

"Is he blackmailing her?" Caroline asked me.

"I believe so, Mrs. Lovechilde."

"So why am I only hearing about this now?"

"We had a word with Lord Pike about pulling his son into line and dropping the threat. But he didn't care. I got the feeling he wants this relationship to work. Even if it takes blackmail." Declan raised his brow.

"He's a gambler. He wants our wealth. That's plain to see." Caroline shook her head. "He'll never be a part of this family. If I have to report him, I will." She looked at Crisp, as though appealing to him to do something, but he remained inscrutable as always.

I kept wondering what this sly character had over such a refined woman as Caroline Lovechilde. Although he conducted himself with the airs and graces typical of wealth, no amount of money, expensive suits, or Rolex watches hid filth.

"What else is on the tape?" Caroline asked me.

"Your daughter didn't go into detail." My chest tightened. Why would she think I'd know more?

Does she know about me and Savanah?

"All I can tell you is that Bram's threatening to upload the footage onto social media."

"Then we must involve the police. They'll have to stop this." Her large dark eyes filled with alarm. This was her daughter's reputation at stake. "They can, can't they?"

"All he's got to do is press a button. They can arrest him. But it will be after the fact," I said.

"In other words, this tape will become public before the law can intervene?" Declan asked.

I shrugged. "I'm not an expert, but I'd be on the phone to your lawyer."

"At least he's being held for the moment. He can't do anything. So, now's the time to act," Declan told his mother.

Ethan, who'd joined us again, shook his head. "This had to happen today."

"Don't worry, darling. The hotel's a triumph." His mother kissed his cheek. "You've done a stellar job."

Declan nodded. "You have, Eth."

I left them and went to Savanah's room.

After I knocked on the door, I heard, "Go away."

"It's Carson."

She opened the door. Her mascara had run, and her big blues drowned in tears.

I wanted to take her in my arms and hold her. Soothe her.

"He's been arrested."

"But that won't hold him for long. He'll still send out that fucking tape." She ran her hands over her hair. "I've made such a mess of my life. I want to die." She fell onto the sofa and sobbed.

I sat down next to her and put my arm around her. "We can get through this." I grabbed the box of tissues and passed her a few.

She blew her nose, and her large blue eyes resembled the ocean. "We? There's a 'we'?"

"I'm here. I care for you."

"That's all?" Tears continued to streak her high cheekbones.

"Isn't that enough?"

She nodded weakly, and I grabbed a tissue and wiped the makeup stains off her face. "It's also very complicated. Your life differs greatly from mine."

"Mm." She looked down at her feet.

"Savanah, you have to press charges, like this minute. Your mother is talking to the lawyer. You should report his physical abuse. There are also today's incidents witnessed by me. He's with the French cops right now, which will last a minute. His father will get that seen to. You've got enough on him to have him locked up."

"He'll get bail and then send out that beastly tape." She covered her face. "Shit."

"They can threaten to sue. From what I'm hearing, that family aren't as flush as they pretend."

She chuckled sarcastically. "Tell me about it. I pay for everything when we're out. Including his fucking drugs." She held her head again. "This is a fucking nightmare. How did I get myself mixed up in this?"

I avoided lecturing her on dating bad boys and how that would never end well.

"If that tape is made public, everyone will hate me. You'll hate me. Shit." She walked to the wall-to-ceiling window and screamed. "I want to die."

From the fridge, I grabbed a bottle of water, unscrewed the top, and handed it to her.

"I need something stronger. Or a cigarette. Or a Xanax. Please get me something. I'm losing it here." She clutched her arms.

Normally I would have tried to talk someone out of sedatives, but I could see Savanah was about to snap.

I embraced her, and her tense body slowly unwound.

"That's better." She looked up at me with a trembly smile. "All I need is you, Carson. You know that, don't you?"

With that wide, searching gaze, she reminded me of a lost child, and my heart ached for her. All I wanted to do was to hold her. Stroke her. Protect her.

"Can I run a bath for you?" I asked.

"That would be nice. Can you wash my back?"

It was a relief to see her lips curl. "I'll see what I can do."

Just as I let go of her, she crossed her arms and trembled again. "You've got to stop him."

Taking a deep breath, I could see she needed more than a bath to calm her troubled state. "Okay. I'll be back in a minute." I paused at the door. "Don't do anything silly."

She fell onto the sofa and held onto her face and shook her head slowly. "But please hurry back."

There was that child again. Who could deny her anything?

But I wasn't meant to be papa. Not going on the guilty fucking erection. This poor woman needed my support. Not my dick.

"Okay. I'll see if there's a doctor."

"No. Just ask my mother. She's always got Xanax. Doesn't go anywhere without them."

That took me aback. Caroline Lovechild was the last person I imagined needing downers.

"Can you promise me you won't do anything?"

She laughed darkly. "What am I going to do? Knot the sheet and hang myself? Drugs maybe. But I don't have any."

"Savanah, don't talk like that. We can fix this."

"And then what? That fucked-up sex tape will end up being viewed by everyone, and you won't want to know me?"

"I'm a grown-up. I can handle it."

"I bet you can. I just hate that you'll see me as a filthy slut."

I frowned. "I could never see you as that. I know this scene, and I also know that a night on alcohol and drugs can make a person do things they later regret. We've all got one of those stories."

Her face brightened slightly. "You've done that? Had a sex tape?"

I shook my head. "Not that I'm aware of. But I've had regrettable sex. Lots of it."

"With a man?" she asked.

My head drew back. I wondered why she asked that. "Nope. I'm into women. One hundred percent." I studied her. "Why ask me that?"

She knitted her fingers. "No reason."

I returned to the function, where people chatted and laughed as though that earlier drama hadn't even happened, and found Caroline

Lovechilde with her boyfriend. He had his arm wrapped around her waist, and they looked very much in love.

"Can I have a quick word?" I asked.

She followed me to a quiet corner.

"Savanah's asked for a couple of Xanax." I gave her an apologetic half-smile.

Her eyes held mine for a moment, and I caught a hint of unease.

She rummaged in her bag and then passed me a tissue. "There are a couple. She knows I won't give her more."

"Do you think she might need to go somewhere?"

"Like a hospital?" She frowned.

"She's really shaken. And she mentioned she wants to die more than once."

Caroline shook her head. "That wouldn't be the first time."

My eyebrows met. "She's tried to take her life before?"

"No. Never. My daughter can get a tad dramatic, that's all. I've contacted my lawyer. Let's wait and hope. We can sue. But the Pikes are already mortgaged to the eyeballs." She touched my hand. "Thanks for doing this. I know my daughter looks up to you."

I took a breath. Another matter needed discussing. "About what I saw that night at the back of the casino..."

When I'd gone to report my disturbing findings, we were interrupted by her boyfriend, and therefore I wasn't able to divulge what I'd witnessed.

"I've spoken to Manon. Apparently, it was a private function. Dancers." Her eyebrow lift told me she didn't believe that.

"One girl looked very young and like she was trying to escape."

Her brow creased, and the blood drained from her face. Caroline had every reason to be concerned because from where I stood, her granddaughter pushed the unwilling girl ahead.

"Is there any way you can actually get inside?" she asked.

"I'd have to be invited," I said.

"Can you send someone else?"

I took a deep breath. "If I were you, I'd involve the law. I know what I saw."

She held her chin, and her hand trembled slightly. It was the most bothered I'd seen her. Even more so than after hearing of Savanah's blackmail. "No. I can't."

Her boyfriend joined us. "What can't you do?"

Her face softened. "Nothing. It's okay. Just talking about my daughter's predicament, which with the help of Carson, we are getting a handle on."

I left the whole Salon Soir scene alone. I could see it was too much for her, and I even felt a little guilty for bringing it up. It did concern me, however. I wished I could tell Declan, but being sworn to secrecy, I prided myself on being a man of my word.

CHAPTER 17

Savanah

AT LEAST MY TRIP to Paris had a nice ending. It took little to seduce Carson into my bed. All I did was lock the door, hide the key, and walk around naked, for him to change from bodyguard to voracious lover.

We even extended our trip by two days, taking in the sights with me on the back of a hired scooter, rubbing against his manly body. There was something about being in love in Paris that made me experience that elegant city for the first time, despite numerous visits.

I even forgot about Bram, who hadn't even texted me, which filled me with the hope he'd finally moved on to his next victim.

Sadly, that was short-lived because I'd only just arrived back at Merivale when he called—or I should say harassed—me. He wanted to discuss something and insisted we meet in London and not talk about it over the phone, which was always my preference.

With a heavy heart, I headed down to see my mother, before leaving for London, to ask about the lawsuit involving that tape, when I heard Manon yelling, "Stay out of it. It's got nothing to do with you."

Instead of interrupting them, I positioned myself by the door.

"Yes, it does," my mother responded. "While you live here, you must behave in a dignified manner, as is expected of a Lovechilde."

"Oh, really? Well then, to do that, I need lots of money."

"You have a credit card. The limit has been increased twice."

"It's not enough. That's why I plan to marry money. And Rey's a billionaire. He'll give me everything and more."

"He's not the marrying kind."

"I'm sure I can change that."

Whether Manon was still a virgin remained a mystery. She certainly didn't act like one. But she was foremost ambitious, with wealth being her endgame.

"Please tell me you haven't slept with him." Sounding distressed, my mother's rare display of emotion made me flinch.

"And what if I have? Would that make you jealous?"

"Why are you like this?"

Good question.

"I'm just going for what I can get. You, of all people, Grandmother, should understand."

"Tell me what's happening at the back of the casino."

"It's just a private club, nothing else."

"Are there young girls in there? Being paraded?"

What?

"It's all above board. Cross my heart." Manon's juvenile pledge sounded so fake I was dying to see my mother's reaction.

I walked in. "She can't help it if she's a princess." I gave Manon a sly smile.

Manon returned the middle finger before turning her attention to my mother. "I'm off to the Salon."

"Are you working there now?" I asked. "What happened to the spa?"

"I resigned. Everyone's so bitchy. I prefer the casino. It's more fun."

Clearly flustered, my mother gestured for us to leave her alone. Not a good time to discuss the sex tape, I'd decided. On a deeper level, I didn't want to bring up yet another murky issue. Lumping my shit choices with Manon's filled me with even more self-loathing for troubling my mother.

Wanting to learn more about that private club, I followed Manon outside.

"How is Salon Soir more fun?" I asked, catching up with her in the courtyard by the servants' quarters.

"Just is. For one, there's entertainment." She lit a cigarette, balancing it on her lips which seemed thicker every time I saw her.

I'd used some collagen filler myself, but Carson hated pumped lips, so I'd given it a break. He'd told me his cock loved my lips the way they were, as did his mouth.

Mm... Anything to keep that man hard and interested.

Manon certainly knew how to make the most of her good looks. Impeccably applied makeup brought out those large, almost black eyes that were exactly like my mother's.

Wearing a skintight top and short skirt, Manon loved parading her assets and attracting a lot of male attention.

Drake chatted and laughed with the gardener when he noticed us.

"What kind of entertainment?" I asked, trying to extract as much detail as possible before he came over.

"It's a private club." She made eyes at Drake.

"Has this private club got a name?"

"Ma Chérie."

"What goes on in Ma Chérie?"

She puffed out a smoke ring. "It's a men's club."

One didn't need to be too bright to read between the lines. "Like a strip club with dancers on poles?"

"Mm... Not quite. More meet and greet." Her dark eyes smiled wickedly like she was dying to share a secret.

Drake ambled towards us, and her face warmed. I knew she liked him, and he made no secret of his attraction.

I raised my chin at him in the distance. "Are you two together yet?"

"No. But we'll see. He's nice."

"He's gorgeous."

Her smooth brow pinched. "Don't you dare fuck him."

I had to laugh. "Look at you being all territorial all of a sudden. I prefer men to boys."

"Oh, he's a man all right."

"I thought you said you hadn't hooked up," I said.

"I haven't. But he's seriously hot." A little smile grew on her full lips. "I'm sure he's got a big dick."

She sounded so immature, I nearly laughed.

I thought of Carson. The mention of a big dick had me firing up. And our time in Paris flashed before me, which had ended with a 'to be continued.'

"You haven't fucked yet, have you?" I had to ask.

"None of your business."

"But a big dick? I mean, it would hurt if you haven't had sex." I couldn't help goading her. She carried on like she was free and easy when perhaps it was all an act.

"You would know. You've probably fucked everyone."

Ouch.

"I've had a bit of experience. I am nearly twenty-nine."

"Yeah. You're old." She wore a crooked grin.

"And you're fucking naïve if you think Reynard Crisp is going to make you rich and famous."

"I haven't fucked him." She puffed out smoke and stubbed out her cigarette. "Yet."

"Careful there. The guy's a worm."

"He's been nice to me."

Drake joined us.

"How are you?" I asked him, tapping his bulky biceps. "You're looking seriously buff."

He smiled shyly. I liked him. He was sweet.

His eyes devoured Manon, and the air seemed to crackle between them.

They made a gorgeous couple, but I was just worried about Drake, given Manon's twisted nature.

With curiosity piqued about Ma Chérie, I left them in their young-adult romantic bubble.

I walked back inside and went upstairs to pack my bags for London with a heavy heart. I wanted to stick around and seduce Carson.

When he returned with the medication, I'd asked for back in Paris, he found me in the bath, and I begged him to stay and keep me company. We chatted about small things, and as always, I liked the sound of his deep, husky voice. He was also a great listener, unlike some of the idiots I'd dated.

No one was like Carson, especially in the way he made me feel.

Just as he was about to leave me alone to take my bath, I begged him to stay and propped myself up above the bubbles so he could see my tits.

His eyes darkened with lust and, pulling up the chair, he unbuttoned his jacket and took a seat.

"You look nice in that tux, by the way. But you'd look even nicer without the jacket."

"Now look, Savanah. I'm here professionally."

"You didn't seem to mind the other night." I referred to him entering my bathroom and letting me suck him off.

I ran my tongue over my lips, and I noticed a bulge growing.

I rose from the bath. "Can you pass me that towel?"

By this stage, his eyes were burning into me. I bent over in front of him. Showing him my naked pussy. I could feel the air thicken, even spark.

I then unzipped his pants. I had him. No protest. That big dick poked out of his briefs, beading with precum.

I licked the salty head, and he groaned, opened his legs a little to let me in, and that was that. To hell with being professional.

With that dirty, sweet reminiscence making me throb, I sent Carson an image that I'd taken in Paris in lacy blue crotchless lingerie. I'd already paraded myself before him while we were there, and with no further comment about being my bodyguard, he sat me on his lap and lowered me onto his hard dick. The intense stretch nearly made me draw blood from my lip.

Setting up the tripod, I created an image of me with my legs slightly apart. I made myself come first.

My phone pinged straight away.

"Nice." He wrote.

I laughed. A man of few words. "Is that all?" I returned.

The balls bounced then stopped and then started again. This went on for a while. "I'm working, Savanah."

"Is your dick hard?" I asked, giggling to myself.

No waiting this time. He responded within a breath. "Yes."

"What's making you hard?" I had to coax smut out of him.

Again the balls bounced about. "Your juicy little cunt. What else?"

My face heated, and I ached for him. "My eyes?"

I had to touch myself. It was hotter than I expected. I imagined that strong, muscle-bound body. Carson licking his sexy lips and holding his heavy dick in his hand, about to stretch me to the limit. His unblinking stare impaling me too.

"You're beautiful, Savanah. Especially your eyes. But your pretty little juicy pussy is staring at me, and I'm finding it hard to concentrate."

"I'm touching myself right now. Do you want to see?" I clicked on his number, and he picked up.

"Savanah." His voice sounded hoarse from lust like he was touching himself.

I positioned my phone and then rubbed my clit. "Can you see that?"

I heard a heavy breath. "Yes."

"Are you touching your dick?"

"Yes."

"Can you show me?" I asked.

"Why don't I just come over? In, say, one hour."

"I have to go to London, like now. I'm already late. But I wanted to seduce you first."

He sniffed. "You're doing that, all right."

"Do you like it when I touch myself?"

"Very much. Too much."

"Too much?"

"You're distracting me, and I'm having difficulty focusing. Like someone is calling out for me right now. I have to go, even though I'd love to see how this finishes."

I laughed. "I think you can guess. I'll send you the photo of me coming if you like."

"If you want."

"Don't sound so enthusiastic," I said.

"I prefer the real thing. And if someone hacks your phone, these will become public."

My stomach sank at the reminder of that wretched sex tape.

I moved my phone to my face and blew him a kiss.

"You're beautiful," he said.

And we left that hot and steamy moment at that.

As I was leaving for London, I saw my mother with Cary in the courtyard.

I needed to tell her about the woman in the car.

But how? She looked so happy. It broke my heart to crash her bliss.

Ethan would know what to do. He was going to drive me to London, and I'd promised to drop in, mainly to see my nephew.

When I arrived at their house, Mirabel was in the garden with Cian, who was tossing a ball to Freddie, looking like pure domestic harmony in front of that picturesque cottage.

"The garden's lovely," I said to my very-pregnant sister-in-law.

"Thanks." She smiled.

Freddie jumped all over me and licked my hand. "Hey, cutie."

I found my brother on his laptop when I arrived. A guitar, sheet music, and notepads scattered over the sofa made the room look messy and lived in.

I preferred that to everything being perfect in its place.

Having helpers meant that we never experienced mess, only the crap in my head, and no amount of domestic help could help clear that up.

"Ah. Good, you're here. I thought I was meant to pick you up." Ethan closed his laptop.

Cian chased Freddie. Wearing his caped crusader outfit, my nephew dangled a mask.

Mirabel laughed. "He's trying to mask Freddie. The dog let him yesterday, but now he knows what's involved, he doesn't want a bar of it."

I giggled. "How's his piano going?"

Mirabel looked at her son. "Do you want to show Auntie Savvie what you learned yesterday?"

Cian stuck his thumb in his mouth and went from wild to adorable and shy.

His mother helped him on the piano stool, and then his little fingers ran through the scales.

"Wow." I looked at Ethan, who wore the proud smile of a father.

"Thea's impressed. He's got a good ear, apparently."

Cian gaped at us with those wide chocolate eyes, soaked in our adulation, and then jumped off the stool and returned to chasing Freddie with the mask.

Ethan laughed. "Poor Freddie. I think he wants to go back to Merivale with the adults."

"Mother's ordered a corgi. A black-and-white puppy. I saw the photos. Very cute."

Ethan collected his bag and then planted Mirabel a lingering kiss that I think involved a tongue.

"Ew. Please." I pulled a face.

They laughed, looking all starry-eyed. I could see they were very much in love.

I pecked Mirabel's cheek and then hugged my nephew, and off we went.

We were halfway to London when I said, "I haven't spoken to Mother about the woman in the car."

"Declan did."

I turned. "Oh?"

"She didn't seem that worried. But that could've been Mum putting on her brave, evasive face."

"They looked pretty loved up today. Maybe Cary's explained, and it's all good," I said.

"I hope so." Ethan shook his head. "The last thing we need is another situation."

"Speaking of drama, are they still working on Dad's case? I hope so because I want that murderer locked up."

Ethan nodded. "They're onto it. A ten-million-pound reward has been listed. Nothing's surfaced as yet."

I sighed. "I won't rest until they find him."

"None of us will."

CHAPTER 18

Carson

I OPENED MY LAPTOP to pay some bills when I noticed an email with the subject: Savanah Lovechilde with an MP3 attachment.

I naturally assumed it was from Savanah and that she'd sent me some sexy video despite it normally coming through my phone.

My dick pushed against my fly in anticipation. She had me hot and bothered just thinking about it.

I'd never been one for sexting, but Savanah clearly enjoyed doing it. And receiving them often resulted in me taking matters into my own hand, literally.

When the MP3 had downloaded, I pressed Play, and there she was with a dick in her mouth. It was on the smaller side, which didn't make watching it any better. The burger I'd just eaten sat uncomfortably in my gut.

I should have stopped it there, but I couldn't help myself. The camera then travelled down her body, and a woman was tonguing Savanah.

Savanah had never alluded to being bi. I guess I'd never asked.

I normally didn't mind seeing a woman eating pussy, but this made my stomach curl. As much as I tried pushing those feelings away, Savanah had become more than just a casual fuck. I'd become attached.

Pressing Delete, I didn't recognize the email, and if Bram had sent that video to me, then he'd sent it to others. After getting over the shock of seeing the woman I was falling for feasting on a cock that wasn't mine, anger took over. This would crush her. And now that I'd seen the tape, it was easy to understand why.

Unsure what to say to her, I ignored Savanah's calls. Instead, I grabbed my jacket and, driven by a fire in my belly, I visited Bram's family home. If he wasn't there, I'd deal with his father, who was an older, just as smug version of his son.

Their Cotswold home was easy enough to locate. After googling Lord Pike, I discovered the family had a website with pictures of their home, which was open for tours. Within an hour I was there, scooting along the lamp-lit cobbled path to the door.

It took a few rings of the doorbells before a man answered the door.

"I'm here to see either Bram or his father."

The butler gave me the up and down. "Your name?"

"Carson Lewis. In charge of security for the Lovechildes."

"One moment." He closed the door in my face.

"Nice one, arsehole," I muttered.

I'd never liked the upper classes and their snooty staff, with their holier-than-thou attitude.

The door opened and from behind, I heard, "Come in."

Bram's father entered the large somber room with paintings of sneering men and glum women.

"How can I help you?" he asked. "I think we met, didn't we, in Paris? You were the one that roughed up my son."

I nodded. "I've come to speak to him."

"To threaten him again?"

I would have loved to wipe that smirk off his veiny face. He had that reddish drinker's nose, just like my dad's.

"He's broken his promise, which means a lawsuit, I believe."

"Oh, so you've come to threaten me?"

"Look, Mister..."

"It's Lord. You'll address me by my title."

Yes, Lord Scumbag.

"Your son has crossed the line. He's lucky that Ms. Lovechilde hasn't laid charges. I've seen the bruises."

"That could be anyone. It's no secret that Savanah Lovechilde consorts with brutes."

"Your son being one of them."

"Now listen you." He pointed in my face and had I been a few years younger, that aggressive gesture would have resulted in his index finger hanging off a tendon.

I stepped away and counted to three—an army technique when faced with rude but harmless types.

Was Lord Pike harmless? To me maybe. But I smelt something rotten in him just by his association with Crisp, and I knew he was a private guest at that venue of sleaze at the back of the casino.

"Is your son here? I'd like a word. Or do I just go straight to the police?"

His cloudy eyes held mine for a moment. I didn't blink. Stonewalling was my specialty.

He puffed out a breath. "What the fuck has he done now?" he muttered, sounding like a father sick of cleaning his son's mess.

Despite lacking sympathy for Lord Shithead, I would have hated to have a son like Bram, whom I'm certain had rubbed the family name in the mud.

"Just wait here." He pointed at an antique chair that looked like dust might fly off it were I to sit.

If I were a director looking for an ideal horror movie setting, then that creepy room, with its dark wood walls and scowling portraits, qualified. There was even a statue of armor, which sort of amused me.

Humor aside, I sensed that this was not a happy home.

I heard raised voices in the background, and a few minutes later, rubbing his head, Bram lumbered out dressed in a velvet dressing gown. I had this sudden urge to laugh. His customary black ripped jeans and loose, half-unbuttoned black shirt were probably being washed by his maid.

"So what's all this about?" he asked. "You woke me up."

I cocked my head. "Let's step outside and go for a walk, shall we?"

He studied me for a minute. "Why, what have you got in mind?"

"We need to talk. In private."

He shrugged. "Should I call security?"

"I value my freedom too much to waste it on your puny arse."

"Did Savvie send you? I hear you're porking her." He pulled a crooked grin, which only made him uglier.

"Just step outside. Or we can talk here in front of your staff."

He rubbed his face and then pointed for the door. Once we were outside, I stood intimidatingly close. "Who else have you sent that footage to?"

"No one. I'm sticking to my word. For now." He smirked. "She knows the score. We're catching up tomorrow for a function."

"So you can make a dick of yourself again?"

"Who the fuck do you think you are, making such snide comments?" He kept scratching himself. A sure sign of heroin addiction. My brother had the same affliction.

"Now that the footage is live, your father will probably hear from the Lovechilde's legal team."

"I didn't send it."

"Someone did."

"Show me." He raised his chin.

I pulled out my phone and scrolled through my email.

"That's not my email address."

"Then you must have sent it to someone. You better find out who that belongs to and shut it down."

He shrugged. "Like I said. No idea. I had my computer hacked. So it's probably someone I don't know. Which means I'm in the clear."

"No, it doesn't. It's still criminal to film someone against their consent."

Slanting his head, he returned a cocky grunt. "You don't know Savvie, do you? She fucking loves the limelight. Even when it's directed at her well-visited cunt."

Rage charged through to my clenching fists. Taking a deep breath, I had this unbearable need to throttle him. I counted to three instead, because one punch would lay out that scrawny worthless piece of shit.

"I'm bored with this conversation. Get off our land, dickhead."

I grabbed him by the scruff of his neck and pushed him out of my way like a piece of garbage. He stumbled back and ended up on his bony butt.

He yelled something, and I walked off with his comment about Savvie revolving in my head.

I had to stop these feelings. Now. No more. We'd had our fun. I was there to protect Savanah, and I'd continue to, but I would no longer lie on those silky, perfumed sheets. No matter how much I wanted to.

And I fucking wanted her all right. With every cell of my body.

Something I'd promised myself never to do. I'd become an addict. Addicted to Savanah Lovechilde. Only, like with everything in my life, I had the will of a bull when pushed.

When it came to self-control, I'd been trained to do without my favorite indulgences. In this case, that ugly comment about Savvie would be my ammo against weakness, helping me stick to my resolve.

It was late when Savanah called. "Hey, why aren't you returning my texts?"

Annoyed at myself for picking up that call, I took a deep breath. She had a right to know what had happened. "Bram's video was emailed to me."

There was a long pause. "Are you there?"

"Oh, crap. You saw it. I bet you hate me, don't you?" Her voice cracked.

Where was that open-minded man I'd prided myself in being? I felt guilty for being so judgmental, but I couldn't get past the image of that cock in her mouth.

How would this work? One gaze into Savanah's limpid, vulnerable eyes melted my heart and made my dick go rock hard.

What was it about a beautiful woman in need of rescue that sent my libido soaring?

"Bram denies sending it. Something about being hacked, which I think's bullshit. Talk to your legal team and get it stopped."

"You saw it?" Her voice sounded like that of a child crying out for love and cuddles. All I wanted to do was hold her and rock her. Draw a line through the filth.

I thought of the porno images she'd sent me of herself. I couldn't bring myself to delete them. They were pure Viagra to my overactive male gland. "By the way, you need to stop sexting."

"You didn't like my little pictures." Just as her voice cracked, it occurred to me that Savanah hadn't emotionally matured. "Can't you come here and hold my hand?"

"You're in London. I'm here at Reboot." I lied because I was driving to my old flat to look for recent signs of my brother.

"Does this mean there'll be no more us?" She sniffled.

"I'm not in a good place right now. Let's talk when you get back."

"You're meant to be protecting me," she said, sounding more like that rich diva that, up to now, had been missing.

"I can protect you physically, but I can't help your actions. Allowing to be filmed while having sex rarely ends well."

"Are you suggesting I wanted myself filmed?" she shrilled. "Fuck, Carson, how can you think that? I didn't want any of it. It was Bram that forced me. He'd slipped me a drug. I don't even fucking remember doing it." Sobs choked on her words.

"You need to hang low. Get your legal team onto this." I puffed. "And try to stay away from men like Bram." That last comment came from under my breath.

"I don't want anyone else. I just want you." She sobbed, and my heart ached.

"You only want me because I'm not throwing myself at you."

"Bullshit. It's deeper than that. Don't you feel it?" she asked.

Yep. I feel it all right. Too fucking much.

"Why didn't you do your job and threaten him?" There was a bite to her tone. "That's what security's meant to do."

"I can't do this now." I closed the call.

To clear my head, I decided to stay in London for a couple of nights. As much as I preferred my new place in Bridesmere—a one-bedroom apartment in a recently refurbished Victorian building—I needed some space. I also couldn't bring myself to return Savanah's many calls. Declan was the only person I'd contacted to ask for a couple of days off.

As I moved around the council flat I'd grown up in, there was no trace of Angus. No empty bottles. No empty pizza boxes or even rubbish lying around.

The jarring difference between my new and former home took some adjusting to and was like daylight when leaving a cinema. The council estate, with its dealers and lowlife, was a far cry from the friendly smiles that came with village life.

Although that flat reminded me of who I was before I fell into this rich and powerful world, spending time at Merivale had taught me that rich people's problems were just like everyone else's. Only they ate better. Drank quality alcohol. And didn't need to steal to buy drugs.

Drinking a beer, I leaned back on my late mother's worn recliner, a chair that had held her cancer-riddled body for that last year of her life. I could even still smell her favorite perfume she wore all my life. A lump formed in my throat. Funny how a scent will do that to you. Suddenly I could see her kind, suffering eyes. It was then that I decided God didn't exist. How could he do that to such a woman who would have given her last penny to anyone in need?

I closed my eyes, inhaled and exhaled, and thought about my mother's rosy cheeks, which would flush when she was happy. I imagined her pride and joy at knowing I was no longer stuck in poverty, and that I'd put down a deposit on a new apartment.

Clearing my head of sad thoughts, I turned on the television. Man U. was playing, and with a six-pack chilling in the fridge and a pizza smiling back at me, I felt quite at home and miles away from the shitstorm brewing in Savanah's universe.

My phone sounded. Seeing it was Declan, I picked up. "Hey, what's up?"

"Savanah's been badly beaten."

"You're fucking kidding me." My veins froze. "Fucking Bram, I bet." Blood rushed through me, setting me into battle mode. I needed this bastard's balls on a platter.

"She's not saying who did it. She's asking for you. That's why I'm calling."

I rubbed my head repeatedly. "Is she okay?"

"She's in hospital. Her face is pretty messed up. She sustained a fair bit of bruising. He's a fucking animal."

My head swirled as though immersed in a cloud of thunder. I wanted to kill him.

"She keeps asking for you. I'm sorry. I know you asked for a few days off."

"It's fine. I'll go now. Just send me the details."

"She told me that someone had sent you the sex tape."

"Yep." I puffed. "I even spoke to Bram at his family home. He denied it."

He sighed. "I think Savvie needs to go away somewhere until the dust settles."

"What about Bram? You're going to press charges, aren't you?"

"Savvie has to press the charges." He sighed. "I believe my mother's on the phone to Lord Pike right now. Anyway, I'll wait until you get here before leaving the hospital. She needs someone around her."

"I'm coming now."

CHAPTER 19

Savanah

IT HURT TO WALK. My mother looked up from her newspapers. Her eyes had gone glassy like she'd been crying. Were those for me? Or for Carrington, who'd left the night before in a hurry? They'd been inseparable for two months, and now he was gone. I'd heard them arguing about something but lost in my horror story, I wasn't paying much attention.

"How are you, darling?" she asked, placing down her paper.

"I'm getting there. I can walk better today." I sat down slowly.

My lower back and pelvis still ached, to be expected after being kicked repeatedly. I must have blacked out after Bram started kicking me because I couldn't remember what happened after that. The staff at the London hotel must have heard my screams because the next thing I knew, I was stretchered off to the hospital.

After they'd banged down the doors of his father's estate, the police arrested Bram, I'd heard while lying in hospital. I wasn't about to deny his involvement.

The pity gleaming from my mother's stare made me want to scream and do something nasty like have Bram strangled. All kinds of ugly thoughts rushed through me now that I'd finally woken out of my painkiller-induced haze.

"I've got a prescription I need to have collected," I said. "Is Janet around? Or maybe someone?"

"I'll arrange that." She studied me a little longer. "I'm sure that with time, you'll be well again."

I exhaled a deep breath. "The doctors think I won't be able to have children, Mum."

Tears slid down my cheeks. They seemed to arrive unannounced like it had become normal for me to cry at the drop of a hat.

She put her arm around me. "We'll get the best advice and doctors. I'm sure you'll be good with time."

Her phone sounded, and she declined the call. It rang again.

"Someone's keen," I said.

"It's Cary." Her voice wavered, and the phone trembled as she lay it down.

I touched her hand. "What's happened? From my window, I saw him leave, carrying a suitcase."

"He forgot to tell me he's still married." She gulped back some water.

"But he told you he was divorced." I gave her a sympathetic smile. Stung by guilt, I should have told her about the woman I'd seen in the car hugging Cary. "How did you find out?"

"Declan did a check on him." She pulled a mock smile. "His interference riled me." She knitted her fingers. "I suppose it's better to know."

Studying her closely, I recognized heartbreak because she appeared as shattered as I felt. I'd witnessed her vulnerability with Cary and how she'd changed. She had spent her life being cool and in control, but with him around, she was lighter, and her eyes looked brighter.

"Will he divorce her?" I asked.

"He says they're like brother and sister. They don't even sleep together."

I nodded. "That's something, I suppose. But why is he still with her?"

"She needs him. She's threatened to kill herself if he leaves."

"But he's been here for two months. You've been inseparable."

Her breath was jagged. "I know. He told her it was a project or something. I don't know. It sounds complicated. Something I don't need." She looked at me and sighed. "Okay. Enough. It was nice. But he's too weak to make that sacrifice for me. I'll get over him."

She rose. "Give me the scrip and I'll take it to Janet."

For a moment, I fumbled because I didn't want my mother knowing it was for Xanax, and that I'd developed a habit. I needed something to help my brain fuzz out the crap filling in empty spaces. Spaces that should have been occupied by positive pursuits, like an arts degree or something more worthwhile than shopping and chasing my next thrill—some damaged soul who might make my skin tingle.

So far, Carson had been the only person to do that. And while I imagined his upbringing was tough, he was by far the most well-adjusted man I'd ever dated.

Despite our two months of steamy sex, we were never officially dating. No one knew about us.

I had to cajole him with dirty talk and saucy texts and images. It didn't take much. He seemed to get hard from just my hand on his. Talk about virile. Talk about super sexy. But above all of that, he made me feel safe.

"Now that I think about it, I might go into the village," I said.

"But you can barely walk, darling." My mother's concern made me want to cry again.

I need those drugs. Like now.

"It's okay. I've got it." I tried to crack a smile. It hurt to even do that. He also punched me in the face. Luckily, my nose wasn't broken.

Fucking arsehole.

I hugged my mother. "I'm sure it will all work out for you."

"By the way, I spoke to Jim, the caretaker. He's expecting you at Lochridge. There haven't been visitors for a while. I think I surprised him."

"I was ten when I visited. Does anyone even go there?" I had memories of the manor that after Ethan had convinced me was haunted, I'd ended up sleeping with my parents.

I'd chosen Lochridge as my latest getaway because I needed space to heal away from people and distractions like shopping and flirting with foreigners abroad.

I was no longer the frivolous, flirty young woman I was before Bram. It was like he'd bludgeoned her out of me. Not worth potentially becoming barren and losing my mind over, however. A therapist would have been the healthier option to hooking up with a man with a sadistic streak.

Going away also meant I'd need a bodyguard, seeing that Bram was on bail and obsessed. "No" seemed to fuel him. He was one of those spoiled brats that wanted what he couldn't have, even when at risk of being locked up for breaching a restraining order.

He still wanted to marry me, which made me want to laugh and scream at the same time. He also kept asking me to forgive him, acting all pathetic and contrite. As if I'd ever want to marry him?

That's what landed me in the hospital in the first place. After he asked, "So we're marrying soon, right? When should we set the date?"

I shook my head repeatedly. Like one would at the suggestion of having an arm chopped off. "There's no way I'm marrying you."

Silly me. I should have kept that to myself. He'd been drinking heavily because his drug dealer hadn't delivered, which was a double whammy, I soon discovered. Drunk and desperate for a hit turned him into a crazed monster.

"Don't mess with someone's head when they're chasing, Bitch."

"I'm not marrying you, Bram. I want you gone from my fucking life. Like now. Do your worst."

Well… he did.

Next thing, I was lying in the hospital battered and bruised.

"Declan visited Lochridge a couple of years ago," my mother said, helping me snap out of that horrible re-run of Bram attacking me.

"That was the last time anyone stayed there," she continued. "He found it run-down and, like with all those old sprawling places, damp and cold. It's now got central heating. The roof leaks have been repaired, I'm told, and the main sitting room and lounge freshly painted and restored. I was meant to go down and inspect it, but life's gotten in the way." She paused. "I've asked Jim to hire staff for your stay."

A flurry of excitement ran through me, thinking of that long trip with Carson as my bona fide bodyguard.

Maybe he'd become my lover again. It had been torture not being with him.

The lurid contents of that sex tape had affected him more than I'd imagined. I would have thought him a little more open-minded. But at least it meant he cared. He made that plain enough when he visited me in the hospital. His gaze held mine forever like he'd never let me go, making me feel loved and cherished. At the mention of Bram, his eyes darkened.

"Are you sure you want to stay away for a month?"

"I'm enrolled in an online design course. And away from all the distraction here, I might make a go of it." I sighed. "And to be honest, I need a break from Manon."

My mother splayed her hands. "Darling, I need her here. Otherwise, goodness knows what she'll become."

"She's already become it. Under your very nose. She's screwing Crisp and working for him at Ma Chérie. Mum, you need to put a stop to that sleaze happening on our doorstep."

She frowned. "She hasn't slept with him, and Rey's reassured me he's stopped pursuing her."

"Yeah, right. And he's donating his billions to charity."

My mother smiled at my irony. "He's not as bad as you make out."

"You obviously don't know him that well."

"I know Rey better than most." Her raised eyebrow wasn't lost on me.

I was dying to know why she kept him close. And how he owned land that once belonged to our family.

She rubbed her long fingernails, something she did when challenged. Over and above everything, however, I couldn't understand why she was turning a blind eye to the young girls entering through the back of the casino almost nightly.

"They might be trafficking underage girls for all you know."

"They're not." She sounded tetchy.

"Then what the hell is going on with those girls arriving in vans? It smells like something rotten."

"They're auctioning themselves off."

I frowned at how cool my mother's tone sounded at that preposterous idea. "Like their virginity, you mean? So it's a sex club for older men to fuck young virgins?"

She winced. "It's a gentleman's club. What a misnomer that is."

"Yeah, it should be called a dirty old men's club." I sniffed.

"I'm told girls dance in skimpy outfits before being auctioned."

"Oh my god. Like cattle." I shook my head in disgust.

She looked defeated despite her resigned tone. Knowing my mother, she would have discussed this sad affair ad nauseam with Crisp.

"They can do it there or online. According to Rey, it's safer for the girls this way because they get to choose, and they sign legal documents to ensure they're paid and protected."

I shook my head. "Regardless. You have to close it down. And what about Manon's part?"

My mother bit her lip. I could see she was under a lot of pressure. This was not her at all. She used to hate me wearing short skirts when I was Manon's age.

"Manon helps the girls with makeup and dressing and offers pep talks. She insists that none are under eighteen. They sign forms of consent. She even showed me."

"She showed you? Shit, Mum, you can't let this happen at the back of Elysium. It's seedy and should remain in London alleyways and not at a luxury destination."

She sighed. "It's Rey's land. I have no control."

"I thought that land belonged to our family."

She shook her head. "It's a long story, darling."

The sadness in her voice rang loud, and with Cary breaking her heart, I decided to lay off and hobbled off to pack for my trip away.

Despite not knowing who'd seen the sex tape since Bram kept pleading innocence, I still felt the need to hide. I'd even considered changing my name. Only I was a Lovechilde. I could never walk away from my name and heritage. It flowed through my veins.

At least Carson had agreed to accompany me. A big paycheck would have helped, despite him saying it wasn't about the money.

The pity in his honey-colored eyes made me want to yell obscenities, but I needed him.

I couldn't even think of sex. Not in my condition. I ached all over.

I even told Carson, "I won't try to fuck you. I can't anyway."

Darkness intensified in his gaze. He mumbled something about killing Bram if he came anywhere near him.

As touched as I was, because it showed just how much I meant to Carson, that terrified me. If he got locked up because of me, I would have lost my mind completely.

Could I do one month with Carson without seducing him? I shrugged that thought away. For now, I needed a driver and someone close so that I wouldn't keep jumping at my own shadow.

He was the only person I could trust to keep me safe, which had little to do with him making my heart flutter each time I saw him, smelt him, or stood close.

LOCHRIDGE SAT ON A hill surrounded by a rugged forest and nothing but the wild ocean. Winds roared through the trees, making them dance vigorously, looking like they might snap.

Carson had spoken little during our five-hour trip to Lochridge. We mainly argued about music.

"It's my car. I choose the music," he'd said with that authoritative, deep voice.

When "I Put a Spell on You" came on, I relented. "I love this song."

"You see? There's a lot about the blues to love."

I smiled. It was nice being together for such a long period. I don't think we'd ever spent that much time together.

Normally, he had me all hot and bothered. But for once, I didn't count down the minutes when we'd get all naked and sweaty. Even though, as always, he looked good enough to ravage, especially in that green polo. His well-developed pecs and biceps strained against the fabric as if trying to break free.

We drove up a rocky track, and as we bounced along in the SUV, he said, "A normal car wouldn't make it up here."

"From memory, we came here in a Range Rover."

"When were you here?"

"Um, when I was little. We only came here once. My dad preferred our house in France or our Torquay house."

"Why did you choose here?"

"You don't like it?" I studied him closely. He wasn't an easy man to read.

"I do. I just wondered."

"Mother suggested it. I think she liked that the house is secluded. Maybe she's worried Bram will find me."

"She doesn't need to worry with me here." His gaze softened, and I wanted to remove my blouse and cuddle him.

Stop it. He's your bodyguard, not your lover.

"It's rather picturesque," he said, as we drove through the iron gates of Lochridge.

"Legend has it they used the manor for a film in the sixties."

"A horror movie?" His dry delivery made me chuckle.

"It's not that bad, is it?" The overcast day did give the grey stone mansion a gloomy aspect. "The village is about three miles away. Surrounded by impossibly thick scrub and bent-over trees, it is rather remote."

As we pulled up in front of the two-story house, I had to agree with Carson about the place looking a little dark. As a girl, I used to love and hate the scary stories that my brothers fed me, eventuating in me sleeping between my mother and father.

"I needed somewhere away from people."

He did a slow turn, taking in the sights. "You've got that here. It's very secluded."

I studied him. Mm… secluded with him for a month. I sighed and felt an ache through my cleft. Was that pain or desire?

Both.

He must have read my mind because his eyes lingered, making me wish I'd worn my sunglasses to hide the black eye which was covered in foundation. Even applying makeup had become painful.

"Is it to your liking?" I watched him taking in the sights.

From where we stood, there was nothing but ocean bordered by craggy cliffs and windswept trees.

The sharp air refreshed and chilled at the same time.

"It's stunning. Is there a path to the sea?" he asked.

"There is. I'll show you after we've settled in."

"I might even get to do some fishing." His eyes had gone a soft amber, and he reminded me of a boy. I wanted to wrap my arms around him and smother him in sweet kisses.

"You fish?"

"When I get the time, I do." He lifted cases from the boot and placed them on the ground.

"I didn't know that. Why didn't you tell me?"

He sniffed. "Because you don't strike me as the fishing type."

He pointed down at my four-inch wedges, which I reserved for uneven ground, like walking through the grounds of Merivale.

"Did you bring some more practical footwear?"

"I brought a few pairs of flats. They're in there somewhere." I pointed at the heavier piece of luggage.

He lifted it, and his muscles strained against his polo, making me all hot and bothered again. "It weighs a ton. You must have brought an entire shopful."

I laughed. "Almost. I like my shoes."

"I've noticed." His eyes had gone into melty chocolate, and that spark of heat again sent a twinge of pain. My clit couldn't throb without my pelvis complaining.

"There's a boathouse that belongs to the family. I'll show you once we've settled."

His face brightened. "Now you're talking. Love boats."

I laughed. "You're such a boy."

He raised my two bags while the other smaller bags slung over his shoulders. "And you're such a girl. I mean, Savanah, really. All of this. It's ridiculous."

"Hello. We're here for a month, you know." The thought of spending a month with Carson invigorated me. Normally, my ADHD would have me running for Europe and hotel swapping. But after everything that had happened, anxiety had kicked my short attention span in the butt.

"Do you want me to carry something?" I marveled at how he managed five pieces of luggage. Those muscles threatened to burst a seam or two.

He shook his head. "I'm good."

Oh... That you are.

CHAPTER 20

Carson

I'D NEVER FELT SO much hatred before. And for a former soldier who'd seen his fair share of human cruelty, that was some admission. Seeing that beautiful face and those perfect eyes surrounded by bruising was like seeing a work of art destroyed by brainless criminals. And Bram was as brainless as he was sadistic.

I could almost understand a man beating another man for some stupid reason, like being drunk and in the mood to hit out at the world, but a woman?

Savanah didn't know that I'd gone to visit Bram's family home again. Soon as I heard Bram was out on bail, I drove to London in the middle of the night, looking for the prick. This time, Bram's old man blocked my entry. Unlike his son, he wasn't an idiot. He knew that if I got a hold of Bram, he'd end up in hospital.

And now there I was, away from London and the temptation to throttle the bastard beating at my chest. My Mr. Nice Guy did not extend to woman beaters.

It was a risk, me there for a month with the woman who'd taken up lodgings in my dick. However, my need to protect her trumped sexual frustration, of which there was plenty. As I was quickly discovering.

Just a whiff of her rose fragrance made me burn for her. I had to keep focusing on the tasks before me, like carrying that ridiculously heavy luggage up a ton of steps to that ghost house.

Savanah's safety was all that mattered. The insanely outrageous sum deposited into my account had little to do with this mission, which I saw as a labor of love.

Savanah had not only moved into my dick but also my soul. After seeing her in the hospital, my emotions went haywire. I'd never felt that kind of fear of losing someone before. Other than my mother, of course. But she deteriorated slowly, giving my emotions time to process the pain.

Despite something telling me that Savanah and I could never make it past that gorging stage, I couldn't control these deeper feelings.

I even went to return the money but didn't because her mother might grow suspicious. Billionaire heiresses didn't normally have relationships with their bodyguards.

"You've got rocks in this luggage," I said, heaving the load up the steep steps.

She walked ahead. "Let me see if Jim can help."

"I'm good." Seeing the extraordinary view, and having never visited Cornwall, I fell in love with what looked like ancient, untouched land.

Savanah knocked on the door. We waited for a while, and after another go, no one answered.

"You don't have a key?"

She shook her head. "That's odd. The caretaker knew we were arriving today. I was there when my mother called him." She pulled out her phone and then looked up at me in horror. "There's no signal."

I lowered the luggage. "Just wait a minute. I'll go around the back and see if there's a way in. I'm sure we can break in."

"But that's ridiculous. Where are the staff?" She looked alarmed.

I gave her an encouraging smile. "Don't worry. We'll sort this out."

The wind had a chilly sting, so I ran back to the car and grabbed my hoodie and a denim jacket.

Seeing Savanah gripping her arms, I placed the jacket over her shoulders.

"Oh my god. Denim. I hate it." She grimaced as if asked to walk around in a rubbish bag.

I laughed. "It looks good on you."

Her mouth curled slightly. "Does it?"

Savanah was such a child. I had to remind myself that she'd lived a different life than most. She was used to having everything whenever and wherever. And she was a fashion victim in the true sense of the word.

"It's a shame you don't like denim because it goes nicely with your eyes."

She clutched onto it. "Well, then. Thanks."

I smiled. "Back in a minute. Don't go anywhere."

"Yeah. Righto. I think I might just head over to visit the neighbours. Not." She rolled her eyes, and I laughed.

As I tramped around the side of the extensive property, I could only assume that the staff were at the back. It was a big estate.

For me, it didn't matter if they were there or not. I loved the idea of being alone. But for Savanah, who was used to servants, it would only stress her more. Even though a good slice of reality, maybe a week of roughing it, wouldn't be bad for her, I couldn't imagine her agreeing to that.

The vegetable garden was weed-ridden, and there was no sign of life. Confirmed by a bolted door.

I tried pushing hard against the back door, but it wouldn't budge, so I headed over to a shed and found a crowbar.

After I prized open the door, spider webs brushed my face, confirming that the place hadn't seen humans for a while.

Moving through the large kitchen area, I made my way to the front, through a large, musty room with sheets covering the furniture and a massive fireplace.

I went to the door and let Savanah in.

She stepped into the entrance, which was a large sitting room.

"What the fuck?" She turned around. "Where are the staff? The place looks fucking run-down." She brushed her face. "Dusty and yuck. Let's get out of here and stay at a hotel. I need a signal to call my mother."

"So, do I bring in your gear?"

She looked pale suddenly. "I can't stay here when it's like this."

"No. I guess you can't."

Savanah gave me a puzzled look. "And you can?"

"You bet. With a little dusting and cleaning, it will be lovely."

"Lovely?" She looked around. "Where are the cleaners? They should have already been here. I guess while they're getting it spick-and-span, we can stay at a hotel." She smiled. "That's what we'll do."

"Okay." I went to bend down to grab the luggage.

She stretched out her arms. "Let me carry the small bags, at least."

"No. I'm good."

"I'm not that unwell." She fisted her hips.

"I know you're not. But I've got this. Come on. Let's head off."

We got down to the SUV when I noticed a flat tyre.

"Shit." I dropped the luggage down.

"What?"

I pointed to the tire. "Must have been the rough ride."

"But aren't these cars meant to handle that?" Her voice went up in register.

I swallowed tightly. "It gets worse. That was a spare. I didn't have time to get another, I'm afraid."

Her eyes nearly popped out of their sockets. "What?"

"I'm sorry." I opened out my hands.

"How the fuck can you not have a spare?"

Although annoyed at myself for overlooking something as vital as a spare, her tone still grated on me. "Hey, mistakes happen."

"You're meant to be on top of this stuff. You're paid to be fucking organized."

Her words stabbed at me. I hated being yelled at.

Taking a deep breath, I counted to three to bite my tongue. "You wait here, and I'll go onto the main road and see if I can get a phone signal for help."

"I'm not waiting here on my own." She clutched her arms and shivered.

"Then come with me. But you need sensible shoes."

She huffed and puffed, and I rolled my eyes. If she hated me, I hated myself even more for fucking up.

While she rummaged through her suitcase, I walked around, seeing if I could get a signal, but to no avail.

As the highway was about a mile up the track, I hoped Savanah could manage.

She found a pair of wedged shoes with a flower stuck on them. Unfit for a rocky path. The shoes were so loud and ridiculous, I almost laughed.

"You don't have a pair of sneakers?" I asked.

"I hate sneakers."

I released a deep breath while maintaining a cool head. "Why don't you wait in the car, then?"

She shook her head. "I don't want to be here alone. Shit. Mum was meant to have it all nice and ready."

Reminding me of a young, lost girl, she started to cry.

"Let me see what else you've got." I softened my tone in a bid to calm her down.

She rummaged through her shoes and held up a pair of sandals with a smallish heel. "These I normally wear to the beach."

"They'll do. You might need socks. It's cold."

"Socks with sandals?" Her face crumpled in shock like I'd asked her to parade in her knickers. "How awful."

"This is not a fashion show. I promise not to look, and it's getting dark. We need to get moving."

She looked up at the sky and pointed. "Shit. It looks like it's going to rain."

Too caught up in the wardrobe drama, I hadn't noticed. A blanket of darkness was heading towards us. "That came up suddenly."

I looked back at the mansion, which, with the darkening sky, looked even gloomier.

"Fuck. Fuck. Fuck." She clasped her head. "I've ended up at the fucking Addams Family's house. Only there are no weirdos for entertainment."

"I don't know. I can do a good Uncle Fester or Gomez after a few drinks." I smirked.

She slapped my arm. "Stop making jokes."

I hoped for a smile, but she looked long-faced and distraught, making me feel like shit again for fucking up.

"Why don't we go inside and set up the place for the night? I'll gather some wood. We can make a fire. I'll dust and clean one room where we can sleep. That will be easy enough. We don't need to inhabit the entire house. Do we?"

Her mouth made a tight line. "I guess not. What about food? I'm hungry."

"Let's go in and see what's there. And first thing in the morning, I'll get out onto the highway and try to sort this out. Okay?"

"I guess."

Not letting her sulky attitude get to me, I carried her luggage back in.

I switched on the lights. "At least the electricity's working. That's something."

She shivered. "Is there any heating?"

"From the looks of things, it's the fireplace. But hey, I can get that going."

She followed me to the back. "It doesn't look like anyone's been here for ages."

"No." I went to the larder and found lots of tins. I picked up one of braised beef and vegetables. "This will have to do for tonight."

"Yuck." She grimaced. "Is there anything to drink?"

I went to the sink and after the water ran for a while; it cleared.

"I think there's a cellar somewhere. I remember playing there when I was young. We pretended it was a dungeon."

I followed her to the back of the kitchen and found stairs leading down to a cellar. "Wait here," I said. "The last thing I want is for you to slip and hurt yourself."

I hurried to my car and grabbed a torch from the glove box. Still angry at myself. I didn't normally forget important details like a spare tyre.

Upon visiting the cellar, I discovered—much to my relief—wine, whisky, and bottles of ale, and therefore, I brought up a bit of everything.

Savanah popped her head into the fridge. "Ew. There's rotting meat in here. And to think my mother's been paying a caretaker."

"I'd say they've been doing something else with their time," I said.

She picked up a bottle of Burgundy. "There better be a corkscrew."

I pulled out my Swiss knife. "I've got one here. Why don't we have a nip of whisky? It will warm you up quicker than wine will."

"Good thinking." She sat on a chair and slumped, looking resigned to a night of roughing it.

I loved an open fire, so after I'd had a quick shot, I rubbed my hands together. "Right. Back in a minute. I'll gather some wood." I grabbed a cane basket by the door. A smaller one caught my eye, and I pointed. "Maybe you can collect some kindling. It will be quicker."

"I don't even know what that is." Savanah wore that confused, worried look that told me to leave her be. I had to keep reminding myself this girl hadn't lived in the real world.

"Don't worry. Leave it to me. For now, maybe remove the dust covers from the front room. Yes?"

She wasn't a woman who was used to doing anything. Least of all taking orders. She released a puff. "Okay. But hey, I'm pissed off with you."

"Yeah. Yeah. I'll keep apologizing when I return."

She rolled her eyes and returned a mock smile.

As it happened, I discovered a shed of chopped wood. So I went around and collected twigs from the adjoining forest. Overall, I felt light and alive. I loved the place. Resourcefulness had been drummed into me in the army, and this was children's play compared to the challenges I'd faced while on tour.

Having endured long stretches at army campsites with very little else but video games and men talking about all the things they missed, patience had also been drilled into me. In any case, I preferred the ocean over the desert, beach scrub over caves, and soaring seabirds over military aircraft.

I returned to find that Savanah had removed the cover from a couch and a table. "Will this do?"

"For now." I dropped the wood by the fireplace and got to work, and before long, a roaring fire brought some welcomed cheer to the room.

"It was meant to be painted and restored." She pointed at the cracked walls.

"I might just check upstairs and set up our sleeping arrangement first, just in case."

She clutched her arms. "In case of what?"

"There's a storm coming, and if the electricity cuts out, we'll be in the dark. I've got a torch. But while there's light, I'll get things ready."

She bit into a nail.

"Are you okay?"

She shook her head. "What do you think? This is turning out to be a nightmare."

I smiled. "See it as an adventure. You wanted to get off the grid. Now you've got it."

"Not to this extent. I've lost all contact with the outside world."

My eyes settled on a phone. I pointed. "There's a landline here."

Her eyes lit up. "Oh my god, so there is." She bit her lip. "I don't even know my mother's number."

I raised the receiver and discovered there was no dial tone. "It's not working."

Her body slumped. The poor girl was seriously out of her comfort zone, and guilt sliced through me for not packing that tyre.

Sticking close, Savanah followed me up the stairs. The rooms were large but dark and a little gloomy.

"God, I don't remember this place being so horrid." She peered into a wardrobe filled with coats.

She pulled out a woman's red coat. "This is kind of cute. Very '60s." She sniffed it. "And musty."

"Give it some air, and at least it will keep you warm." I removed the duvet and gave it a good shake.

"Should we sleep up here?" I asked.

I glanced at the double bed, unsure of what to say. We weren't meant to be sleeping together. Up to now, she'd been the initiator. Not that I minded. Women taking the lead were kind of sexy. But that was in the past with Savanah and I had to stick to my role as a bodyguard and not some smitten ex-lover.

"No. It's creepy and freezing. Near the fire would be better."

I had to agree. The damp, dusty room was not very inviting.

"And the bathroom's too far. At least there's one downstairs that's not too terrible," she added.

"There are two mattresses downstairs. In the servant's quarters. They'll be easier to drag out. Should we do that?" I asked.

Rain pummelled the windows, and the howling wind made them rattle.

"Anything. Just let's go back downstairs." She gripped her arms.

"There aren't any ghosts." I chuckled.

"Oh, there are. I'm sure. I sense these things." She clutched onto the red coat.

I stretched out my hands. "Here, why don't you put it on?" I took the coat from her and helped her into it.

"It smells a bit. But it's warm." She stood before a mirror.

"It suits you." I knew her well enough to know that would matter. I wasn't bullshitting, though, because red suited her.

Everything suited her. She was gorgeous. Even in this difficult situation, Savanah still looked radiant. Her thick dark hair was messed up like I'd run my hands through it.

We returned to the kitchen, where I piled wood into the potbelly stove.

"At least there's a shed of chopped wood. There's enough to last for a week or even more." I poked at the fire.

"A week or more?" Her face crumpled in horror as she pulled up a chair at the large wooden table.

I laughed. "Oh, Savvie."

"Savanah to you."

"Well, pardon me." I pulled a posh voice, and her mouth curved slightly.

"That should warm up the kitchen." I rose from the stove to inspect the cupboards, where I found candles, tobacco, torches, and a cigarette lighter.

"Oh my god. I want one." Savanah looked longingly at the packet of cigarettes as a child would a bag of sweets.

"I thought you'd given up." I placed the items on the table.

"I had. But this is stressful." She lunged for the pack.

"Knock yourself out." I poured myself another shot of whisky and held up the bottle. She nodded, and I poured some into her glass.

She took the drink and lit up a cigarette, and as smoke poured out of her mouth, she sighed with relief. "Oh, that's better."

I hated passive smoking, but I wasn't about to complain.

She raised the pack. "Do you smoke?"

I shook my head. "Nope. Never. My mother died of smoke-related disease."

"Oh really. Lung cancer?"

"No. Throat cancer."

She puffed away, looking interested and concerned at the same time. "That's so sad. I know so little about your life."

I exhaled a breath. "There's not much to know." I gulped down the drink and then rose. "I'll drag the mattress into the front room. Yes?"

She nodded slowly. "Is there just the one?" She wore a suggestive smirk, which made me smile.

Give me flirting over whining any day.

"There are single mattresses from what I've seen."

She puffed out smoke. "We really are roughing it."

I smiled sympathetically. "We'll have this sorted by tomorrow. It will only be for a night."

Her face brightened, which put me at ease at last. I hadn't realized how on edge I'd been.

"It's kind of interesting. And I love open fires. It's warming up at least." Removing her coat, Savanah still wore my denim jacket. "I guess I should give you back your jacket."

"No, keep wearing it. It suits you."

She gazed up at me and held my stare. "Really?"

I'd already told her that, but Savanah loved to milk compliments, and I didn't mind. "It goes with your pretty blue eyes."

"I'm not exactly a peach at the moment. All battered and bruised."

"Sorry. I forgot you were in pain, and here I am getting you to do things."

"No. It's okay. I'm feeling better. Not so much pain today. I haven't even taken a drug." She chuckled.

"That makes me glad." I thought about my mother and how she took painkillers like sweets that turned her into a zombie. They not only numbed her physical pain but emotional pain, which resulted in her remoteness towards us in the end.

She held my gaze and frowned. "Why do you care if I take them or not? Although my mother keeps at me about my Xanax use."

"I don't blame her, Savanah."

"Call me Savvie, if you like." She flashed me a conciliatory smirk.

"Okay." Her eyes held mine again, and I fiddled. This was becoming a little complicated. I wanted to hold her and care for her, but I also wanted her as a woman. "Pharmaceuticals are just as bad, if not worse than street drugs."

She shrugged. "To be honest, after everything that's happened and is happening, I couldn't give a shit."

My heart went out to her. I could see she needed to speak to a professional. A suggestion I would leave for another time.

I left her at the table smoking, to organize our bedding.

I soon discovered that the single-bed mattresses had bedbugs, after catching mites jumping when I raised the sheets. Someone had sprayed the double-bed mattress, which I could still smell so that it was clear of the little biters.

Back to complicated. I rubbed my head. The double mattress was all we had. I dragged it out and positioned it in the front room and then found clean sheets and pillowcases in the cupboard.

Savanah followed me around. "Are we sleeping on that? Together?"

Despite being tempted, I wasn't about to remind her how we'd fucked mindlessly for close to two months.

"I *can* exercise control when needed." I raised an eyebrow, and she smiled.

CHAPTER 21

Savanah

HE RAN HIS HAND down his face. "There are single mattresses, but I'm afraid they've got bedbugs."

I scrunched my face. ". Fuck that."

"Don't worry. It's a big mattress. I promise to behave."

Carson seemed to enjoy this hell, whereas I felt so out of my skin, I did not know who I was anymore. I was helpless. I needed him there, yet I wanted to hit and scream at him for forgetting that fucking tire.

I watched as he made the bed. The roaring fire helped. The room was no longer bleak and damp.

Carson went to the kitchen, and I followed. Despite the improved ambiance, I hated to be alone in the room. That childhood belief in the house being haunted probably lingered.

"You must be hungry," he said, looking for something in a drawer.

I rubbed my belly. "Starving. But I don't know if I can bring myself to eat that." I pointed at the tin he'd opened.

"Well, I'm game." He smiled.

Thunder struck, and I jumped. Carson headed back into the front room and, like a puppy dog, I followed at his heels.

From the large window, we watched cracks of lightning illuminate a grey, angry ocean.

"That's fantastic," he said. "I love a storm over the sea."

"I do too when surrounded by twenty-first-century comforts," I said.

He pulled a subdued smile. "Don't worry. We're fine here. We've got everything we need."

I followed him back into the kitchen and watched him move around with ease like it was his home.

As he stirred the pot, he pointed at a cupboard. "Can you grab a couple of plates?"

I went over and found a plate and returned it to the table.

The Burgundy remained unopened and despite a few shots of whisky, my body craved more alcohol. "Could you do the honors?" I pointed at the bottle.

He pulled out a contraption with lots of bits to it and miraculously opened the bottle. Something told me that Carson could resolve most things. A comforting thought despite this stubborn resentment towards him for putting us in this mess.

To be reasonable, it wasn't completely Carson's fault, since Jim the caretaker was the baddie here.

Despite my shitty attitude towards him, I found myself more and more attracted to Carson. I loved how my comfort meant everything to him, and how resourceful he was. There was nothing he couldn't do.

He stirred the pot and then added more logs into the stove's furnace, which proved a turn-on. A pang of desire shot through me on seeing those flexed muscles straining through his polo as he lifted logs.

Who would have thought watching a man toiling away could be such a turn-on?

"Are you okay?" Carson must have noticed my wince.

"Um. I get the odd twinge here and there."

His eyes darkened. "If I get my hands on that prick…"

I regretted bringing up my ordeal. Bram was the last person I wanted to think about.

"Where's your plate?" Carson scanned the table.

"I don't want to eat that shit." I stuck to my guns despite the aroma making me hungrier.

He shrugged. "You should have some."

I found a couple of glasses and poured out the red wine. I took a sniff.

"The wine smells okay."

He took a sip. "It tastes even better. It's a good drop."

"And you would know." I inclined my head.

"I've had enough dinners at Merivale to appreciate a decent wine, yes."

"Hmm…" I sipped the wine and was pleasantly surprised. "It must have been ordered for one of my family's visits."

"When did they come here?"

"Like twenty years ago. I was little." I watched him eat, and my stomach pleaded with me.

He stopped eating and looked at me. "It's not that bad."

I took a cracker from a packet Carson found in the pantry and dipped it in his stew. The meaty gravy made my stomach pine for more.

"I guess I can have some."

He sprung up, looking pleased like my eating meant everything to him. A sudden sense of guilt flushed through me for acting like a sulky diva, motivated by some childish need to punish him.

THE STORM INTENSIFIED, AND the howling wind rattled the doors and windows.

"I can run a bath for you." Carson lounged in a leather armchair. The light emanating from the roaring fire gave his face a warm glow.

As the hypnotic flames danced, I relaxed for the first time that day.

"Maybe tomorrow after the bath's been cleaned. I hope I'm not too smelly." I sipped on my wine, which had made me so pleasantly tipsy that I'd almost forgotten all about tomorrow and how we'd have to navigate our way to a phone signal.

I watched Carson stoke the fire and add more logs. I would have been hopeless without him. But then, I wouldn't be there.

"I don't know why I let my mother convince me to come here."

Sipping on a whisky, Carson looked like he belonged there. "It's magic. I've never sat in front of a large open fire like this before."

"Really?"

He smiled. "We sat around bonfires in the army, but never in a mansion."

"We have them at Merivale. Mainly for effect, since we also have central heating." He gave me one of his searching stares. "Why are you looking at me like that?"

He shrugged. "Just marveling at your privileged life."

"It's not always great, you know."

He stretched out his long, muscular legs.

"You do look rather content, sitting there."

"What's not to like?" He stared into my eyes, and a sudden ache in my vagina made me reposition myself.

Is this man right for me?

My heart needed to guide me, not my libido.

Carson definitely had top billing with my libido. But lost somewhere among the rubble of my recent fall from grace, my heart was another matter.

"Why are you looking at me like that?" he asked.

"Because every time you undress me with your eyes, my clit throbs." I couldn't help myself. Sexy talk with Carson felt as natural as shopping for lurid lingerie. And wine helped.

His eyebrows shot up. "Am I that obvious?"

"Yep. You've got that same hooded stare as when you're fucking me."

"It's not intentional. Must be a subconscious thing." A slow, sexy smile grew on his face. "Probably at the mention of your throbbing clit." His eyes softened to a shade of honey. "Do you want me to put it out of its misery?"

The throb intensified, only this time there was no stabbing pain, only need.

"Bram made a mess of my vagina."

His playful smirk turned into a dark glower. "Fucking cunt. If I get a hold of him, I'll rearrange him."

"He's not worth going to jail over." My sober response hid the sudden fear gripping me. I would have lost my mind if Carson got locked up on my behalf.

"What do the doctors say?" His voice softened, and I breathed again.

Despite us descending into the dark topic of vendetta, Carson's concern was touching.

"I probably won't be able to give birth." My voice cracked.

Silence filled the room as if someone had hit a mute button. As tears burned, Carson stared into my eyes. His lips were tight and his eyebrows pulled together as if he truly wished to help. In that unblinking, bordering-on-pained gaze, I not only read deep concern but also a restless need to fix this—to rip Bram apart.

No one else knew this, other than my mother. I couldn't bring myself to share that heart-shattering prognosis.

Tears kept pouring out, washing over my cheeks. Turning to stoicism as a crutch, I hadn't even cried on my mum's shoulder while sharing this dark outcome. I acted like I didn't care if I gave birth or not.

But it mattered.

A lot.

Being robbed of motherhood felt like losing a baby.

He kneeled at the side of my chair and put his arm around me.

"You're a strong, healthy woman, Savanah. There's a lot the medical profession can do these days."

"I don't know." Tears kept coming like I'd burst an emotional artery.

He rose and walked away, returning with a box of tissues, and passed them to me.

I blew my nose and wiped my face. "At least it doesn't hurt to pee anymore."

He paced while rubbing his neck. "I can't stand it. I need to see this fucking guy."

I leaned over and grabbed his arm, which was so muscle-bound that a sizzle of desire travelled through me.

Maybe the wine had numbed away the pain from that attack, but then why did I feel so much throbbing and tingling desire?

"That's why I came here, away from everything, to think about my future."

He sat again. "And what does that look like?"

I knitted my fingers. "That question makes me want to pop a Xanax. Even the therapist couldn't get an answer from me." I chuckled coldly. "Everything seems so unclear. Blurry. I don't think I've gotten over losing my dad." I swallowed back a lump. "Before Dad died, I skipped through life, taking things for granted. At the back of my mind, I just assumed that one day I'd marry and have children."

"Do you want that?" he asked. "Or is it because everyone expects that from you?"

"Well, I'm of the nonconforming kind."

He smiled sadly. "That's what makes you special."

I lurched my head back. "Really? So it wasn't my long legs and sexy bedroom eyes after all?"

He sniffed. "Oh, they will win hands-down each time. You're fucking gorgeous. But..." He stroked his lower lip. "I like that you're not just looking for Mr. Right. There's more to you."

"Is there? Then can you point me to her? Because most days I feel like an empty shell. And I am searching for Mr. Right. Only now, who will fucking want me? I'm barren."

Tears ran down my face again. Just saying that out loud had twisted a knife deeper into my heart.

"Oh, Savvie..." He gave me an uncertain smile. "I can call you that?"

"Yes. Of course, you can. I'm sorry. I just wanted to hit you."

"Mm... I wouldn't have minded." His eyes shone with a wicked grin.

As jarring as that shift in mood was, I welcomed it because I needed a break from all this self-reflection.

"Oh god, not you too. You're not wanting me to go all dominatrix, are you?"

"Me too?" He studied me. "How many men have you been with since we started to..." He played with his fingers, and I noticed a shy look.

"Fuck." I finished his sentence, claiming my role as the brazen one in this dynamic. "Nothing like that. Just that Jacinta, a friend of mine, has met this guy who likes to be beaten, with her in leather."

Carson laughed. "You'd look hot in leather, but at the back of my bike, gripping onto my waist. That's as far as it goes. I meant I could handle you hitting me if you wanted to, given that I was trained to take punches, and therefore make a good human punching bag."

"That's crazy." I laughed. "I didn't know you owned a motorbike."

"When I get back to Bridesmere, I'm planning to buy one." He went serious. "Touching on that earlier subject about children—not all men need to become fathers."

"Do you?" I asked hesitantly. This was the deepest conversation we'd ever shared, and with Carson's gaze looking all soft and caring, my heart grew like a balloon.

"Nope. Love is more important. I mean, I like kids. But there are so many around."

I took a moment to respond. "So, fatherhood's not on your to-do list?"

"Nope. I can take it or leave it. I live in the now and adjust my life accordingly. I can't think too far ahead."

"I wouldn't have taken you for the spontaneous type. You strike me as someone with a clear sight of where you want to be."

"If only life was that organized."

"You sound sad," I said.

"I'm not. I'm here. Loving this fire and talking to a beautiful woman on a soul search." He ran his hands down his face. "I also feel like shit for getting us into this predicament when I was meant to be protecting you."

"Don't worry. I'll punish you in other ways." I steamed up at the thought of teasing him.

"Mm... look forward to that." He sniffed.

I pointed. "There. You see? You do like it. You're a closet S and M freak."

He laughed. "Nope. Promise. Not one for whips and rubber suits. Although a little spanking on that very pert, fine arse of yours makes me hot."

I laughed. He'd already done that once, and it had turned me on.

You're off sex. Remember?

GETTING READY FOR BED, I made Carson come with me to the bathroom so I could brush my teeth, and when I returned to the living room, I pulled out a dozen different nighties, which were more silky negligees.

What was I thinking bringing these along?

Had I intentionally packed sexy nightwear for Carson? Or was it just a habit?

Carson stripped down to his briefs and his T-shirt, and as I stared at that perfect masculine specimen, I wondered how I'd ever sleep.

Especially with that bulge that seemed to grow as he watched me trying to choose what to wear to bed. My lacy negligees were arousing him.

He went to his overnight bag and brought out a long-sleeved T-shirt and tossed it to me. "I think you'll be more comfortable in this, won't you?"

I smiled. He was right. This was hardly the place for a silky nightie, and besides, it was freezing. I placed the red coat close by.

"Turn around," I said.

"It's nothing I haven't seen before." He lowered onto the mattress, which was on the ground close to the fire that, thinking of everything as Carson did, he'd screened off.

He rolled on his side to give me privacy, and I loved how his long-sleeved T-shirt felt on my body. Especially his scent.

Once in bed, I moved my legs vigorously to get warm.

The thick rain pelted down, and the roaring wind made the windows rattle, more so than earlier.

"I'm so glad you're here." I wrapped my arms around him and snuggled in tight.

"I love the sound of rain at night," he said.

"You're so warm. You don't mind if I huddle up close?"

"No. It's nice."

His warm, hard body made me feel so safe. I was relieved that there was only one mattress. Otherwise, my earlier petulance may have robbed me of this deliciously cozy moment.

"I'm sorry if I acted like a spoilt brat earlier. I'm just out of my comfort zone. But tomorrow we can live it up. Yes? We'll go to the village and perhaps find somewhere nice to stay."

"Sure."

"Am I sensing disappointment?" I asked.

"Not really, but I was rather looking forward to that boat and some fishing."

I slapped him. "You're such a boy."

A very big boy.

The heavier the rain and more ferocious the winds, the more I squeezed onto Carson's solid muscle-bound body, loving how he felt against me. I'd never felt so safe with a man before, and after everything I'd experienced, Carson was the only man, other than my brothers, whom I could trust.

If only he wasn't so fucking hot.

I ran my hands over his rock-solid stomach.

There was a sizzling sensation between my thighs, and for the first time in two weeks, it was warm and inflamed and not stabbing at me.

"This reminds me of the first night. Remember when you stayed with me at Mayfair?"

"Pretty unforgettable."

His dry response intrigued me. "What do you mean?"

"Just that."

"Did you want to fuck me?" I walked my fingers down his stomach, and he flinched.

Was he scared of me touching his dick?

I knew I wanted to. Like badly.

"What do you think?" he replied.

"At the time, I read your rejection as you being unattracted."

"A man doesn't bone up over a woman he doesn't want to fuck."

His erection grew in my hand, and the veins throbbed in my palm, making my mouth water.

"You seem pretty hot right now."

He moved my hand and turned around, showing me his beautiful face in the soft light emanating from the embers. "Savvie, if you keep doing that, I'm going to come."

"That's okay, isn't it?"

"I like to return the favor."

"You can if you like." I smiled, loving where this was going.

To hell with pain. Give me nine inches any time.

His breath on my face made me feel his heat.

He ran his hands over me, settling on my breasts. We looked into each other's eyes and then our lips touched, brushing and exploring in that sweet, cushiony warmth. His tongue parted my lips, and I surrendered to a warm, moist dream.

Carson was the best kisser I'd ever experienced. And as his hands ran up and down my body, I was on fire.

I slid down his body, kissing him all the way down, before filling my mouth with his cock and sucking like mad.

"Fuck. That's nice."

I clasped onto his firm butt and gorged on his dick until my jaw ached.

"Savvie, I'm going to come." His voice was heavy with lust.

I moved my lips up and down his veiny, velvet shaft until he shot deep into the back of my throat. I drank his dick as though dying of thirst.

"Fuck." He held me tight. "That was insane. You give great blowjobs."

"Wasted talent?"

He pulled away and, wearing a frown, studied me. "No. I mean, I love your lips on my dick."

I laughed. "Don't panic. I'm too rich to go around blowing men for money."

"Thank Christ for that." He sounded worried.

"Why would you think that of me?"

"I don't. It's just what you said." He kept holding me tight.

His fingers touched my cleft, and I winced.

"Too much?" he asked.

"I'm all hot and throbby."

"Let me lick you. That should ease any pain."

He parted my legs, and before I could say, "yes, please," his tongue was lapping over my clit, and he sounded like he was devouring a banquet.

Warm swelling made my pelvis rise to his mouth. A fierce need to orgasm had become my only pain. My toes curled, and I screamed, scratching into his flesh while bathed in a golden light.

Then he just continued to ravage me, one orgasm after another, all merging into one almighty release that seemed to last forever.

I fell on my back and laughed.

"That was fucking wicked. Oh my god, I don't think I've come that hard before."

He wiped his creamy lips. "You're delicious."

I laughed and fell into his brawny arms. I wouldn't have changed a thing. Even sleeping on the mattress on the floor in front of an open fire would be a moment I'd never forget.

"I'm loving this suddenly," I said.

"Yeah. It's special." He sighed. "Out of adversity, sometimes magic happens."

"I guess you're right. We'd be in a pleasant hotel by now."

The contradiction from that comment made me giggle. Earlier, I'd wanted nothing but my normal comforts, and now here I was, slumming it and loving it.

Carson was right about being open to possibilities.

"I'm sorry we can't fuck," I said.

"That's okay, Savvie. Soon you'll be able to, I'm sure."

"Will you fuck me then?" I asked, breathing him. He always got this erotic, manly scent after coming.

"With pleasure." He kissed me sweetly on the lips.

Carson's dreamy, meaningful stare held mine, and I fell asleep with a smile.

CHAPTER 22

Carson

WITH THAT PERFECT ASS poking at my cock, I had to relieve myself if I wanted to walk properly. One better. Savanah ended up sucking me off for breakfast, as she sweetly put it.

I returned the favor and feasted on her pussy. Her release dripped on my tongue and made my dick go hard again.

Savanah had me in a state of constant arousal, especially as she spread her soft thighs wide, almost provoking me to enter her.

"Aren't you still sore?" I ogled her wet pink slit, and my dick hit my navel.

"Let's try. I'd love to feel you inside of me." She fondled her tits, making her nipples spike and my brain shut down.

Entering her slick, tight pussy using one finger, I withdrew after she flinched. "Sore?"

"No. Please, fuck me." Her sensuous, breathy tone made my pulse race.

"I'd love nothing more. But I also don't want to inflict pain."

Her pretty eyes smiled back at me. "I can take it. And that kind of pain is nice."

As though to prove a point, she parted her legs even wider and then fucked herself with her finger, her eyes burning passionately into mine.

Blood engorged my dick. Coated in cum and saliva from when she'd blown me earlier, my cock went steel-hard in my hand.

"You're a serious turn-on, Savvie."

She ran her soft hand over my cock, making it throb. "And so are you. I love your dick."

"Is that all?" I asked.

"I love you."

I searched for that customary cheeky grin, but her face didn't move.

What was that ache in my heart? Or was that warmth flooding me with a feeling I'd never experienced?

"Why did you stop?" Her eyes smiled back at me. And there it was. As I suspected, Savanah uttered those words as though she referred to liking my jacket or something just as mundane.

Although it may've been a game to her, for me, hearing those three powerful words robbed me of speech.

I cleared my throat. "I... wasn't expecting that."

Her smile turned sad and even heartfelt. Her eyes glistened, and again I was left speechless. "I do love you, Carson. You're the only person I trust outside of my family."

I took her in my arms and kissed her tenderly. My way of returning that love, because coming from my lips, that word felt foreign. Like it would leave me open to something I wasn't ready for.

Taking control, she held my dick. "Mm... you're so wet."

"That's your doing. You're a seductress, Savvie."

"Am I just?" She giggled and then held my dick in her fine, soft hand again. Even that one little action was a red-hot turn-on.

Taking control, she placed my throbbing dick at the entrance of her pussy. She opened wide and then arched her pelvis to meet mine with a thrust.

"Oh..." I grunted, and my heart almost leapt from my chest. It beat so fast. "How is that?" I gasped.

"Nice. I think."

"You think?"

"Just fuck me."

"I don't want to hurt you."

She hissed as I entered her, and I stopped.

"Please, go on. I like it. It's pleasurable pain." She moaned as I circled my dick slowly to stretch her.

"You're just a very small girl." I groaned at how good she felt.

"Small?"

"Your pussy is tight."

"Is that a turn-on?" Her eyes sparkled. Savanah loved to talk about sex, and that was fine by me because it only made me hotter.

"I can't tell you how much." I let out a breath.

Her groans kept making me stop. But she pushed onto my ass for me to continue.

The fleshy folds of her pussy sucked on my shaft and squeezed it tight. Her slick walls tugged at me with every stroke until my cock swelled to blowing point.

For someone who normally went all the way, I had to think of anything but her rosy erect nipples and how much I loved her aroused, hooding eyes, the deeper and harder my dick pounded.

As a thundering climax rushed through me, I lost all control. It might have been all the tension surrounding Savanah's attack, and my fuck-up with the tyre, but I blew so hard my brain almost left my skull.

It took some time to remember who I was.

After my senses returned, I repositioned myself and held her.

"Are you sure I didn't hurt you?"

"No. I mean, it's still a little tender."

"You didn't come, did you?"

"No. But I was close." She smiled sadly.

"You know that if I see Bram, I'm going to want to kill him?"

"Would you really kill for me?"

"I would."

"Then you must love me," she said.

As someone more inclined towards action rather than words, I responded with a kiss.

Yes, I do love you. I just don't know how to say it.

"So, what are we having for breakfast?" I asked.

She pulled a scowl, which I could only assume related to my swift redirection of conversation. "There isn't anything, is there? Only tins of food. We can have a cup of tea, though, can't we?"

I stretched my arms and then stood up. "There's flour and powdered milk."

"No eggs though," she said.

"There are powdered eggs." I put on my briefs. "I think I'll try that shower."

She got up and gripped her arms. "Me too. It's freezing."

I STEPPED OUTSIDE TO check on the sky. The rain had set in. It hadn't stopped all night.

We were up high, but I wondered about the road and whether it might be flooded.

I found a raincoat and ran to the shed and grabbed some logs, wrapping them in the raincoat, and then I got the potbelly stove going in the kitchen for breakfast.

"I can't believe my parents didn't modernize with a stove." Savanah stood by, watching me load logs into the furnace.

"This will do, and there's also a wood-fired oven for bread."

"For bread? You're going to bake?" The shock on her face made me laugh.

"I'm not just a pretty face." I grinned.

She chuckled. "So I'm discovering."

I found an electric jug for tea, and Savanah brightened up. "Goody. That means a cup of tea."

I laughed. Yesterday it was all about shoes and five-star restaurants. Today it was a cup of tea. Maybe this situation was good for her after all because if anyone needed a dose of reality, it was Savanah.

I whipped up some pancakes and placed them on our plates. Then, holding up a jar of homemade raspberry jam, I said, "Look what I found."

"Yum." She stared down at her plate as though seeing a miracle. "I'm starving, and these look great."

I lavished jam on her pancakes and mine, feeling quite pleased with myself. I hadn't cooked for a while, and I quite enjoyed it. Especially seeing Savanah's pretty face light up.

"I also found ground coffee and an espresso."

Her eyes widened with glee like I'd discovered a gold mine.

With breakfast eaten and the coffee brewed, Savanah looked quite content as she clutched her cup. "So, shall we go out and try to get a ride to the village?"

"In this rain?" I frowned.

She'd changed into a dress suited for a night out in London. "Maybe we should wait until it stops, I suppose."

"Have you got any jeans or comfortable clothes?"

She touched her dress. "This is comfortable."

"But you're shivering, Savvie."

"I've got some leggings. I'll pop them on. They'll look kind of weird with this, though."

"I preferred you in my T-shirt, to be honest," I said.

"You don't like my clothes?" She looked disappointed like I'd criticized something dear to her heart.

"You're not only the most beautiful, but also the most stylish woman I've ever known. I'm just talking about comfort here."

She slanted her face. "What a nice thing to say."

Without a stitch of makeup, Savanah looked ravishing with those rosy cheeks and her bright eyes brimming with anticipation.

"I am a little cold, I must admit. When we go to the village, I can buy some warmer clothes."

"We're not going to the village in this rain, Savvie." I rubbed my face. How will we do this?

I could easily entertain myself. I had a book on military history that I enjoyed sinking into. How would I keep Savanah occupied?

Her face scrunched, as though she was trying to solve something. "Oh, well. I guess I best try to change into something a little more comfortable."

We returned to our makeshift bedroom, and as I added more logs to the fire, Savanah laid out her extensive collection of clothes.

"You brought a lot of clothes." I grinned.

"I don't enjoy wearing the same thing twice."

"You must need a large room just for your clothes." I poked at the embers to fire them up before adding more logs.

"I give them away to charity shops."

"That's generous."

I headed back into the kitchen and to the storage room, where I put on a pair of wellingtons and a heavy-duty raincoat and hat.

Never far from my side, which I kind of liked, Savanah grimaced. "Are you seriously going out there?"

"I'm going to get as much wood as I can. You can help if you like." I pointed to another raincoat and boots.

She looked at them in horror.

"You know what? Don't worry. I've got this. Have you got a book or something?"

"I have." She bit her lip. "I've also brought my sketchpad."

Now that took me by surprise. "You draw?"

"Don't look so surprised. I attended art school for a while."

"I'm not surprised. You've got a lot of flair, Savvie."

I left her there at the door, watching as I tramped into the thick downpour, trying to avoid the mudholes.

CHAPTER 23

Savanah

WHO WOULD HAVE THOUGHT I'd be sitting there getting all aroused by seeing Carson stoking the stove for our daily survival?

Clutching a cup of tea, I watched on, entertained as this muscle-bound hottie worked up a sweat. His checkered shirt looked like it might pop buttons as he threw heavy logs into the furnace.

He caught me ogling, and a subtle smile grew on his sexy lips. "What?"

I shrugged. "I'm just getting off on watching you laboring."

He sniffed in that dismissive way of his. "Your turn will come soon. How's that cup of tea coming?"

"Ooh... Aren't we getting bossy?" I poked my tongue.

If truth be known, I liked him bossing me around. Once I would have resisted, even protested, but this experience had changed me. He even ordered me to clean the bath after I refused to use it, which caused a huge argument. As a result, we both scrubbed away and ended up in it making love.

The pain in my body had subsided too, and despite my initial whining over the lack of modern conveniences, I'd grown fond of having to think about mundane things like stoking the fire or making cups of tea. Even washing dishes. Carson had me doing chores I'd never done before. It always started with an argument, but then he'd spank me playfully or say something silly. I even provoked him on purpose.

Isolation had done me the world of good, and three days into our stay, I'd even gotten used to canned food.

Carson cast his attention on my drawing pad. I'd turned the kitchen table into my makeshift desk, mainly because the light was ideal.

"Do you mind if I look?" He cocked his head towards my pad.

I shrugged. "It's just a project I'm doing for my course."

"You're enrolled in a course?" His eyebrows shot up.

I laughed. "Don't look so shocked."

"I'm not. I'm just interested."

That was him. Interested in everything I revealed about myself.

Another big tick.

He had lots of those.

Gold stars, if I had to mark him.

Carson kept surprising me. Over and above everything, however, he proved to be a man with a beautiful soul who was also an amazing lover.

He also didn't take my shit.

And these cute minor battles always descended into passionate sex against a wall or me bent over a table and him punishing me with his cock pounding into me and making me cry like a bitch in heat.

That was the entrée. In bed, we made love. Or so Carson described it as that. It felt like lovemaking for me too. I'd never had a man massage me every night.

After licking me to the point of madness, he'd take me nice and slow, his gaze unshifting as though searching for my soul. We'd move in perfect rhythm, and he'd fill me to bursting point. His shaft seemed to thicken the deeper he penetrated, scraping sizzling pleasure points until a roaring orgasmic firestorm took possession.

"I was meant to finish the course last year." I laughed at my relentless procrastinating. "They asked me to practice drawing things around me, just to loosen up my hand. I'm not sure why because I'm studying design, which involves using software."

He flicked through my drawings, which made me feel a little bashful. "They're not very good," I said.

"I disagree. They're great. I could never do that."

Apart from sketches of chairs and still life, I'd drawn a picture of Carson, and even a self-portrait.

"Do I look like that?" he asked, tilting his head to study the image of his face.

I laughed. "I told you I'm not that good."

"No. It's well executed. Just that I look quite weathered."

I studied him with a growing smile. "Ooh, is that a hint of vanity?"

"Well, I am human. I can't imagine anyone wants to look older."

"True. But you don't look older. You look rugged, which I find very sexy. Give me that any day to smooth-faced men."

He chuckled. "I'll be sure to hang out in the sun more often."

I held his stare and went serious. "Does it matter to you? How I see you?"

He chewed on the side of his lip. "I think so. I mean, you're drop-dead gorgeous, and I'm just a regular guy."

I frowned. "I wouldn't describe you that way. Girls look at you all the time."

"Do they?" His lips curled in a sexy grin, and I wanted to slap him.

"Are you fishing for compliments?"

"Nope. I meant it. I'm not sure why women like me."

"Well, you're tall, well-built, got cute brown eyes. And you're..." I stretched my leg and massaged his bulge with my foot.

He returned a hooded gaze and then moved my foot delicately. "I've got to get some more wood before that turns to wood." He grinned. "Anyway, you've got a ton of talent." He flicked a page and paused at my self-portrait. "Can I have that?"

"It's not very good. I look unhappy. And it's only a quick sketch."

"Doesn't matter. It's beautiful." He stroked my cheek. "It captures you well. You're amazing, Savvie. You need to harness this talent."

Tears burned at the back of my eyes. No one had ever said that to me before. My family always tried to encourage me, but I'd never had someone say I possessed some kind of special gift.

I chuckled tightly. "And I thought my only talent was shopping and clothes."

"Oh, you've got talent in many areas." He gave me a crooked smile. "You look great in anything, Savvie."

My cheeks fired up. "Now you're making me blush."

I touched the vintage Dolce and Gabbana jeans that I'd found upstairs in a closet, which fitted me like a glove. They must have belonged to my mother. Her collection of cashmere turtlenecks came in handy too. I'd also grown fond of an oversized flannel shirt, which probably belonged to my father. I even slept in it.

It was as though this new costume saw me playing a new role—no longer that girl who wouldn't be seen dead in mass-produced clothes.

In retrospect, and with the benefit of distance, I cringed at how elitist I'd been.

I preferred this new, earthier version of myself.

Or was it because of Carson pinching my ass and telling me how hot I looked in jeans?

"Thanks for the encouragement," I said at last. "So you were going to teach me how to bake bread, remember?"

He laughed. "I'm not exactly an expert, but I thought it would be nice to have some fresh bread."

I nodded. "Oh god, yeah. I'd love some." I stood up and stretched. "Tell me what I can do."

He moved into the pantry and scooped out flour from a sack onto a tray. "Just sit and chat. Tell me silly stories." He grinned.

"I don't know any." I leaned on my elbows on the table, as content as a cat in the sunshine.

"You were on fire last night," he said, giving me his gorgeous smile that made me want to strip naked.

"Oh, yes. You got me drunk, remember?"

"Um, from memory, it was you that kept asking me to go to the cellar for more wine."

"It was fun, though, wasn't it?" I inclined my head. "And I can't even remember what I talked about."

"Oh, just cute stories about your life growing up."

"That must have bored you to death. Sorry. I talk too much when I drink."

He shook his head. "No. I like what comes out of your mouth."

"Mm…" I leaned back in my chair. "I think you just like my mouth."

His lips curled slowly. "It's a pretty sexy mouth, all right."

If I wasn't so eager for some fresh bread, I would have reminded him just how sexy my mouth could be, but I held off on sucking his dick until late in the afternoon. That seemed to be our mutual feasting hour.

I watched as he sifted the flour. "You seem to know what you're doing."

"My mother used to make bread when we were young." He smiled shyly.

"You never speak about your life growing up."

He poured a sachet of yeast into the flour, followed by warm water.

"There's not much to tell."

"How old were you when your mother passed away?"

"I was sixteen." He continued to mix the flour, his eyes on his hands.

"Is your dad still alive?"

He shrugged.

"You don't know?"

"I haven't seen him for years."

"You haven't gone looking for him?"

"No. I figured if he wanted to see us, he would've done that by now."

I searched his eyes for signs of emotion, but he remained cool. It was Carson's coping mechanism. He liked to hide his feelings, but he wasn't cold. Far from it. Tactile and demonstrative, Carson always stroked my arm or hair. I'd never known a man to show so much affection.

"You've got a brother you mentioned once," I said.

He nodded while kneading the dough. "He's still alive. Just in hiding somewhere."

"Really?"

"He's not a good person. He's always hung out with criminals and is a drug addict. I've tried to help him." He took a breath. "He jumped bail, and I lost everything. I've given up on him. I kept trying to get him to rehab, but he's a lost cause." Carson worked the dough harder and harder the more he spoke.

"You seem upset. Sorry to bring it up." I cupped my cheeks, watching him work.

"I'm fine. I've had to learn to let go." He shaped the dough into a loaf and then placed a cloth over the tin.

"You're not popping it into the oven?" I couldn't believe how effortlessly he'd produced it.

"No. I'll leave it to rise for an hour before baking."

I smiled. "You're not just a pretty face."

He pulled a face at me. Even an ugly expression looked hot on him.

"I'd say that tomorrow the roads should be clear. We'll be able to make it into the village. You can stay here if you like while I arrange a hire car."

My heart sank. I'd hoped it would remain flooded for a few more days.

He studied me. "What's that look?"

I played with my fingers. "I'm going to miss this."

"So will I." His gaze lingered.

I couldn't get enough of him.

Going by Carson's hungry kisses, passionate groping, and that penis that rarely went soft, it seemed like Carson felt something for me.

Pure lust, yes, but something more too.

CARSON LAUGHED WHEN HE saw me. "It looks like you've fallen into the sack of flour."

Brushing back my hair, I giggled.

When Carson left to check on the state of the road, I decided to surprise him with a cake, having stumbled on a recipe book. By the time I'd gotten the mix into a baking tray, I'd made an almighty mess.

I went to open the oven door when Carson stopped me.

"Don't touch that. You'll burn yourself."

I held onto the cake tin and looked at him, puzzled.

He stared down at it as though it was something unreal. "You really made that?"

I laughed at his shock. "I did."

He got a cloth and opened the oven door and placed the tray inside the oven.

"I'm impressed." He grinned.

"You haven't tasted it yet. But it was fun in a complicated way."

He touched my face and wiped it, leaving a trail of tingles. His fingers had this magic aftereffect.

"You've got flour all over yourself."

He hugged me tightly, which was a first. Normally, the cuddles happened at night after a few drinks.

Being in his arms felt like the safest, most comfortable place in the world. It wasn't always about sex, either, despite how hot he made me feel.

There was something quite profound about being around Carson. He had me digging deep like I could be that person I always thought I could be, if only I knew where to look.

"What's the score?" I hoped the roads were still flooded.

"The road's clear."

I sensed unhappiness in his tone. "You're not happy about that?"

He rubbed his neck. "I was looking forward to doing some fishing. The sea's calm today."

"Then let's do that and stay another night."

He frowned. "You wouldn't mind?"

I laughed. "I was born by the sea. I love it."

"I'm talking about going out on the boat."

"I'd love to do that too. Normally, we go out on the family yacht on the Riviera. But hey, a speedboat can be fun."

He kept looking at me as though trying to understand something.

"What?" I spread my hands.

"I almost forgot you were that daughter of a billionaire, which is why I couldn't exactly chat you up."

I slanted my head to study him. I loved the way his eyes softened when he was out of his comfort zone. "Did you want to seduce me?"

"I wouldn't be a man if I didn't. You're an exquisite woman."

Warmth cascaded over me. "Lucky I'm not that shy."

"Your little warm hand proved that in Mayfair."

"I hope you didn't think I was loose."

He laughed. "Oh, you were very loose. Deliciously so."

"Mm… I'll take that as a backhanded compliment."

"Savvie, you're sexy and beautiful and crazy." His eyes fell into mine and then his lips caressed my cheek.

"I'm no longer that same rich, entitled girl." I twisted a lock of hair in my finger.

His eyes lit up. "You're going to work?"

"Oh god, no. I'll be thirty soon, and then I'll come into a billion pounds."

He rolled his eyes.

"What? You'd prefer me destitute?"

Shrugging, he let out a sigh. "Not to that extreme. This is all so strange. I never expected to fall for someone rich."

A big smile grew on my face. It felt like sunshine pouring over me. "You've fallen for me?"

His gaze held mine while searching for the right answer. He nodded faintly like it was a tough admission.

"Why are you looking so sad?" I wanted to fall into his arms and kiss him all over, but he was confusing me.

"I'm just not sure how this will work and whether I'm just a plaything. A novelty."

My brows gathered. "Fuck, Carson. Do you think I'm that shallow?"

"Well… no." He rolled his lips, something he did when pressed. "But Savvie, since I've known you, you've dated a lot of men."

"I liked you from the moment we met. You must have seen that." I knotted my fingers. "And if I hadn't thrown myself at you, you wouldn't have asked me out, right?"

"I would have tried to hit on you from the moment I laid eyes on you, Savvie, but it was complicated. And I thought..." He took a deep breath and sighed.

"You thought what?"

"That you were too beautiful for me."

I laughed. "Have you looked in the mirror lately?"

He returned a tight smile. "I thought I was just another man you flirted with."

I rolled my eyes and let out an exasperated sigh. "Shit, Carson. You think I'm some empty-headed bimbo."

He raised his palms in defense. "Hey, I never said that. I've never seen you that way."

"How have you seen me, then?" I inclined my head. "What was your first impression."

He ambled into the adjoining room and returned with a bottle of whisky. "Do you want some?"

Nodding, I took the glass, and our fingers touched.

A smile grew on his face, and I almost forgot the intense discussion we'd been having.

But as he sipped his whisky pensively, I still felt on edge and impatient for a response.

"Well?"

"You take my breath away, Savvie. I find it hard to speak sometimes when I'm around you. I feel seriously out of my depth. Inadequate, mentally speaking." His mouth twitched into a half-smile.

"Oh my god. I don't want you to feel that way. We've been equals here, haven't we?"

He nodded. "But this is neutral ground, and you've needed my help, which I like." He paused for my response, but I wanted to hear more. "I can't even imagine how I'd fit into your life. At night, it's amazing. I love being in your room, watching you parade in your sexy lace numbers, and sending me wild. I mean the day-to-day stuff."

"If you wanted me, you'd try." I went to walk away when he stopped me and pulled me into his firm chest. Of course, I melted.

"I've never spent this much time with a woman before."

My eyes widened. "You've never had a girlfriend?"

"I've had girlfriends. I just haven't spent extended periods of time with them, nor have I shared conversations like ours."

"That's because there's no distraction, and I'm the only person here."

"And you like to talk," he added with a smirk.

I slapped his arm. "Hey. I don't talk too much, do I?"

He shook his head. "It's more my shortcoming than yours. You've got a pleasant voice and you make me laugh. I like you best, however…"

Expecting something sexy, I smirked. "How?"

"When you're all vulnerable. When you need me."

Huh?

That really threw me. "Are you saying you're turned on by my damsel-in-distress act?"

He studied me closely. "Has it been an act?"

"No. I only called you when I needed you. But I sensed you wouldn't see me unless it was about protection."

"That's my role, Savvie."

I nodded slowly as I finished my drink and rose.

If I were being totally honest, I loved knowing I could turn to him, especially when I needed him, which went beyond my many dramas.

Shifting the mood a little, I pulled a grin. "Although you don't say a lot, you seem to like to talk about things that interest you, like fishing and…"

He slanted his handsome head. "And?"

"What you're going to do to me." My mouth curled slowly.

"Mm… I like the sound of that." He touched my arse. "And I love touching you."

"Is that all?" I goaded.

"Oh, there's a lot more. Like…" He fondled my breasts. "Like your perfect tits and…" He ran his fingers down to my pulsating sex. "And how you taste. Can't get enough of that." He ran his tongue over his lips.

He tasted my lips slowly, and I became a puddle again.

Holding onto one another, we walked into the room that we'd made our own and fell onto the bed, where he devoured every inch of me, making me see stars.

Yes, I was in love. And maybe he was too. I just had to ride this warm, delicious wave and hope to find him there with those steady hands to guide me.

CARSON HAD TAKEN OFF for the village early in the morning. While I waited, I went through my luggage looking for sensible village clothes and settled on a pair of leopard-skin, high-waisted flares, and a green cropped cashmere jumper. Imagining Carson's dry response to my clothing choice made me smile. He didn't quite get my fashion obsession. Something I'd never thought about until I met him. I'd certainly never worn the same clothes over three days.

Apart from the jeans I'd grown fond of, there was an oversized Scottish woolen jumper I'd appropriated from my parent's bedroom, which belonged to my dad. Wearing it had made me feel close to him, tugging at my heart whenever I took a deep smell of the wool, an action that had Carson looking puzzled.

"It belonged to my dad," I said, a lump forming in my throat.

His eyes softened, and he held me. No further explanation was needed. He just understood me better than most. And I seemed to cry at the drop of a hat since that awful experience with Bram.

This rawness helped me look deeper into myself. As the layers came off, I discovered things about me I liked, which had little to do with wardrobe choice.

Everything about our rich scene was cosmetically airbrushed, in that our souls had been buried by the collagen fillers.

Were we really going to leave?

A dark cloud drifted over me. I wasn't ready to face anyone, and this was to be a one-month getaway. I also wasn't ready to be separated from Carson.

I pushed that thought aside and tried to think about now and not tomorrow, something I was always good at. I hardly looked beyond two hours.

Bram must have knocked on some dormant part of my brain. Not that I believed his attack had done me good. Or had it?

I wouldn't have been here. I would probably be in London lunching with Jacinta or Sienna, talking about the latest Balenciaga range.

That phone signal, however, couldn't come fast enough, so I could call my mother. She would have been worried sick after not hearing from me in days. Just as that thought arrived, a car drove in, and I hurried out to meet Carson in the Range Rover he'd hired.

"That was quicker than I expected."

He looked me up and down, and a smile grew on his bearded face.

"What?" I chuckled.

"You're back to your fashion best I see." He stroked my exposed navel. "Sexy. A bit chilly though, isn't it?"

My nipples tightened. The cool air had little to do with it. Carson's eyes hooded as they roamed up and down my body and settled on my nipples.

That man could make me come by just looking at me.

"I couldn't exactly go to town in my father's oversized jumper. While we're there, I'll shop and find some village wear. There are boutiques, I hope. Last time I visited, I was probably more interested in getting an ice cream than finding the latest Stella McCartney must-have."

He smiled. "I'd be happy to buy you an ice cream. If only to watch you devour it."

I slapped his arm. "You've just got blowjobs on your mind."

He frowned. "No. I've got eggs and bacon on my mind. Can I invite you to a nice big hot breakfast?"

"Oh, yes, please," I crooned.

AFTER WHAT HAD BEEN four days of isolation and nonstop orgasms and me baring my soul to a man that had taken my heart, I found myself in Port Ives. It felt odd walking around a village but also nice to sit in a café and order breakfast.

"I never thought I'd love the smell of bacon and eggs so much." I bit into a slice of crispy bacon. The salty, oily flavor set my taste buds firing.

"I'm with you there," Carson said.

After breakfast, I called my mother.

"Savanah." She sounded alarmed. "I've been worried sick. You haven't returned my messages, and Declan's been calling Carson. I even called the local police. They informed me that the road was flooded and suggested that you probably didn't have a signal. I was just about to send them to the house to check on you."

"I'm great, Mum." I smiled. "I haven't had a signal. I'm in the village. The roads have only just opened."

"You sound well, sweetheart."

"I am. But hey, Lochridge is a mess. Jim was nowhere to be seen. There are dust covers everywhere. We found rotting food in the fridge. It was pretty dreadful. No central heating like you'd arranged."

"Oh my goodness. I'll get the police onto him."

"There could be a reasonable explanation." I wasn't about to admit that I enjoyed the novelty of roughing it.

"Oh my. So how have you managed?"

Um... Sleeping with my security guard. Hundreds of orgasms. Who needs modern conveniences?

"Um... I've managed." I smiled.

"At least you sound upbeat. Better than when you left."

"I feel great, really. I've been getting around in the jeans that you left here years ago and Dad's fishing jumper."

"I'm so happy to hear from you. I've been so worried."

"It's all good. So, what's been happening?"

"Mirabel had a baby girl."

"Oh, really? I'll have to call Ethan."

"Do that. Her name's Rose."

"That's so nice. A girl in the mix," I said.

"I think so."

"And what else?" I wanted to ask after Cary, but I sensed from her tone that something was amiss.

"I'm hosting a tea party this afternoon. I must keep moving."

"What about Manon and that sleaze bar?"

"I'm staying out of it, darling. Reynard has reassured me it's all legitimate."

"And Manon?"

"She's her own person."

"But she's living at Merivale."

"It's here or with Rey. I'd prefer her close."

"Why are you protecting her? And if she's on with Crisp, then let him take care of her."

"She's not with him, she's assured me. She's young, and I need her close. At least she's behaving. She's even set up an office here, and she's keeping herself busy and is even treating the staff with a little more respect. Maybe that's all she needed all along, something to focus on and a stable environment."

"But Ma Chérie is bringing us into disrepute," I persisted.

"Let's talk soon. Are you coming home?"

"I might stay a couple more weeks."

That was new to me. I just thought of it, and fuzzy warmth flooded me.

"But it sounds so uncomfortable, and there's no staff. And to think, I sent Jim twenty thousand pounds, along with the monthly caretaking fee I've been paying him for years."

"I don't need staff. We're doing our own cooking. It's really nice. And I'm drawing."

"We?"

"Well, Carson's here."

"Mm... It sounds intimate."

"Have you spoken to Cary?" My mother's talent for evading questions taught me well when it came to subterfuge.

"He keeps calling me."

"Is he going to leave his wife?"

She sighed. "It's complicated, darling. Anyway, I must run. I'm so glad you called. Let's talk again soon."

"It might be a day or two, given the lack of signal."

"Bye, sweetheart."

"Bye, Mum."

CHAPTER 24

Carson

THE BOATHOUSE WAS A dream come true, and after I cleaned the motor, I pushed the boat onto the water's edge.

Savanah arrived with sandwiches and a flask of tea. She'd embraced domesticity to such an extent that when staff arrived, she asked that they clean but leave by day's end, much to my relief. I'd grown fond of our privacy, and I was comfortable around the kitchen, and Savanah expressed eagerness to learn to cook. Not that I demanded she help, but the novelty of learning something new had fired her up. The look of wonder on her face after she'd made an omelet was priceless.

We'd even moved into the master bedroom, which came with a fireplace that the staff went to the trouble of stoking before leaving.

We'd been there for three weeks, and these were our last days.

Savanah stepped on the boat wearing clothes she'd bought in town, which included a sensible jacket, a beanie, and a new pair of low-heeled boots.

As we sat at the water's edge eating sandwiches, she poured tea from the flask.

"You're good at this," I said.

"Well, Fiona helped." She pulled a guilty smile. "But look, I baked this." She opened a container with slices of cake.

The sweet aroma made my stomach smile. "I'm impressed. You'll be able to open a cake shop soon."

She giggled as she often did when I made impossible suggestions. This girl was a billionaire. Something I'd forgotten these past weeks. Savanah had become so down-to-earth and willing to learn that my heart swelled.

I took a bite of cake. "Delicious. You're really good."

"That's what you said last night." Her teasing smile made me laugh.

I rose from the seat outside the boat shed. "Are you sure you want to go out on the boat?"

She nodded and opened her backpack and brought out a sketchpad. "I thought I could take some pictures and make a few sketches."

With her long dark hair in a ponytail and her face clean of makeup, Savanah had never looked more beautiful.

"Why are you looking at me like that?" she asked.

"Because I'm thinking of abducting you and keeping you locked up here with me."

"Oh?" She inclined her pretty face in a challenge. She ran her tongue over her lips, and my jeans tightened. "And how will you do that?"

I helped her onto the boat and then carried on a fishing rod and a bucket filled with water.

"I could always lock you up in the bedroom."

"Naked?" she asked.

"I can give you a shirt. But no underwear. Of course."

"And what would you do if I tried to escape?" She smirked. Savanah loved these little games we often played.

"I'd strap you down and fuck you until you couldn't walk."

"Ooh, that sounds hot."

Her hand landed on my dick, rubbing around my zipper, and the bulge grew in her hand.

"Mm... what have we here? Is the thought of me tied to a bed being fucked raw turning you on?"

I walked my fingers under her blouse and squeezed her tits gently. "You could say that."

She pulled down my zipper and took my cock in her hand. The cool sea air wasn't enough to stop it from going steel hard.

Without saying another word, she took my dick into her mouth and sucked on the tip. I closed my eyes and forgot where I was.

Luckily, it was a secluded bay, and as I leaned back, indulging in the delight of her expert sucking, I knew this would be one of many sexy moments shared with Savvie that I'd remember forever.

Her soft, warm lips moved up and down my shaft, setting me on fire.

I fondled her tits, and it didn't take long for her to drink every drop I shot into her.

"Oh, Savvie, what are you doing to me?" I groaned in ecstasy.

She wiped her lips and giggled. "I love sucking your dick. You know that."

I held her in my arms, kissed her tenderly, and in a hoarse whisper, I uttered, "I love you."

She raised her face to mine. "What did you say?"

I smiled awkwardly. Those words had never left my lips before. Yet they felt so natural at that moment, especially as her luminous blue eyes trapped mine.

"I love you, Savvie."

She bit her lip, and a tear followed, falling on her rosy cheek.

I held her tight. "I'm sorry for making you cry."

"I love you, too, Carson. I don't want this to end." She smiled sadly. "I want us to stay like this forever."

Yes, please.

I pulled the cord and started the boat. We chugged along, slowly.

The day was still, and the sun rippled on the water, turning it into wavy green glass.

Savanah kept looking at me. It was clear she wouldn't let that powerful confession slide. What could I say? Um... I'll marry you and we'll live happily ever after at Merivale?

"Let's just see how we travel."

"Does that mean that you can't see yourself with me unless we're here?"

"I didn't say that." I steered the boat to deeper waters.

This woman can read my fucking mind.

She held up the flask. "Tea?"

With the sun beaming down on her, highlighting red streaks in her silky brown hair, and her wide, captivating blue eyes smiling back at me, Savanah had truly stolen my heart.

"That would be nice, angel."

BEING AROUND PEOPLE AGAIN took some getting used to. I missed Lochridge and not having Savanah around me day and night.

As someone who'd identified as a lone wolf, I'd never been a clingy person. The army might have bludgeoned self-sufficiency into me, but it hadn't prepared me for losing my heart to a woman with whom I couldn't normally expect a long-term relationship.

Since returning a week ago, Savanah had shared my bed every night, and our need for each other had grown.

Apart from the sex, which was still at its raunchy best, having Savanah around with her sketchpad or just chatting about things, with her feet up on my ordinary furniture, brightened my day.

Back to my role as CEO and occasional personal trainer, mainly due to a lack of experienced staff, I went through the books and stared in wonder at how popular Reboot had become.

"At this rate, we'll need to hire more staff," I said to Drake, who returned a somewhat baffled expression. "What's the issue?"

"All my clients are women."

With those Harry Styles looks and that tall, buff body, he had his share of admirers.

"You'll have to stop pumping iron and looking so appealing, Drake," I joked.

He wore an embarrassed smile. "I'm a fitness junkie. It keeps me out of trouble. Chases the blues away."

Mm... Been there, done that. Sex with a gorgeous, needy girl wasn't too bad either.

"Good old endorphins." I sniffed. "You must like all the attention these girls are giving you."

"I guess so. It's hard to concentrate when they bend over wearing very little."

"Enjoy it."

"They come here for you too," he said.

Yep, I had my female clients that seemed to enjoy wearing low-cut crop tops and gear that left little to the imagination.

"We need to employ more trainers. And Declan's keen to start up the youth program again, which is my area of interest."

He nodded. "I'd like that too."

Savanah turned up looking flustered, and after she gave Drake a quick nod, she turned to me.

My next appointment, Louisa, turned up at the same time. Dressed in her usual skimpy fitness gear, she loved parading her body, especially her tits, which spilt out of her tiny top. She also spent most of our session talking about her erotic romance novel obsession, even remarking on how I'd make an excellent cover for one of her books. I laughed at that, despite living in my own erotic romance with Savanah.

Savanah gave Louise a forced smile before turning her attention to me. "I need a quick word."

Turning to Louise, I cocked my head towards Drake. "He can get you started."

Drake was wiping down the equipment when I approached him. "Can you get Louise started on the treadmill? I'll be back in five."

He nodded, and I left them to it.

"What's up?" I asked as we stepped outside.

"I tried texting you." She looked worried. "Now I can see what's been occupying you."

My forehead creased. "I'm working, Savanah. That's all it is."

She frowned. "You don't look happy to see me."

"I am. But I'm with a client."

"Do they all look like her?"

"I'm not interested in her. If that's what you're getting at."

She bit her lower lip and had that girl-lost look about her. "I can't go ahead with the court trial. It will break me. I'm going to drop the charges. Mother thinks I'm crazy. She's begging me not to."

"I agree with your mother. Bram needs to be locked up. He's dangerous."

"Can't we stick to a restraining order? I spoke to the lawyer, and he advised we could put together a list of stipulations."

I shook my head. I understood her fear well enough. No one wanted to face their assailant.

"Maybe have the trial with only your counsel present."

"I just want it gone. Like forgotten."

"Are you fucking serious? This guy put you in hospital, Savvie. If you don't do something, I might."

Her eyes widened. "Oh no. I couldn't lose you. Please don't go near him. He'll get you locked up. I can't do without you."

My heart swelled as a sad smile grew. "I can look after myself, Savvie. Don't worry."

I stroked her cheek, and her face softened.

"The guy's a fucking monster."

"Will you come with me to the lawyers? Can you help me with this?"

Her big blue eyes shone with that fragile, lost expression that could bring me down to my knees. Protecting her meant everything to me.

I draped my arm around her, pulling her in tight like I wished to transfer some of my strength. "I'll do whatever you want, Savvie. You know that."

Every night since our return, Savanah stayed in my apartment. She'd even offered to upgrade my living arrangements, which, being fiercely independent, I rejected.

"Can I come over tonight?" She bit her lip.

"Of course. I'll cook us a nice big steak." I smiled.

Her lips trembled into a smile. "I'd like that. So you'll come with me tomorrow?"

I nodded. I couldn't deny this beautiful, half-broken woman anything.

She went to go when she said, "That woman wants to fuck you. I hope you don't get all hard around her. She's got enormous tits."

For someone close to thirty, Savanah sometimes reminded me of a teenager. Sometimes someone even younger. "Savvie, why would I go for her when I have you warming my body every night?"

"She seems hot for you, though. She might offer to blow you or something."

I knitted my brows and studied her expression to see if she was kidding. She remained serious. "God, Savanah, I'm not that type of man."

"But you were, weren't you? You said you were wild once."

I kissed her gently. "Tonight. And look, Savvie, don't worry about anything. Although I would consider pressing charges."

Two hours later, I received a call from Caroline, summoning me to Merivale. As I walked along the forest to the hall, I wondered how Savanah's mother would take me dating her daughter, even though for now, we'd decided to keep this relationship between us.

Declan and Ethan were in the office when I arrived, and Caroline pointed to a seat and got straight to it.

"I know you're close to my daughter. It's no secret that she has a deep affection for you."

I had to smile at that old-fashioned definition of attraction. Whether Savvie's mum knew that we were sleeping together was another matter. In many ways, it irked me. Like I'd betrayed her trust by taking advantage of her daughter.

Had I?

It was Savvie who kept lunging for my dick. I was just responding as any hot-blooded male would do around a beautiful girl. But she was fragile, too, and this bond we'd formed was deepening by the day.

Declan gave me one of his "I'm here for you, mate" nods. I was sure he knew. Savanah opened up to her brothers about most things.

"We've been discussing Bramwell Pike. After spending most of the morning begging Savanah to go through with the charges, she won't budge. She's talking about a restraining order instead. Has she said anything to you?"

I took a deep breath. "She mentioned it, and of course, I tried to talk her out of it."

Caroline returned a faint, but grateful smile. "That's why I asked you here: to convince her to press charges. I fear what he might do. And there are those dreadful sex tapes."

"You've seen it?" My forehead hurt from frowning. I hated what it might mean for Savvie to know that her mother had watched that sickening footage.

"No." She tapped her fingernails together.

"A friend of mine saw it," Ethan said. "He destroyed it. But we're thinking that there might be more out there. At least if Bram's put away, he can't keep rubbing our sister's reputation in the mud."

"But didn't you threaten to sue?" I asked.

Caroline nodded. "That's in place. But that tape was sent around before we even knew it existed." She sat forward. "Can you turn her around? I'm aware of how important you are to her."

I chewed on my cheek. She must have known about us. It wasn't easy sneaking around small places like Bridesmere. "I'll do my best."

She looked over at her sons before returning her focus to me. "I need you to do some more surveillance at Ma Chérie."

"Like last time?"

She nodded. "This whisper of underage girls is not going away and is extremely concerning." Her expressionless gaze held mine.

"Maybe you should send someone inside," I said.

"It's by invite only." Her eyebrow arch spelled exactly what that meant—a brothel for men buying virgins.

I took a deep breath. "Okay. I'll head out late tonight."

"And if you can try to talk to Savanah about pressing charges."

"She's just terrified of the media turning the trial into a circus."

"That is a problem. I'll have another word with Lord Pike. I can't imagine he wants to see his reputation in tatters."

"Perhaps he can send Bram to LA or somewhere far away," Declan suggested.

She nodded slowly. "That's an idea."

I headed back to Reboot with a heavy feeling in my gut.

CHAPTER 25

Savanah

SIENNA AND I TOOK our seats just as the auction began. Elysium needed more art, and in my newly appointed role as buyer, I was there to bid for a collection listed in their latest catalogue.

When my mother gave my selection her nod of approval, I sensed her relief at my finding a focus. It was amazing what love did for one's motivation, and thanks to Carson, I'd finally found some inspiration. Being in charge of art acquisition fitted me as well as a pair of Manolo must-have shoes.

Sienna, who I hadn't seen for a while, met up with me for breakfast, and I invited her along to the crowded auction.

When a tall man in a designer suit strutted by, Sienna leaned in and whispered, "He's hot."

"We're here to buy art. Not pick up rich daddies. And try not to make a noise when the bidding starts."

She giggled. "He's hot, though, and he gave me the eye. You must have seen that."

I shook my head. "You're incorrigible."

Adrenaline pumped through me, and with a million pounds to spend, I had my heart set on a series titled *Twilight*.

The collection arrived on stage for bidding. Propped up on an easel, the six oil paintings featured monochromatic works in blue, depicting the sky, with each canvas intensifying as the night crept in.

When I won the bidding, I nearly jumped out of my seat, pumping a triumphant fist, but I composed myself and, despite the big smile on my face, channeled my dignified, cool mother instead.

My father would have loved this collection. When I was young, we often visited galleries together. He seemed to prefer smaller, independently run studios, where he made some struggling artists' day by giving them much more than their asking price.

"That was a steal," I whispered.

"Gorgeous." Sienna's attention headed for the attractive older man seated in the next row.

"The art or him?" I cocked my head.

"Both." She ran her hands down her ruler-straight hair.

"Meet you in the foyer." I rose. "And behave."

I slipped into the office and scribbled a cheque for two hundred thousand pounds and arranged delivery of the art.

Sipping champagne and ready to pounce, Sienna waited for me in the reception room, ogling the distinguished man in Armani.

On a recent night out, Sienna and Jacinta had admitted to being ready for marriage and children. They'd changed their tunes, but then, so had I. I wanted that too.

For the first time ever.

And now, I may never have children. Though I tried not to think about it, the thought of never being a mother gnawed at me like an unrelenting ache.

It came as no surprise to find Sienna fluttering her eyelashes at the dripping-in-charm Pierce Brosnan lookalike.

"This is Marcus," she said as I joined them. She opened her arm out towards me. "This is Savanah."

He turned to me. "I see you bought the *Twilight* series."

Unable to hide my joy and squaring my shoulders with pride, I nodded. "The collection's for our family resort."

"Here in London?"

"No. Bridesmere."

"Oh, are you a Lovechilde?" He smiled.

"How did you guess?" Sienna chuckled.

His gaze lingered on Sienna for a moment before returning to me.

"I attended the opening of Elysium," he said. "I've since stayed there twice. Can't stay away. Especially now." His eyebrow arch piqued my curiosity. "That collection will look fabulous there."

"Yes. I think so." I smiled, buoyed by my win. It felt that way, considering the art had come in lower than expected.

"I'll be there tomorrow." His attention turned from me to Sienna. "I'm invited to a soiree hosted by Reynard Crisp, whom I'm sure you're acquainted with, given his affiliation with your mother."

I glanced at Sienna and took a moment to respond. "So, what event is this?"

"Ma Chérie is hosting a night, I believe."

"A night? Do you mean those cattle auctions?"

Sienna turned sharply to me. "Huh?"

His eyes held mine for a moment. We both knew what he meant.

Sienna looked from him to me. "What am I missing here? Is there some kind of party involving livestock? And if so, where can I get an invitation?"

I chuckled. "You'll be too old." I watched Marcus closely to see if he would elaborate or hide beneath that veneer of sophistication adopted by many in our wealthy clique. It would start with a little humor, light chit-chat glossing over their darker sides, as though being of a certain pedigree made it right to take advantage of anyone for the right price.

"Hey, I'm not even thirty yet," she protested.

"Do you want me to tell Sienna what goes on at Ma Chérie?" I inclined my head.

He opened out his palms. "I was invited to a game of twenty-one, followed by a burlesque show."

"It's a brothel, from what I hear."

My brazen response made Sienna's eyebrows raise. "Wow. Really?"

Marcus returned a crooked smile. "It's legal and licensed, I believe. Although strictly members only, Ma Chérie is nothing but a meeting place."

"Describe it as you like. Our family's in the throes of having it shut down."

That was false, given my mother's refusal to discuss that sleaze hole.

He stroked his neck. "From what I hear, it's tasteful. The girls are more than happy to partake, and many lives are improved as a result."

"Mm..." I rolled my eyes.

"Now if you'll excuse me." He left us to finish our drinks.

Sienna and I headed to a bar, and as she linked her arm to mine, she asked, "What the hell was that about? I wanted to get his number, and you kind of insulted him."

"Sweetie, I wasn't kidding when I said you're probably too old for him. Ma Chérie is a virgin auction venue."

Her mouth opened. "Hence that cattle call reference. I thought that virgin-selling only happened via agencies and the net."

"Evidently, these little clubs have sprouted around the blue-blood scene, so that girls in skimpy gear can parade themselves and have men bidding for them."

"Ew. That's desperate, isn't it?"

"It is. However, if the girl consents and is happy with the arrangement, who are we, privileged little things, to judge? I just don't want it near Merivale or at the back of Elysium."

She nodded pensively. "So true. We're lucky. We just threw away our virginity to some useless boy that we liked the look of."

"Am I sensing regret?" I asked as we slid into a bar and grabbed a table by the window.

"No. But if only I knew what I know now. That kind of thing."

"Yeah. Tell me about it. On TikTok, David Bowie said that the fascinating thing about growing old was that you become the person you always should have been."

"Ew. With fucking wrinkles." She grimaced.

I laughed. "But really, I have so many regret fucks."

"Yeah. Me too."

"My biggest regret is still hanging around like a fucking maggot on rotting meat."

"Oh, Savs, you're not rotting meat." She giggled.

"No. I'm not physically decaying, but my soul's not faring that well knowing he's around."

"But you've got your nine-inch hottie keeping your toes warm at night. That must remove some of the angst."

I nodded wistfully. Sienna was right. With Carson around, even Bram and that atrocious sex tape were just tolerable.

AFTER LEAVING SIENNA, I was about to hail a cab for Mayfair when I sensed someone following me. I turned but didn't see anyone. Shrugging it off, I thought paranoia had played tricks on me, since watching over my shoulders had become a habit.

Bram was meant to be in LA. That was the deal after I'd dropped charges, despite everyone, including Carson, begging me not to.

As I travelled along in the taxi, I kept turning behind me and noticed a cab on our tail.

"Is that car following us?" I asked.

The driver looked in the rear vision mirror. "Not sure, lass. I'll keep an eye out if you like. Is someone chasing you?"

"Not as such." I exhaled a nervous breath.

The cab delivered me home, and I climbed out. Just as he drove off, I noticed a shadow, and the next minute, Bram stood before me.

As I screamed, he placed his hand over my mouth. "Don't. I will not hurt you. I just needed to see you."

Under the dim streetlamp, he looked like he'd been sleeping rough. Although his hair was typically messy, his eyes, resembling dark, hollow pits, screamed in desperation.

"You shouldn't be here. I've got a restraining order on you."

"I just want some money."

Scratching his arms, he looked scrawnier than usual, like he was all skin on bones. He'd clearly fallen victim to his addiction.

"I've still got copies of that video, you realize? Give me something and I'll go away."

"What about the deal that was made? And I don't have any cash on me."

"Transfer some. Now. I can wait."

On the pretext that I was about to transfer some funds, I scrolled through my phone and sent Carson a text. "Help. Bram's here. I'm at Mayfair."

It beeped back.

Bram grabbed my arm roughly. "Who are you texting? Transfer the cash now." He squeezed my arm, and I cried out. "Shut the fuck up. Now, Savvie."

"It's dark out here. I can't see what I'm doing." I was close to tears. "Just let me go inside. I'll be able to arrange the funds for you there."

Noticing Alfred at the doorway, Bram said, "I'm not an idiot. You'll call the cops. I want it now. If that money's not in my account within half an hour, that sex tape's going out to social media and all my contacts, which are half of yours too."

"You'll be arrested," I said.

"They won't know where to fucking find me." An evil smile flashed before me. It was the most animated he'd looked so far. He pointed in my face. "Get it done. Or else." He slipped off into the shadows, and I raced up the stairs.

Alfred looked worried. "Is everything all right?"

"I'm fine."

I ran into my bedroom and called Carson.

He picked up straight away. "I'm driving in now. I'm an hour away."

I sighed. This was to be our one night off. But I couldn't go one night without needing him, and this time it wasn't because I wanted him in my bed.

"He wants money. I'm about to transfer some to him. He's threatening to send the video to the fucking media."

"You should have pressed charges, Savvie."

"I'll send him ten thousand dollars, but that will be it."

"I wouldn't send him anything." He sounded justifiably annoyed at me. I know I should have been stronger, but what no one knew, including Carson, was that I would have snapped had I walked into that courtroom. Or even if I hadn't attended, just reading about it in the media would have broken me. Even a Xanax habit couldn't have improved that.

"But he's threatening to send out that video."

"I'll be there soon. Do nothing until I arrive."

"But he's threatening to release the footage within half an hour. I'll pay him this once and then we can involve the police. I promise."

"If that's what you want." He puffed.

"Are you pissed off with me for dragging you out here?"

"No. I mean, I was working for your mother, casing Ma Chérie, but I explained the situation. She seemed pretty worried about you."

"I love you, Carson."

I closed the call and transferred ten thousand pounds into Bram's account.

WHEN I WAS ABOUT to enter my mother's office, I heard her talking to Crisp, so I paused at the door to listen.

"I want it shut down."

"Caroline, I own that land."

"That burlesque bar, as you call it, is bringing disrepute to our name. People still associate that land with the Lovechildes, and these establishments of yours are disturbingly close to Elysium."

"Casinos have always been the playground for the rich. Look at Monte Carlo."

"I've never seen thugs loitering around the French casino, which I've visited more than one occasion."

"The casino's invite-only," he said. "They're not thugs. They're wealthy patrons. New money. Mainly tech billionaires who are following this ugly tattooing trend. It's hard to distinguish some from lowlifes." He chuckled. "You know that better than most, given Savanah's choice of boyfriends."

"I don't want Pike anywhere near us. His son is wreaking havoc on my daughter's life and reputation."

"Then she should have gone ahead with the trial and not dropped all charges. Besides, Conrad has now distanced himself from his son."

"Whichever way, I don't want Lord Pike anywhere near Merivale, or Elysium, for that matter. Can't you see how bad it looks? Just by association. By now, everyone knows about this ghastly sex tape scandal. And Pike parading amongst us only perpetuates gossip."

"I'm sure he knows he's persona non grata here at Merivale, but concerning Salon Soir and beyond, Conrad is a close friend. And let's remember, Caroline, I own you."

There was a deathly silence, and my body froze.

He stepped out and, on seeing me there, grinned. "Sneaking around listening to people's conversations again, I see."

I stuck up my middle finger at him.

He returned his signature uncompromising smirk. "Have a nice day, Savanah." He stopped and turned. "If you ever need a new career, there's a producer I can introduce you to." His raised eyebrow spoke volumes about what kind of film industry he referred to.

"Fuck off."

Manon swanned in just as I spat that out.

She chuckled sarcastically. "You look all hot under the collar. Must be that girl-going-down-on-you act. I didn't realize you were a lezzie. I might have to lock the bathroom."

I went to slap her when my mother arrived.

"That will be enough." Fuming, she switched from me to Manon.

"Step in there and close the door," my mother instructed Manon, before turning to me.

"Throw her out," I shrilled, wanting to scream and then hide in a cave somewhere.

"I'm talking to Manon now." She slammed the door; such was her fury at me and probably Crisp and Manon too.

I leaned against the wall, with a thousand voices yelling in my mind, just as Ethan walked in holding Cian's little hand with Freddie tagging along at his heels.

I kneeled down and hugged my nephew, followed by a pat for Freddie.

"Good timing, Eth. Let's talk somewhere outside," I said.

He held up his finger. "One minute. I just want a quick word with Janet about the menu for our party."

"What party?"

"You didn't get the invite? Sunday. Rosie's christening."

"Oh, yeah, of course. The christening. How is she?"

Looking the proud father, Ethan had stars in his eyes. "She's beautiful."

Cian tossed a ball, and Freddie chased it, nearly knocking over a pedestal with an antique vase.

"Not inside," Ethan said sternly.

Cian looked up at me and gave me a cheeky smile.

"He's the spitting image of you. He even plays ball inside like you used to."

He sighed. "Yep. He's naughty. It takes having children to realize how hard we made it for our parents." He chuckled.

If I had a daughter, I'd advise her to stay away from bad boys. But that wasn't ever going to happen, I thought, sighing to myself.

Ethan removed the ball from Cian's clasp just as he was about to toss it to Freddie again. The canine leapt in anticipation.

I giggled at that welcomed bit of amusement after all the heavy crap going on around me.

While I waited for Ethan in the garden, I called Carson. "Hey."

"Hello, angel. Are you okay? I'm just with a client."

"Let me guess: a woman in her thirties, all hot and bothered?"

He laughed. "Don't know about the bothered bit, but yeah. We're still meeting for lunch in an hour?"

"I'm looking forward to it. I miss you."

"I only saw you three hours ago," he said.

"Are you tiring of me?" Not joking this time, and feeling raw, I meant it.

"Never tire of beauty."

"Aw... you're so nice." I smiled, and suddenly all the bullshit no longer mattered. "I love you, Carson."

"See you, gorgeous."

I wondered if he'd ever tell me he loved me again. Despite that one time at Lochridge, since returning home, those words had not left his lips.

Ethan joined me and tossed the ball to Freddie. Cian ran along with the tenacious pooch. As we watched on and chuckled at how determined that little chubby-legged boy was, I recounted how I'd heard Crisp reminding our mother of his ownership.

Ethan shook his head. "Declan overhead something along those lines a while back."

"We have to bring in the police to stop Ma Chérie. Mother's got Carson casing it. He told me how some girls looked quite young."

His brow pinched. "Shit. That's appalling. And now with Rosie, I can't have this filth around here."

"He's calling it a burlesque bar."

He sniffed. "Euphemism for a sleaze bar more like it. An insult to the art form. I used to enjoy the odd show in London. Very artistic. And Mirabel is doing this whole burlesque act in her new video." His eyes lit up with wonder.

"I'm dying to see it. I love her new song. She's so amazing." I smiled.

Freddie dropped the ball at Ethan's feet, and he picked it up. With both dog and Cian standing in readiness, he tossed it, and off they ran, child and dog.

We laughed.

"Cian hasn't worked out he can never get that ball where Freddie's involved."

I laughed. Thanks to my cute nephew, I almost forgot about dirty-old men's bars and regrettable sex videos.

CHAPTER 26

Carson

ETHAN AND MIRABEL HOSTED a garden party to christen their daughter on a perfect sunny day at Merivale, with an abundance of quality food and drink, as always, delivered on gleaming silver trays.

The garden felt surreal with its fluttering butterflies and fluorescent-winged insects playing in its rainbow of flowers, making me question whether those were standard or magic mushrooms in the omelet I'd eaten for breakfast.

Like the other functions I'd attended, I listened to all kinds of discussions about money, or how someone's kid's excesses would send them bankrupt, and whispers about who was bonking who, and so on. Everyone seemed to love a good scandal. Their eyes would light up. But then, from my experience, people didn't have to be rich to get off on gossip.

I preferred chatting with some of the older guests. I was particularly taken with ninety-year-old Gerald, who'd grown up in London during the Second World War. He talked in great detail about the blitz and the Battle of Britain. He might have been talking about *Star Wars* in the way he described the bombings over London and the eye-watering bravado of young, inexperienced pilots and how they saved London from the Nazi scourge.

Having met him at the other Lovechilde functions, I always said hello, and then we'd get lost in conversation. Fascinated by my experience with the SAS, he asked all kinds of questions about modern armaments and technology's role in modern-day defence systems, an area I was well-versed in.

Savanah rocked Rose, Ethan, and Mirabel's beautiful baby girl, in her arms. She must have sensed me watching because she peered up and smiled.

I excused myself from a couple who'd been chatting about the sad state of Man U. now that their coach had departed. Not one for football talk, I just nodded. I think they assumed I was like most people from the suburbs since I didn't dress in designer, despite Savanah's best efforts to drag me shopping. I had to stop her in her well-intentioned tracks by reminding her I was a cargo pants or jeans man, and that would always be me.

"But you look hot in a tux," she argued.

I laughed. "For a swanky affair, but not day-to-day wear."

"I guess that would be hilarious seeing you at Reboot training all those randy cougars in a bespoke suit."

"Randy cougars?" I frowned.

"They're a little older, from what I saw."

"They're mainly there for Drake," I informed her as I shook my head at the floral shirt she dangled before me.

"You're so safe," she lamented.

"Savvie, you know me by now, don't you?"

She smiled tightly. "I do."

"Then you have to take me the way I am. I'm not that guy who wears cravats or fitted slacks that sit on the ankles, sock free."

She cuddled me. "I know. And you look hot in jeans. Can we at least shop for some designer jeans?"

"Levi's," I declared. "Checkered shirts and Levi's. Just like John Fogerty."

"Huh?" Her brow creased. "I don't know him."

"'I Heard It Through the Grapevine.' Remember that song I played in the car? You've heard it a few times. You told me you liked it."

"You want to dress like an American?" She looked puzzled.

I laughed. "Come on. Let's get that ice cream."

And that was our little shopping expedition in London. It always ended up at a bar or an ice cream parlor. Anywhere but a boutique or Harrods.

I even made her promise that she wouldn't drag me shopping for clothes again. That disappointed her, but in return I promised not to drag her to motorbike showrooms.

She shook my hand. "Deal. You do alpha male things, and I'll stick to being a girl." Her eyes searched mine. Given our different worlds, I sensed she needed to know that we could work.

In the bedroom, we were compatible to a fault. A fault because we'd spend hours fucking and cuddling and just being.

It was nice.

Better than nice.

I'd fallen for her.

Declan and Theadora joined me along with their three-year-old son, Julian, who seemed fixated on a very cute corgi pup.

I greeted them. "Nice day."

Declan hugged me. "Glad you could make it. We like having you here."

Why was he saying that? Was he reading my insecurity about being the guy from the wrong side of town mincing with wealth?

That's how I felt at these functions, but all it took was a few beers and Savvie saying silly, amusing things to drop those useless thoughts.

"Julian, don't pull Bertie's tail." Shaking her head, Theadora turned to me. "He thinks the puppy's a toy."

"Bertie does look like a toy," I said of the black-and-white pup. I bent down and rubbed the canine's little belly. "How old is he?"

"He's six months," Declan said. "I bought him for my mother. She's always wanted a corgi."

"Black-and-white's unusual," I said.

Theadora picked up the pooch and rocked him in her arms. "He's so adorable, though." She gave Declan a pleading smile.

Declan regarded me. "Thea and Julian are constantly at me to get a pup."

Savanah joined us. She took my hand, and my face heated. I hadn't told Declan about us, but going on his smile, I gathered he already knew. Savanah kept little from her brothers.

"We're dating," Savanah said to Theadora and anyone else who might have been interested.

That's where we differed. I was extremely private, while Savanah loved to talk about anything and everything.

I sighed silently. Yep, we had some issues to iron out. Namely me not blushing every time she grabbed my arse publicly, or told her girlfriends, with me present, how I'd made her come by the bucketful.

I even lectured her on keeping me out of salacious conversations with her girlfriends.

"But we love talking about sex," she argued.

I shook my head and laughed.

Although I was in for an interesting ride, I'd become attached and devoted to her. It wasn't just desire either. I worried about her too. Which, added together, spelled love.

Theadora kissed my cheek, followed by a hug for Savanah. "Congrats."

I returned an awkward smile. It sounded like we'd announced an engagement.

Bubbling over, Savanah, having consumed a few champagnes, was her happy, sociable self, which I loved despite her unfortunate inability to edit words.

It had been a week since her confrontation with Bram, and we'd gotten past that.

I'd visited Pike again, and since then we'd heard nothing. Much to my relief because I was bursting to take that bastard down. I didn't like gratuitous violence, but when it came to protecting people I loved, that was another story. Sacrifice came easily to me. It would always be Savanah first.

As I watched her express herself with her hands waving about, her long, lustrous hair free, and in a purple curve-hugging dress, my heart swelled the size of a balloon. I felt like the luckiest man alive.

I just had to remind myself to keep this real between us. That I'd still be that security guard slash Reboot CEO and occasional personal trainer saving to run his own security firm.

As that guy who'd always insisted on buying dinner or drinks for dates and girlfriends, I faced a challenge, given that I didn't enjoy taking.

Declan stood close. "I heard you saw some underage girls entering Crisp's private venue."

"From where I stood, in the dark, mind you, she was trying to run away. Manon whispered into the girl's ear, and it took some time to coax the girl inside."

Theadora shook her head. "I can't believe this is happening right under our noses." Wearing a look of urgency, she turned to her husband. "You've got to close it down."

His disturbed frown was understandable given his wife's experience in a London equivalent of Ma Chérie.

Ethan tinkered with a glass, and welcoming the interruption, I turned in his direction.

"To everyone, thanks for being here on this glorious, sunny day. The family is being summoned, and anyone else who'd like to be in a few happy snaps of our gorgeous little daughter's day."

As the photographer positioned everyone, I turned to Savanah. "You should join them. There aren't enough good-looking people in that photo."

Savanah laughed. "They're all genetically blessed, aren't they? Children included."

Bertie joined the group, and Theadora raised the dog before her son lunged for the popular pooch, while Ethan's son picked up the Jack Russell. The poor animal didn't look too pleased. I sensed he wanted to be left alone to scout for rabbits.

Savanah laughed. "What a great photo."

I had to agree. Ethan, wearing a loud purple jacket over a pale-green shirt, looking the proud dad—albeit an eccentric one—held their baby. Matching her husband in a wild display of color, Mirabel reminded me of someone from a '70s flower-power album, wearing a long green dress with flowers, and her waist-length hair blowing in the wind.

Savanah gestured. "Are you coming?"

"In the photo, you mean?" I frowned.

She nodded. "Don't be shy."

"I'm not. But your mother..."

"Don't worry about Mummy. Compared to all the dickhead boyfriends I've had, you're royalty." She giggled.

"I'll take that as a compliment."

"More than a compliment." Her eyes shone with sincerity and, taking her hand, I dropped the coy act.

I placed my arm around Savanah's waist, and she whispered, "I love you, Carson."

I turned to look at her. Her eyes had a sheen of moisture. "You're not going to cry, are you? You're supposed to look cheery for the camera."

She smiled sadly. "I'm always saying it, though." She stared deeply into my eyes, searching for an answer. "Is it because you're not sure about us?"

Just as I was about to speak, Caroline joined us, and I greeted her with a nod.

I kissed Savanah on the cheek. "I'll be back in a minute. Your mother wants a word."

"Don't let her spook you."

"I don't spook easily." I leaned over and kissed her. "I love you too."

As the sun warmed over us, we locked eyes. I knew with all my heart that I wanted to spend my life with this woman.

Whether she wanted that, I couldn't say. Savanah changed her mind as often as her clothes, which was about four times a day. Her desire for me had grown, however, and it wasn't just this constant need to fuck either. We'd also become affectionately attached.

I followed Savanah's mother into the library with endless rows of antique books. One could almost feel their brain cells expanding just being amongst those dark-wooded shelves, which I imagined being filled with an eternity of knowledge.

Caroline sat at the desk, and from party host, she'd effortlessly morphed into CEO.

"Do you think we can send someone into Ma Chérie?"

Here I was thinking she was about to discuss my relationship with her daughter. Her launching straight into my security work jolted me back to the real world.

"You want me to recruit a young girl to do undercover?"

She nodded. "Can you find one? And by all means, not a word to Manon or Savanah."

"I rarely speak to Manon unless she's hanging out at Reboot."

"Manon visits the gym?" She wore a puzzled frown.

"Not to work out. She comes to see Drake."

"Are they together?" Her dark eyebrows gathered.

Shifting about, I felt uncomfortable suddenly. Drake had spoken in private about his attraction to Manon, but it wasn't my style to divulge our private conversations.

"I'm sure they're not."

"He's got another girlfriend?"

I took a deep breath. "He's young. He goes out." I didn't wish to spell out the fact that Drake had women coming from all corners. Mainly older ones.

"She likes him," she said, almost to herself.

"Maybe."

"I wouldn't mind, to be honest." She sighed. "My granddaughter worries me."

"It looks like she's on Crisp's payroll." I rubbed my neck.

How did we get onto this subject?

"As long as that's all she is."

Knowing how 'out there' Manon was, I sympathized with Caroline.

"Manon's her own person. She's like nineteen going on thirty. She strikes me as ambitious, but I don't get the feeling she's throwing herself at Crisp."

She studied me. "I hope you're right."

I could see her granddaughter's welfare meant everything to her, which raised my respect. Not only had that mudslinging video threatening her daughter's reputation challenged her, but she had this feisty granddaughter mixing with a man whom I wouldn't trust with my worst enemy.

"I cornered Conrad Pike," I said.

Her brow pinched. "And? Can he at least put a stop to that disgusting tape?"

"He reassured me that Bram was in France."

"Okay."

"Don't worry. He won't go near your daughter again. I've turned it into my life's mission." I smiled.

"You're inseparable, I believe." She played with a gold pen. "Are you serious about her?"

I took a moment to answer. Only because I wasn't sure how she would take my response.

I nodded.

Expressionless, her uncompromising stare made me flinch.

Had I betrayed her trust?

After all, she'd paid me to protect her daughter, not shag her and somehow fall in love in the process.

"So, what's your intention?"

I went to speak when she added, "I only ask because Savanah's fragile, especially since her father's death. Her choice in men, as you know, has been deplorable." She tapped her red sharp nails together. "But I've noticed a pleasing change in her. Her course is going well, which doesn't surprise me. She's a creatively talented girl, who, until now, has rarely stayed the course. This wealthy lifestyle, I'm sure, contributed to her inability to focus, but there's also been something broken in her. She's suddenly brighter. Happier. Almost that girl she was before falling in with the wrong crowd, so to speak."

I nodded, listening to a report about the woman who'd stolen my heart.

She continued, "I'm only saying all of this because I think you've been a beneficial influence on my daughter."

I breathed a silent sigh of relief. "Savvie's warm, intelligent, and boasts a ton of talent. She's unique, and I admire that."

"I know that. It's what makes her special but what also gets her into trouble." A tight line formed on her lips. "So, what's your plan? Are you sticking around?"

"I'm not going anywhere."

"Would you be prepared to marry her?" She inclined her head. As always, Caroline Lovechilde was hard to read.

Is she wanting me to marry her daughter?

Or is she asking for another reason?

I scratched my chin as I asked my heart that question and then my head. The two were opposed.

I went with my heart. "I'd marry her tomorrow if she'd have me."

A flurry of purple raced in, and before I knew it, Savanah had her arms around me.

"Sneaking around eavesdropping again, I see," her mother said with a grin.

"I only just caught that last bit. The best bit." Savanah bubbled over with excitement like we were about to go on a trip around the world. She wrapped her arms around my neck, close to strangling me with affection. "Do you mean it?"

I looked from mother to daughter.

What just happened?

The past few months flashed before me. We'd been inseparable, and apart from Savanah occasionally giving me the shits with her "I want it now" act, which had become less frequent, we lived well together. She talked, and I liked to listen. I also loved cuddling in bed at night. I'd never slept so well.

The thought of spending a lifetime with this stunning woman sent a wave of pleasure through me, even though I hadn't planned on tying the knot with anyone.

"I'd love to marry you if you'd have me."

I took her hand, and Savanah leapt on me for a hug.

Yes, she was a child. But I loved that about her.

I looked at her mother, wondering whether this was what she wanted.

"Do you approve?" I had to ask.

Caroline nodded very slowly, as though that idea was growing on her.

"Let's announce our engagement here." Savanah danced on the spot.

CHAPTER 27

Savanah

JACINTA WALKED THROUGH HARRODS with me. "I can't believe you're engaged. I didn't even get the invite."

I chuckled at her downward smile. "No one did. It just happened. One minute, I'm at my brother's christening, and the next, all the guests are toasting our engagement."

"Have you set a date?" She paused at a rack of skirts.

"Not yet. I've been too scared to bring it up with Carson."

"Why?" She frowned, holding a skirt against her body.

I sighed. "I'm reluctant to burst this dreamy bubble. My mother might've pressured him. I overheard her asking him what he planned to do with this relationship."

Jacinta stroked a leopard-print scarf and chuckled. "That does sound like a little pressure."

"Exactly. That's why I'm seeing this as a kind of cooling-off period. Only he's been just as affectionate and sweet." I smiled like a woman overdosing on bliss. "We're staying at Mayfair for now, while Carson sets up his security firm."

"He doesn't need to do anything though, does he? I mean, you're filthy rich, Savs." She picked up a red Louis Vuitton handbag. "This is soooo nice."

"Here, let me buy it for you as my getting-engaged-and-exploding-with-joy present."

"Oh, no, it's like three thousand pounds."

I headed to the register and paid for the bag and passed it over to Jacinta.

She hugged me. "I should be the one buying gifts."

"Don't worry. I'll be sure to drop hints about things I love." That suggestion was ridiculous. I needed nothing. Just Carson.

"I could kill a G and T," I said.

Just as we hit the street, I saw Carson talking to a young blond woman.

I froze.

As Jacinta turned to see what had grabbed my attention, I dragged her to hide. "That's Carson."

"Oh, so it is." She looked puzzled. "Why are we hiding? And who's that girl?"

"Good fucking question. I don't want him to see me."

"You're trying to catch him out?"

"Well, look at them."

"She could be family," Jacinta said. "They're not doing anything."

With long blond hair and a full figure, the stunning girl waved and then left Carson.

"Shit." My body, along with my spirit, sagged. From gliding along on top of the world, I'd crashed into a thorny bush.

"I'm sure there's an explanation," Jacinta said.

After Carson disappeared around the corner, I had this powerful urge to text him and make demands. I took a deep breath instead. Something he'd taught me to do whenever I jumped to conclusions and ranted and raved before learning the facts.

Instead, I decided to ask him face-to-face at Mayfair.

"Did you see how pretty she was?" I went on, as we sat down and ordered a drink at our favorite little bar.

"I'm sure there's a valid explanation. Don't worry. From everything you've said, and the vibe I got from him, he's not like that."

"To be honest, I know little about Carson other than he was in the army, and he's got a brother who's a drug addict and involved in criminal gangs."

"That sounds colorful." Jacinta sipped her drink. "Don't worry. I'm sure there's a reasonable explanation. Let's talk about your wedding. Something nice."

AFTER LEAVING JACINTA, I cut across an alleyway to hail a cab when Bram stepped in front of me and startled me.

I hadn't seen him since that encounter in Mayfair and had even stopped thinking about him, in the hope he'd finally gone.

It shouldn't have come as a surprise; Bram was London through and through. He'd even once admitted to a fear of flying, and that he loved London.

"Oh, for heaven's sake," I muttered under my breath. "What now? You were in France, according to your dad."

"I'm back. I missed my little cash cow."

I rolled my eyes.

Cash cow? Really?

"I'm not giving you another penny, Bram. Now fuck off."

He pushed me against a wall. And despite the odd passer-by, that tiny lane was a perfect location to be murdered in broad daylight.

He poked into my ribs. "It wouldn't take much for me to post that video on the dark web. That means it will go viral and live on forever so that your children..." A malicious smile grew on his once handsome face, which grew uglier each time I saw him. "Oh, that's right. I made sure you wouldn't be able to procreate. My little gift to humanity. A few less spoiled little shitheads to crowd the gentry." His malevolent chuckle froze my heart.

What could I say? He might have a knife. I would never get rid of this monster, and I'd be forever known as that rich girl who got caught with a cock in her mouth while being tongued by a girl.

I suddenly understood why some people took their lives due to bullying. If it weren't for Carson, I might have done just that. Only as I stared into those hollow eyes, I refused to allow him to control or intimidate me. I could do anything. I had money. I had resources.

"I'll send you another ten thousand," I said with resignation. He stood so close his fetid breath made me want to puke.

"Why don't we make this a regular thing? You set up a direct debit and post me ten big ones a week." Revealing his yellow teeth, he chuckled.

I released a deep sigh of frustration. "Are you ever going to leave me alone?"

"Probably not. You're good for it. You're rich."

"So were you."

He pulled an ugly scowl while wringing my wrists.

"Ouch," I cried.

A man walking by stopped to help, and Bram said, "Tonight, or else. I meant it. Weekly." He ran off.

"Are you okay?" the stranger asked.

I nodded, despite tears falling down my cheeks.

"Do you wish me to call the police?"

I shook my head. Knowing Bram, he'd still send that soul-destroying tape somewhere.

Clouded by all these dark thoughts, I drifted along. Instead of catching a taxi, I ended up walking past boutiques I'd normally pause at, checking for the latest range, only now it was all a blur.

After an hour of walking, my feet ached. Heels hadn't helped. I'd become accustomed to flatter shoes since returning from Lochridge. Carson preferred me shorter. He enjoyed tucking his chin over my head. I smiled sadly at that sweet random thought, having almost forgotten about him with that sexy blonde.

I was so lost in my thoughts that I nearly walked straight into Manon and, oh god, (could it get worse?) Bethany.

My evil half-sister's back.

Maybe she'd never left. Every time Bethany came up in conversation, my mother would quickly shut down.

"Oh" escaped my mouth.

"That's not a nice way to greet family." Bethany looked stunning in a red Chanel suit. Her long dark hair, in soft waves, framed the same milky complexion as my mother's.

"The last time we met, you were being dragged away by the police," I said.

"They couldn't pin anything on me." She still sounded like she'd come from some council estate, unlike Manon, who was secretly taking elocution lessons, encouraged by my mother, who couldn't have her granddaughter sounding cockney.

"I hear you're marrying that hunky Carson," Manon said, wearing her competitive I-want-what-you-have face.

That could have been me being paranoid, but I'd noticed her flirty smiles. It was no secret that Drake was her crush, but Manon loved to be the center of attraction.

"I wouldn't have thought he was your type," I said.

"They're all my type. Depends on what they can do for us." She glanced at her mother, and Bethany remained stony-faced. Her mask was still in place.

"Are you returning to Merivale?" I asked Bethany.

She laughed coldly. "I don't wish to upset Mummy dearest. She has nothing I want now. I'm pretty set up. I've got my nice Edwardian home in Highgate."

"Getting it all cozy for when Will gets out of prison." I didn't hide the darkness in my voice. Will killed my father despite some other beast doing the deed.

"I've moved on. I'm now with a lord." She looked at Manon and grinned, as though she'd won a prize. "He's loaded."

"So Will ruined his life for nothing?"

"He had me for fifteen years. I wouldn't say that's nothing. I once charged you know."

Manon shrugged as though this disturbing insight into her mother's past was part and parcel of being alive.

"Okay, then." I turned my back to them. I couldn't bring myself to even wave goodbye.

Somewhat disturbed by this encounter, I watched them walk off. Nouveau riche gutter: that's how I would have described Bethany.

When I arrived back at Mayfair, I found Carson on his laptop.

He rose and gave me one of his warm, lingering hugs, followed by a kiss that always flushed me with warmth.

CHAPTER 28

Carson

It killed me to lie to the woman with whom I planned to spend my life.

"But who is she?" Savanah kept pressing.

Just my fucking luck: she'd spied me with the girl I'd hired to play an auctioning virgin. We were spotted at the front of the drama college where I'd originally scouted Tiffany, who I sensed would appeal to hungry, rich sleazebags. It pained me to know that girls had to resort to selling their innocence.

I didn't get the whole virgin appeal myself. I'd always preferred experienced women. As a randy teenager, I quickly discovered that the inexperienced girls weren't too pleased with my uncommonly large dick. That soon changed once I started fucking older, more experienced women. They couldn't get enough of it, much to the pleasure of my turbo-charged libido.

Savanah's brow pinched as she waited for my response.

I knitted my fingers. "She's Angus's ex. She wanted to know where he was." Under pressure, that was the best excuse I could muster. Ridiculous as that was because a girl like Tiffany would have nothing to do with my drugged-out brother.

"Oh. I thought you'd lost touch with him." Savanah sat next to me on the sofa.

"I have. But she asked to meet me."

"She knows your number?"

I took a deep breath to give myself time to lie more. My stomach curled. This wasn't me. I didn't bullshit.

I thought about that unsavory establishment, which I was just as determined to see closed as the Lovechildes. I didn't want that grime near our lives.

"She must have gotten it somehow; I didn't ask. I only agreed to see her because I thought she might know something more about Angus. Like his last whereabouts."

"From where I stood, she seemed upset or emotional about something."

I revisited my exchange with Tiffany, who wasn't so much being emotional but coolly explaining that she'd agree to be a plant if I gave her a nice place to stay in the village, clothes, and a fat paycheck.

"Savvie, I'm not interested in her. I want you."

I turned to her and gazed into her worried blue eyes. "Is that why you're looking so freaked out?"

She headed to the bar and poured herself a G and T. "Can I get you one?"

I shook my head.

I knew Savvie well. Whenever she poured a large measure of liquor it meant that something heavy was going on. I only hoped she hadn't turned this whole Tiffany affair into something bigger than it needed to be.

"I saw Bram."

The blood drained from my face. "Did he hurt you?"

Tears streamed down her face, and I held her. Savanah's body shuddered in my arms.

I pulled away to look at her. "What did he do? Fuck, Savanah, we need to put this cunt away." Wearing her lost, wide-eyed stare, she sniffled. I returned a tight smile. "Sorry, vulgar language."

Shaking her head, she broke out of my arms. "No, he is a cunt, all right." She gulped down half of her drink. "He wants ten thousand pounds a week from me."

"What? Forever?"

She bit her nail. "I imagine so. He's threatened to send the tape into the dark web."

I rolled my eyes and groaned. "Shit. Then the footage will be shared with whomever, and you'll have very little control."

She fell onto the sofa and buried her head.

I joined her and placed my arm around her.

"I'm fucked. If I pressed charges, he'd still do it. Don't you see?"

"Leave it with me. I'll find a way."

Her eyes drowned in a pool of tears, and her lips quivered on mine as I kissed her.

"I hope you won't resort to murder."

I shook my head. "I won't jeopardize my life with you, Savanah."

Her mouth trembled into a sweet smile. "Even though I may not give you children?"

That was the first time she'd brought up our marriage. I even wondered if she was having second thoughts. Whereas for me, the idea of us together as man and wife had only strengthened.

"Being with you is all I need to be happy." I gave her a warm smile.

She wiped her nose, and then her face brightened a little. "You didn't just agree to marry me because my mother pushed you?"

I shook my head. "It came as a surprise, to be honest, but when I said it, the thought of marrying you felt natural. Are you having doubts?"

"No fucking way. I want this. I want us."

I opened out my arms, and she fell into them. We kissed passionately, and then she separated from my hold.

"Where are you going?" I asked.

"I've got a little surprise for you. Just give me a few minutes and then come into the bedroom."

I breathed out the stress that had taken grip, and instantly my dick woke up. It rarely took long around Savanah.

"That sounds a little wicked." I grinned.

"Oh, it's that, all right." She swanned off, and I grabbed myself a bottle of water from a double-doored fridge that supplied us with all kinds of treats.

The cook had taken the night off, and I was about to order a pizza. The thought made my taste buds fire. But then, the thought of eating Savanah's pussy as the first course made my mouth salivate more.

Her bedroom, which had become our room, always lifted my mood with its lavender rose scent.

I found her on the bed in a blue lacy number. Propping myself on the silky chair, I undid my fly as I prepared to watch Savanah perform one of her sexy little dances.

She pointed at my jeans. "Take them off. Shirt too."

Her bossy tone only made me hotter. I opened my legs a little as my dick tented my briefs.

Like always, Savanah stole my breath with those long, shapely legs and perky ass that I loved to rub against.

"Mm..." Her seductive gaze fell on my growing cock. "I see you like this."

I pointed to the bed. "Open your legs for me."

"What will you do to me?" Acting coy, she placed her finger on her lips.

Loving these little games, I smirked. "What do you want me to do to you?"

Answering that question with a pose, she parted her thighs widely. In her crotchless panties, she revealed an inviting pink, glistening slit.

"Remove your briefs. I need to see your big, hard cock."

Following her command, I stripped naked and then sat again.

"Fuck your finger." I held my dick. Precum dampened my palm as Savanah fingered herself. "Are you wet?"

"Very." Her finger moved in and out. "I'm thinking about your big dick fucking me raw."

I joined her on the bed. "That can be arranged."

She licked the head of my cock, and it went rock-hard like we hadn't fucked for ages, which wasn't the case. We'd only fucked that morning.

I parted her legs roughly and licked her until her juices dripped down my tongue, and she cried for me to stop.

"Slide on top of my cock so I can watch you."

She lowered onto my dick slowly, making my eyes roll to the back of my head.

"Oh god, your pussy is so fucking delectable."

Her eyes misted over, and a groan escaped her parted mouth. "Love the stretch."

"Can we fuck hard?"

"Oh please," she purred.

Sucking on her nipples, I rubbed my face on her tits as she bounced up and down, her firm little ass in my clasp.

If only I could get a photo of her face when she was about to come. I would have paid a fortune. Her heavy-lidded eyes, rosy cheeks, and dark strands splashing over her face made for one erotic image.

She moved faster and faster. Our bodies were sticky and on fire as I guided her over my shaft.

Flexible like a dancer, she moved in and out as the friction intensified between us.

Her fingernails scratched at my arms as she screamed out my name. Her pussy walls spasmed all over my cock, drowning it in her creamy orgasm. I followed close behind and came like I hadn't come for ages.

Every time we fucked, it was like the first time for me.

We fell on our backs, and I wrapped my arm around her and drew her close to me.

As she laid her warm cheek on my chest, she uttered, "I love you."

"I love you too." Those words had become natural to me.

THE FOLLOWING MORNING, I was up early. I'd located the perfect office to run my security firm. I'd already signed up a handful of my former SAS mates, which meant we could go elite—politicians, royalty, and highfliers who needed security. No bouncing at clubs.

"You do realize that once we're married, you won't need to do anything," Savanah said as she buttered her toast.

"You don't know me that well, do you?"

She gave me a weak smile. "Are you pissed off with me for saying that?"

I poured milk into my tea. "A little. I'm already struggling with you buying me all these things. Half of them I don't want."

"Oh?" Her face was slanted. "Like the Ducati?"

I exhaled. I loved my new bike. Top range. I would have gone for something more modest, but Savanah, who'd come with me, had noticed my face light up as I stroked that magnificent machine.

"Of course, I love it. It's just that taking's difficult for me."

"But a security firm? What if someone guns you down?"

I swallowed a mouthful of muesli and wiped my mouth. "You have a colorful imagination. I won't be going out on jobs. I'll just oversee the operation and make sure I match the client with the right fit."

After finishing my breakfast, I stood up and stretched. I had something else to do, which had little to do with my business. "I have to run."

"I'm going back to Merivale today. Mother wants me to help with Elysium and organize a guestlist for a function," Savanah said.

"I'll be there later tonight."

We locked eyes as we often did when I became mesmerized by her beauty. I think I found it hard to believe that someone as stunning as Savanah wanted to be with an ordinary man like me.

"What?" she asked, giggling. Savanah knew me well enough to recognize my attraction.

I took her into my arms and kissed her warm cheek. "Just that you're beautiful, and last night was fucking hot."

"Which part? Me putting the lolly in my pussy and then popping it in your mouth?"

"Mm... That too." My dick moved again. This woman had me on fire.

She touched my dick. "Well, well, well. That blowjob in the shower wasn't enough?"

"It was more than enough. Just that you're fucking sexy. Too sexy. I lose my mind around you. I can't even remember what I had to do."

Wearing a bathrobe, she stretched her legs out on the chair so I could see her naked pussy.

I took a deep breath. "You're a fucking minx."

Lifting her from the seat, I drew her in like a flower. Her scent always made me float like I'd stepped into a garden of roses. I pressed my lips to her pliant, moist mouth, and she melted into me as my tongue tangled with hers.

Difficult as it always around this addictive woman, before I sunk into lust, I pulled away. "I really have to go."

"Tonight then." She brushed my cheek and smiled sweetly.

I held her gaze.

"What?" She giggled.

"Nothing. I'm just a lucky man."

She adjusted my collar. "And I'm a lucky girl to have you in my life."

I pecked her lips, and then before passion swept us away again, I made a dash for the door, wearing the smile of a very satisfied man.

Savanah might have been wild and creative in bed, but she also gave me lots of affection—something I'd been missing since my mum passed away.

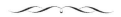

AFTER SIGNING A LEASE for an office in East London, I planned to go in search of drug dealers who might point me towards Bram, since his father had given me nothing. I also needed to find my brother, who I thought about every day.

When a call came from a London hospital, I went pale, assuming it was about Savvie. I soon heard the name Angus Lewis and learned that my brother, having sustained multiple stab wounds, was close to death.

Although it came as no surprise, given the lowlifes he consorted with, it still rocked my world to hear that my baby brother had been mortally wounded. My heart sank as I pushed on the pedal. I became desperate to see him for a last time—to apologize for failing him.

I should have stopped him from fucking up his life.

But then, Angus had never liked to listen, even when faced with the prospect of not making it past thirty.

When the call came, I'd been on my way to my old flat. I wanted to speak to the dealers that loitered around. To see if they'd seen him and to ask about London dealers so I could find Bram. The junkie scene was a small one, I'd discovered, and there was nothing money couldn't buy, including information.

As I drove frantically through the thick London traffic, a call came from Tiffany, who I'd planned to meet at Bridesmere later that same day.

I clicked on the console and took her call. "Hey. I can't get there until tomorrow."

"The B&B hasn't gotten my booking," she said.

A car cut me off, and I beeped my horn. Thinking on the run, I said, "Stay at my apartment. I'll text you the address and caretaker's number. He'll give you a spare key. Give me half an hour. I'm driving. Oh, and pardon the mess."

"When will you be here?" she asked.

"I'll text you. I should be there tomorrow at the latest."

I parked my car in the underground parking bays at the hospital, and five minutes later, after proving I was family, they directed me to a ward room guarded by police—a stark reminder of the prison sentence that awaited my brother should he survive.

"Can you give us some privacy?" I asked the young cop, who looked half-asleep, as guards often did.

He regarded his older partner, who, after checking me up and down, gave me a curt nod.

Angus had tubes coming out of everywhere. His skinny arm filled with track marks hung pathetically by the bed as a tragic testimony of a wasted life.

He looked like a stranger. I had to remind myself that was my baby brother. The same boy I'd played, fought, and clowned around with. We slept in the same room until my mother's death.

A lump in my throat blocked my speech.

His eyes opened and, upon seeing me, he reached out, and I took his bony hand.

"Who did this?" I asked.

"Some fucking Turk selling on our patch. The cops won't get him. They never do."

Drug wars were as nasty as wars on the battlefield, it seemed.

"Are you in pain? Are they giving you enough relief?"

He nodded. His heavy eyelids barely lifted. At least this time he didn't have to rob, or goodness knows what else, for that desperate hit of pain relief.

A small fucking mercy.

"I'm so sorry, Angus..." Emotionally unprepared for this, I had to curl my lips inwards to stop them from trembling.

"No, man. You bailed me out, and I lost your money. I'm the one that should fucking apologize." His eyes were glassy and aged. I read regret.

I took a deep breath to stem the emotion choking my vocal cords.

"I've got something to tell you." He crooked his finger. "I don't want the pigs hearing."

I moved my chair and leaned forward, given his staggering breath hampered articulation.

"Dad made me promise to never tell you. He was part of the street gang I joined when I was fourteen. I only went there to get away from the pedos."

I frowned. "You were sexually abused?"

"Not as such. They fucked my mate, though. He was prettier." His mouth curved slightly. "I was next, though, so I ran away. Found Dad. He was selling drugs, and I begged him to let me stay. He didn't want me there at first, but I became useful... you know... doing errands."

"By errands, you mean selling?"

"I had to survive." He paused for a raspy breath. "Anything was better than that hellhole."

"Why didn't you tell me?" My heart snapped at hearing about my young brother among men who deserved to have their balls chopped off.

"You'd joined the army."

He was right. I started young, volunteering at sixteen.

"Is he still alive?" The last time I saw my father, I was fourteen.

"Nup. Took a bullet in the heart. I held him." A tear streaked his sunken cheek, and equally crushed, I suddenly found it hard to breathe.

Angus's chilly hand touched mine. I guess that was his way of consoling me.

"He was ashamed of you knowing about his drug dealing. He was proud of you for joining the army." His mouth tugged at one end. "He'd started young. Just like me."

Clearing my throat, I asked, "Was he on drugs?"

He shook his head. "Nuh. Just booze. He liked the horses. And he pimped a few girls." He pointed to the side of his bed. "Do me a favour. Press that button for me."

"Painkiller?"

He nodded.

"Shouldn't a nurse administer it?"

"Yeah, but they're stingy."

He closed his eyes as I pressed the button.

"There's something else." His voice had gone slurry. "You're going to marry a rich girl, I hear."

"How do you know that?"

"I saw something on FB, I think." He touched my hand. "I'm happy for you. You were always the one that got ahead."

I studied him for signs of resentment, but his mouth formed an uneven smile.

"I've always looked up to you, Carson."

I couldn't say anything. I wanted to ask about the dealing web so that I could find that scumbag hassling Savanah, but scrambled emotions had robbed me of words.

"There's something else," he said. "There's a drug cartel operating near where your rich family lives."

I sat up. "Bridesmere?"

"They're smuggling through the port there to a private casino at the back of some posh resort."

My brow contracted. "How do you know?"

"I just do. I want you to know because I don't want your kids, my nephews or nieces, being around scum."

Tears pooled in my eyes. I wiped them before he could see.

He closed his eyes. "I need to sleep, Bro."

I squeezed his hand. And then kissed him on the cheek. "I've always loved you, Angus."

He squeezed my hand back and then it went limp.

I felt his neck. He was gone.

I walked out like a zombie. I couldn't even breathe without sobbing.

Was it his death or hearing how my father was too ashamed to see me that had turned me into a block of ice?

All of it.

A sad life lost. My brother, through no fault of his young heart, had run to our father for protection.

I turned off my phone, and heading off into my cave, I returned to the flat I'd grown up in. Balancing a photo album on my thighs, for that was all I had left of my flesh and blood, I stayed the night with a six-pack for company.

CHAPTER 29

Savanah

CARSON WASN'T PICKING UP his phone or answering my texts. He always answered within an hour or two, and now that night had arrived, I became worried sick.

What if he's in an accident?

Would they know to call me?

I jumped into my mother's car and headed to the village to see if he was at his apartment, just in case he'd fallen asleep after returning from London.

He'd been pretty shaken by Bram's latest threats, and my overactive imagination created all kinds of horror scenarios like Carson being stabbed or shot. The drug scene always came with guns and violence. Drug addicts did anything for a hit. Even kill.

After parking the car in front of the redbrick Victorian building re-purposed into apartments, I rang the buzzer.

When he picked up, I sighed with relief. "Carson."

"He's not here."

A girl?

"Who's that?" I asked.

"Um... Tiffany."

My heart pounded. "Are you family?"

"No. I'll tell him you called by if you like."

"No need."

I leaned against the wall.

What the fuck?

I couldn't let that go. I needed answers, so I buzzed again. "This is Savvie again. Can I come up?"

The door opened and instead of waiting for the elevator; I ran up two flights of stairs.

A beautiful blonde answered the door. She might have been around twenty. Big boobs, slim, and gorgeous. Blood drained from my body. She was the same girl I'd seen him talking to.

"Who are you?" I asked.

"I'm Tiffany."

"I mean, what's your connection to Carson?"

Taking her time to answer, she shifted on the spot. "I don't really want to say."

I just stood there like an idiot. My legs shaking.

"Look, we're just friends." She smiled meekly. Tiffany had obviously noticed me freaking out. I'd never been good at hiding my emotions.

I left her standing at the door, biting her bottom lip.

Was this Carson with a girl on the side while planning to marry me because I was rich?

That being the case, why couldn't he stop fucking me? How did he have anything left for her?

Fuck.

When I returned to Merivale, I found Cary and my mother lost in a deep conversation on the chaise lounge in the red room. My mother wore an almost embarrassed smile.

Who was this imposter? What has she done to my normally self-assured mother?

She must have noticed that I'd been crying because her frown deepened. "What's happened?"

I turned to Cary. "Have you left your wife?" I hated hearing that fly out of my angry mouth. Did all the men in our lives have ulterior motives?

"Can you give us a moment?" she asked Cary.

He stretched. "I might just go for a walk. It's a pleasant night."

As they shared a moment, the air seemed to fizz with electricity.

I followed her into the office.

"That was rude." Back to her fierce best. My mother pointed at me. "You have no right to judge him without knowing the facts." She sounded frustrated and sad at the same time. "Especially after the rubbish you've brought here."

I bit my nail. "Carson's not rubbish."

"I'm referring to all your other lamentable and pernicious liaisons."

Bram's latest demands flooded my brainwaves, and I slumped into a heap on the chair, cupped my eyes, and sobbed. "I'm seriously in trouble."

Her anger faded, and her brow creased with concern.

"Bram's blackmailing me."

I told her about the threats and how he'd bailed me up in a London alleyway.

She shook her head. "I have to put a stop to this. Now." She puffed. "Okay. Leave it with me."

"What can you do? Other than have him knocked off."

Not even a look of shock. I waited for her to tell me to stop talking nonsense.

"Don't worry. We'll sort this out. Leave it with me," she repeated.

I wiped my nose, and then, taking a deep breath, I stood up. "I'm sorry for bringing trouble to the family."

She put her arm around me, and I cried in her arms. Something I never did. With my father, yes. Plenty of times. But not with my normally distant mother.

"Carson's not answering my texts. He's in London." I stepped away and sank into the armchair again. "When I visited his village apartment, a stunning young blonde answered the door. She wouldn't tell me what she was doing there, either. Like she had something to hide."

"Savanah, it's probably easily explained. Don't jump to conclusions. I wouldn't."

"Well, you might not let something like that worry you, considering you're seeing a married man, but I'm not about to marry a man who might have a girlfriend on the side. We're rich, Mother. Men gravitate towards us for our bank accounts."

Her eyebrows met. "That's a simplistic, if not pessimistic, view on relationships. I'm sure Carson has a reasonable explanation. Talk to him first. Okay? And Cary came to talk to me. That's all we're doing. So please try to act civil."

I left her and headed outside for a cigarette. I still had a stash which I hid inside a ceramic box by the door.

After lighting my cigarette, I stood at the Mercury fountain and smoked pensively when a deep voice came from behind.

"May I bother you for one?" Cary smiled apologetically.

I passed the pack to him and the lighter. "I've never seen you smoke."

"I do on occasion." As smoke exited his lips, I studied his handsome face and could understand my mother's infatuation.

With that combed-back, greying hair, fitted tweed jacket, and tall, slender stature, Cary gave off that look of refinement that matched my mother perfectly.

That's where we differed. An image of Carson with his checkered shirt rolled up at the sleeves, exposing his tattooed muscular arms, made my heart sigh. Give me alpha males any day. Alpha on the outside, beta on the inside. That was Carson, a hundred percent.

A sweet giant of a man who could crush a walnut with his fist.

That silly thought made my face crack as I smiled to myself.

Stop dreaming. Who's that blond girl?

"I'm sorry if my being here is causing some distress." Cary's eyes had that genial warmth, which made it difficult to remain critical. I reminded myself of Will, who also had that quality. Only Cary had more personality, in that he liked to talk.

"I'm worried about my mother. Her last relationship didn't end well. And I'm sure she told you about my father."

He nodded. "Long-term marriage can be complicated. Even when passion fades, one's sense of duty never ceases."

My ravenous relationship with Carson, and how we couldn't stop fucking, came to mind. I wasn't that naïve to think we'd always engage in hungry sex, but I liked to think that he'd still make my pulse race and that he'd hold me every night.

"I take it you're still married." I stubbed out my cigarette and coughed. It tasted awful despite the nicotine high.

"I am. And I'll remain so. Caroline understands. I explained it to her. It's just that we're in love."

I frowned. "Who, with your wife or my mother?"

"Your mother. I'm head over heels in love."

"Love conquers everything, they say. Isn't that enough to overcome difficulties?"

"In a perfect world, yes. Only... sometimes it's not so straightforward. Not when you're dealing with a frail person who you promised to love 'in sickness and in health.'"

"It's admirable that you want to uphold your promise. However, divorce happens all the time."

He looked down at the ground and ran his fingers through his thick greyish hair. "My wife has terminal cancer."

I was taken aback, and my heart went out to him. The depth of sorrow was clear in his eyes. Even an excellent actor couldn't have shown that look of despair.

"Oh. I'm so sorry." I took a moment to consider this situation between him and my mother. "Then why go around saying you're divorced?"

"I was smitten and thus made a feeble, if not regrettable, attempt at winning her attention." His mouth curled up at one end. "And my wife has asked to keep her condition private. But I can't stay away from your mother, either. We're in love." His dark eyes shimmered with sincerity.

"I understand you can't leave your sick wife when she's in that state, but you were here for a month."

"It's only been a recent request by my wife that I remain there, close. Before that, she was with her family. She didn't want to stop me from living my life, but she's since had a change of heart. Which is fine by me. I'll do anything to make her feel comfortable and loved."

"That's so sad."

He smiled tightly. "This is a flying visit. I have to go back, as you can understand. I just needed to see your mother to explain."

"When you left, she was broken-hearted."

He smiled sadly. "That's nice to know. I mean, I don't like to hear she suffered, of course."

I smiled. "It's okay. I get it."

"Oh, well, I best get back inside. I have to leave first thing in the morning."

"Sorry for being rude earlier."

"Think nothing of it." He kissed me on the cheek and off he went, leaving me with all kinds of sad, swirling thoughts.

CHAPTER 30

Carson

I CRAWLED OUT OF my cave late morning. Accepting that life went on, regardless of a heavy heart, I headed straight to Merivale, mainly to see Savanah, but also because Caroline had asked to see me urgently.

Janet answered the door and told me that Savanah had gone to London, which struck me as strange. She also hadn't answered the text I'd sent, apologizing for failing to return her calls, and that I'd fallen into a rabbit hole of grief because of my brother's passing.

As always, Caroline sat at her desk. Her hair was up in a bun. Her eyes were bright and even a little cheerful, which, after the depressing events of the past day or so, I found refreshing.

Only Savanah had me worried. Knowing she was in London with Bram on the loose raised my temperature.

"Shut down the undercover mission."

My brow creased. "Okay. Can I ask why?"

"Savanah met the girl you'd recruited. And now she's got all sorts of ideas going on in her head."

Shock creased my brow. "How?"

She told me how Savvie visited my apartment and met Tiffany.

No wonder she's not taking my calls.

"On your request, I kept it a secret, and evidently Tiffany didn't divulge either. That's why I'm calling it off. This girl's cover is blown and, well..." She played with her gold pen. "I'm going to have to turn a blind eye, so to speak."

"Everyone wants that place shut down, Mrs. Lovechilde."

"Call me Caroline." She nodded slowly. "I know. I'll think of something. Tell Savanah about the girl if that will help." She removed a checkbook and scribbled five thousand pounds. "Give this to Tiffany and send her back."

Rubbing my neck, I lingered despite Caroline having finished with me.

"Is there something else?" she asked.

"Look, um... some information has come my way. It's pretty serious." Her brow pinched.

"I believe there's a drug cartel operating from the casino."

The pen dropped from her fingers. "What?"

"Apparently, drugs are being smuggled via the local port and are distributed from the casino."

"Your source?"

I took a moment to answer. Guilty shame took a grip, which was like adding salt to a wound because the pain of my brother's death intensified.

"My brother passed away last night. And well..." I took a deep breath. How would my potential future mother-in-law take my being affiliated with a crime family?

I knitted my fingers tightly. "I know this sounds bad, and I had absolutely no part in it..."

"You can speak plainly." Her eyes held mine. "And I'm sorry to hear about your brother."

"As a drug user, my brother hung out with the London underbelly. He revealed last night the existence of a drug syndicate running from here. Having heard about my relationship with Savanah, he felt a need to warn me. He spoke of a casino behind a resort near Bridesmere as the headquarters of a major drug cartel."

She released a breath. "That doesn't surprise me."

I frowned. "Really?"

"Anything with Reynard behind it is likely to throw up dark matter."

That strange analogy to cosmology distracted me for a moment. "But isn't he a close affiliate?"

"Not by choice," she muttered under her breath.

Savanah often complained about how Crisp had something over her mother, which was now confirmed, going on Caroline's sudden dark admission.

"Leave it with me." She swiveled her high-back leather chair and stared out the window.

Despite her closing the discussion, I remained. "These people are dangerous, Caroline. If they learn that their cover's blown, they won't stop at anything to remain a secret."

She turned to face me again. "What have you got in mind?"

"I'll think of something. But I wouldn't tell anyone. Least of all, Crisp."

"That's sound advice." Her eyes warmed. "I'm glad you're part of our family."

My eyebrows rose sharply. Caroline had never as much as kissed my cheek. "That's if Savanah doesn't throw a wobbly."

"She'll be fine. I'll explain it to her. And please don't tell her about the drug dealing."

"I wouldn't dream of it." I gave her a knowing half-smile.

She looked understandably shaken as I left her office.

CHAPTER 31

Savanah

SIENNA SWANNED IN, DRESSED in white flares, a tight white shirt, and a gold belt. I had to look twice. She normally went for loud colors.

"What's got you looking so Liz Hurley?" I asked, beckoning the waiter.

"I'm off to the Riviera. Got a flight to catch in three hours." Her voice bubbled over with excitement, making me smile.

Once we made our order, I asked, "So what's happening?"

"Remember I told you about Mason, that older man I've started seeing?"

I had to think back to the last few calls we'd shared. It was difficult to keep up with Sienna and her revolving door of lovers, and although I couldn't recall, I nodded.

"We're off to Greece on his yacht." Her excitement made me crave that high one felt when looking forward to spending alone time with a sexy man.

That three-week stay at Lochridge seemed like ages ago despite it only being a couple of months back. Drifting in the boat, with Carson fishing and me either reading or marveling at the configuration of migrating birds in the sky, was one of many beautiful memories that filled me with warm nostalgia.

Sienna wore a sad pout. "What's wrong, Savs? You look miserable. Last time we spoke, you were blissed out after multiple orgasms."

"I've just had a rough few days, that's all."

I told her about finding Tiffany at Carson's apartment.

"But Carson explained, didn't he?"

Nodding, I played with my rarely-ever unpainted fingernails.

Carson had driven to Mayfair to explain Tiffany's presence in his apartment, and despite learning of her undercover role darkness still engulfed me.

"Hey, that Lolita bar is very un-Merivale. How skanky is that?" Sienna pulled a face.

"Tell me about it." I sighed. "That's why my mother resorted to getting an actress to expose it. It pissed me off that Carson didn't say anything. Like I'd somehow blow her cover." I exhaled. "The make-up sex was kind of worth it, though. I came so hard I cried." I chuckled.

"Then what's the issue? You're still getting married?"

"I am." I sighed. "I feel so fucking worn out by everything. And I'm not sure if I feel like a big affair."

Her jaw dropped as though I was about to marry in a dress bought from a charity shop. "Hello. Designer wedding gown. Gorgeous photos. Quirky, mystifying gifts. Friends. Party. Need I spell it out?"

"I know. I know. That's how I should be feeling. But I feel fucking flat. It's not the wedding as such. It's fucking Bram."

"Oh... the video." She grimaced.

"You've seen it, haven't you? Everyone fucking has." Depression poured over me again, like a bucket of thick grey paint that was going to take harmful chemicals to remove. Or, in my case, endless packets of Xanax.

"Try to let it go, Savs."

"I can't. He's blackmailing me. He's making me pay ten thousand pounds a week."

"Fuck. That's a lot. But everyone's seen it."

I squirmed. Bury me under a rock, please. "He's threatened to put it on the dark web."

"Oh?" She looked puzzled.

"It will send the footage onto a ton of porn sites."

"Can't you sue?" Her horror mirrored mine after Bram further detailed what being on the dark web would mean.

"Mother's tried that, but Lord Pike's estate is bankrupt."

"Really? But I saw his daughter, Jassie, in Dolce and Gabbana at Cirque practically bathing in Moët."

"Jassie's dating some hotshot banker. So it's probably his money."

"Then have Bram locked up. I mean, he has no right to send that video out."

"The police can't find him. Only the fucking vampire always finds me when I'm alone in an alleyway or when it's dark." I sighed heavily. My heart weighed me down. Just the thought of that psycho ex and his evil, sinister eyes made my blood freeze.

"But what about his bank account?"

"Crypto." I bit into a nail, and Sienna slapped my hand.

"Stop that."

Sipping on my drink, I tossed that upsetting video aside and talked about my wedding instead.

Jacinta and Sienna had been my obvious choice for bridesmaids.

"So, have you both agreed on dresses?" I asked.

"Please don't ask us to wear the same outfit. That's soooo last century."

"I wouldn't dream of it." I giggled.

Talking about clothes at least gave me a break from the whole Bram affair. Although the thought of losing ten thousand pounds a week left an ugly taste. Carson cracked his knuckles, and his face turned dark and ferocious whenever I spoke of Bram. I could almost smell the adrenaline, which freaked me out because I couldn't risk losing the love of my life to prison. If it meant keeping Bram at arm's length and Carson staying away from the law, then blackmail was a small price to pay.

Sienna must have noticed my bleak face again. "Lighten up, sweets. Think wedding. Forget that fuckwit."

Easier said than done.

How could I look at the wedding guests, on what should have been the best day of my life, knowing that some of them had seen me starkers with a dick in my mouth?

With that heavy thought stalking me, I went back to Mayfair, dropped some Xanax, and turned off my phone.

A CONSTANT BEEPING SOUND woke me. Forcing my heavy eyelids to open, I heard my name coming from a distance.

As I lifted my lids slowly, a tall, solid figure came into focus.

Carson took my hand as a nauseating medicinal stench made it to my nostrils, alerting me to being in hospital.

"What happened?" My throat hurt as I spoke.

"You overdosed." Carson's hazel eyes echoed with concern.

"How?" I asked.

He looked bewildered. "You didn't do it on purpose?"

While searching my memory, I finally realized the implication of that question. "No. Of course not. I just had a few drinks and took some Xanax."

"Savvie, they had to pump your stomach."

I sat up and the pain raced through me like someone had stabbed me in the gut. "Seriously? I don't recall a thing."

He exhaled loudly. "Why didn't you speak to me?"

"Does my mother know?" It hurt even to panic. I'd sworn to my mother that I'd stopped popping Xanax.

"I'm not sure. It happened last night, and luckily, the hospital found my number on your phone."

"Shit. I hope she doesn't find out. Please don't tell anyone. I've got enough shit to deal with."

He held my hand and gave me one of his fear-conquering smiles. I could deal with anything with that beautiful man showing me love.

Carson stayed with me all day, taking calls and working from the ward with his laptop balancing on those sexy, muscular thighs. He was heartwarmingly considerate. He even spoke softly to not disturb me.

"Hey, sweetheart, you don't have to stay if you're busy. I understand," I said.

"From now on, I will stick close. I don't want that junkie finding you ever again."

"He wouldn't come here," I said.

He wore his "I'm not budging" face, and I closed my eyes and rested.

They discharged me a few hours later, and we headed back to Mayfair, where we stayed until I'd fully recovered.

One month later…

Cary held my mother's hand as they sat by the pool, sipping on tea and enjoying the sun.

Will that be me and Carson in twenty years?

I hoped so.

I'd never seen my mother so in love. My heart warmed just seeing them so close and intimate.

One month after his wife passed away, Cary moved to England and spent most of his time at Merivale. They'd become inseparable. I could tell he wasn't taking advantage of my mother because of the love in his eyes whenever he looked at her. One didn't fake that kind of affection.

Declan and Theadora arrived with Julian, who, at four, was looking more like his father. Bertie, my mother's corgi, followed along with a bone almost bigger than him dangling in his mouth.

Carson and Declan hugged, while I kissed Theadora and hugged my nephew.

It was the morning of my wedding.

Following tradition, along with my mother's wishes, the ceremony was to be held at Merivale.

When Ethan and Mirabel arrived with their children and Freddie scampering at their feet, the garden came alive, filled with children, laughter, dogs, and general good cheer.

My brothers, along with their energetic sons, tossed and kicked the football. It was something they'd always done as children, then as teenagers, and now as adults.

Ethan and Mirabel's little Rosie, now fourteen months, waddled about trying to catch up. She was so cute with that red hair.

Although I couldn't stop giggling at my brothers and children acting all silly, nerves still invaded me. I felt a panoply of emotions, from elation and a touch of sadness to everything in between.

Watching Rosie stumbling about reminded me how I would never have a little girl of my own. Tears pricked at my eyes, and I took a deep breath while channeling heart-warming thoughts, like spending a lifetime with Carson.

That was all I needed. And I had a great family. I loved my sisters-in-law and my niece and nephews. I'm sure there would be more children to enjoy, and they'd already brought so much light and laughter to Merivale.

I just wished my father had met Carson. He would have approved. Not that my mother disapproved. She had formed a good relationship with Carson, who was always respectful and dignified around those older than him.

I hovered about, watching the crazy sports taking place on the vast grounds of Merivale. Carson had joined in and was leaping in the air to catch the ball, looking all athletic and sexy, which made my panties sticky again. That might have been because, for the first time since dating, we hadn't had sex for breakfast. Since it was our wedding day, we went with tradition.

Theadora sat down next to me on the filigree cast-iron bench. "How are you feeling?"

"I'm kind of nervous, to be honest."

She gave me a sympathetic smile. "I hope you like what we're going to play for the service. Mirabel's singing something she wrote especially for you. It's very poetic and sweet."

I shook my head in wonder. "That's so amazing. I can't wait to hear it. And they'll capture it on film."

"Are you really okay?" Theodora slanted her head and wore a concerned half-smile. She read me well. People who'd had their own demons were good at spotting struggle.

"The whole Bram experience has shaken me."

"He was found dead. Overdosed, I hear."

Declan came up and, having heard Theodora's comment, said, "He won't be missed."

My brother's cool, matter-of-fact response to Bram's passing should have shocked me, but it didn't because all I felt was relief when I heard he'd overdosed.

"I can't help but wonder if it was an accident." I'd already voiced this opinion with Carson, who just shrugged it off a little too quickly, making my mind wander into all kinds of territories.

Theodora shook her head. "Try not to think about it. Especially today."

My brother held his wife's hand. They'd been married five years, and they still acted like a love-struck pair.

Noticing my growing smile, Declan opened out his hand. "What?"

"Look at you two. You're still so loved up."

Theodora chuckled. "Don't sound so surprised."

"Just most married couples don't go around holding hands," I said.

Declan gazed lovingly at Theodora and stroked her cheek before turning to me. "We're not most married couples."

His arched brow and Theodora's little blush revealed passion.

Will Carson and I be all loved up in five years?

I looked over and saw my handsome husband-to-be kicking the ball with the children.

"Carson's a good man. You'd be hard-pressed to find someone more selfless," Declan said. "He was always there for his mates on the field. Risking his life. I'm proud to have him as a brother-in-law."

"Now you're making me cry." My lips trembled.

Theadora hugged me again. "He loves you madly. You've found your piece of paradise, Savvie."

A tear slid down my cheek. "Thanks, Thea. I'm just going inside for a minute."

As tears threatened to erupt, I hurried inside to hide.

Despite tears of joy, I also mourned not being able to have kids. And there was a touch of fear too. What if everything came crumbling down? I couldn't deal with another drama. I'd had too many in that brief spate of time, and anxiety seemed to have attached itself to me.

For someone who'd skipped through life, I could never have imagined carrying such a heavy load, especially on my wedding day.

If only Bram had never happened. I would still be that fluffy girl flicking through fashion magazines, what shoes to wear my only concern. But then, having fallen madly in love with a man whose soul was as beautiful as he was had helped me realize that only love mattered. Not the latest Balenciaga must-have or some viral juicy gossip.

I wiped my eyes, and on entering the front room, found Manon giving Janet a hard time about something.

Turning to me, Manon pulled a smarmy grin. "I thought you'd be at the Pond having a facial or something to remove those dark rings under your eyes."

I stuck my middle finger up at her.

Despite not being able to control Manon's appearance as a guest at my wedding, at least my mother promised that Crisp wouldn't be attending the ceremony. Unfortunately, his nonattendance didn't extend to the weekend party, however, given that everyone in the area had gotten an invitation.

Pushing aside niggling issues, I took a breath and invited the euphoria from a future with Carson to absorb every cell in my body.

I stepped into my bedroom, and my eyes landed on the pale-pink Givenchy gown hanging ready for my special day.

After leaving the hospital, I took a trip to Paris with Sienna, where we embarked on a three-day shopping spree. That was the longest I'd been without Carson, and even a drink along the elegant boulevards of Paris couldn't stop me from missing him.

My mother entered my room. "Are you okay?"

"I'm just nervous, I guess."

"You're having second thoughts." She looked surprised.

I shook my head decisively. "I love Carson." I faced her. "You like him, don't you?"

She embraced me. Something she didn't do that often, but since Cary had arrived in her life, my mother had become more demonstrably affectionate.

"He's a good man who brings strength and protection. One can't underestimate how important those qualities are in a man. A man who can fix things." She smiled.

"Cary doesn't strike me as the handyperson type," I countered.

She chuckled. "That's not what I meant by fixing things."

I sighed.

"What is it then?" she pressed.

"You know how Bram overdosed and was found dead in some back-street in London?" I paused to catch my breath. "Well, I was visited by a detective."

Her brow pinched. "Why didn't you tell me?"

I slid my finger over my ruffled gown. "Do you like it?"

"It's stunning."

"Do you think I made the right choice?"

She studied me again, closely. "Are we talking about the dress?"

I nodded meekly.

"Pink is a favorite color of mine. And yes, you've made the right choice. Both in dress and husband." She held my eyes. "So what did this detective ask exactly?" My mother knitted her fingers, which caught my attention.

"He wanted to know about my relationship with Bram."

"Did you tell him he was blackmailing you?"

"I didn't tell him anything. Just that we were dating for a while."

Carson walked in, and my mother turned to him. "Have you heard about the detective?"

He nodded.

I quickly put my dress away. "Can't have you seeing my wedding frock."

He smiled at me.

"So you didn't mention the tape?" my mother asked.

I shook my head.

"He was found without his phone." Carson's response roused my curiosity.

"How do you know?" This was the first I'd heard about the police investigation.

He rubbed his neck. "I inquired."

"Does that mean that whoever has that phone can find the video?" I asked.

Carson's glance over at my mother wasn't lost on me. "Savvie, it's over. Don't worry about anything. That tape no longer exists."

My mouth had grown dry. "How can you be so sure?"

"Carson's right, darling. It's over." Wearing a comforting smile, my mother touched my hand.

"But the detective wants to speak to me again."

"That's best left to our lawyer," she said.

I nodded. Something didn't sit right. But I couldn't allow this to fog my special day. Bram overdosing, although sad for him and his family, had arrived rather neatly before my wedding, which made me wonder whether it was a coincidence or something a little more arranged.

Carson, remaining tight-lipped following my discussing the detective's visit and my mother's "It's for the best" comment, kept spinning around in my thoughts.

CHAPTER 32

Carson

"I DO," LEFT MY mouth without a moment's thought.

Captivating and beautiful, Savanah looked like an exotic creature in her pink ruffled gown. I couldn't take my eyes off her.

We kissed, and a tantalizing rose perfume wafted over me.

I fell into her deep blue eyes, knowing with all my heart and soul that I would love this woman forever and beyond.

In husky, honeyed tones, Mirabel sang about love taking us to paradise as I held Savanah close to my heart. Her soft hair was under my fingers, and her warm cheek pressed against my lips.

Her hand trembled as I slid the gold ring on her finger. Gazing into her shining eyes, I returned a supportive smile, determined to make her feel secure, loved, and protected.

At the "you may kiss the bride" I took Savanah into my arms, and as our lips touched, I had to control the urge to involve my tongue, reminding myself to keep it nice and clean for London's elite. The more raucous roars came from our lot, and it was Savvie that pressed herself tightly against me.

She whispered, "Mm... What's that I feel? One night without, and you're ready to pop."

I laughed.

I could never have imagined this. Me in a designer tuxedo with my fingers buried in the silk of a gown that cost the equivalent of my former annual army pay.

None of that mattered.

Only Savanah mattered.

I would have loved her if she was the poorest woman on the planet.

In many ways, I wish she was because I wanted to give her everything.

My love.

My devotion.

My fidelity.

My soul.

EPILOGUE

Manon

LIKE ALWAYS, REYNARD FOLLOWED me around like a hungry dog. His smell sickened me. As if heaping expensive cologne hid sex smells. He smelt like my mother's third husband, another slippery character who possessed the same snaky eyes as Crisp. But he never came near me. I was always in control, and besides, my mother had other plans for me.

According to her, having a bum that poked out and large boobs was a commodity. At thirteen, I didn't understand that word. My mother had insisted that the best education for women like us was to learn how to take advantage of our physical assets.

She always harped on about my looks being my only value, like I was incapable of anything but being fondled for money.

I planned to change that by showing her and the world that I was more than just tits and a vagina.

My beautician's work proved that. Clients at the Pond still asked for me. Nice as it was being recognized for my makeup skills, I had bigger plans than just making women look beautiful. Plans that didn't involve fucking old men like Reynard Crisp.

My grandmother hated the thought of Crisp fucking me. Not that she used those words. She was too posh for gutter language, which I liked because I wanted to be her one day—wear designer, speak with big words in a posh accent, and give orders.

Having listened to my mother's bitter rants about how her biological mum had abandoned her, all of my life, I thought I'd hate Caroline

Lovechilde, but I didn't. I'd come to not only admire her but also grow a little attached. I hid that, though.

That would make me look weak, and the last thing I wanted was for the world to see me as one of those girls who cried at the drop of a hat.

Compared to my cold mother, who couldn't give a shit about me, my grandmother's constant looking out for my back meant the world to me. She'd even promised to match Rey's offer if I didn't sleep with him. She never used those words, but I wasn't stupid. I could read between the lines. We all knew what Rey wanted. My grandmother more than anyone, because I figured she'd slept with him when she was my age—a thought that left a bad taste because I hated the idea of her with someone like him.

Yes, I'd gotten attached to her.

That she let me stay despite my crappy behavior also meant everything to me.

I think I'd been testing her.

Her offer was a huge win for me. I would have even settled for less. Rey seriously creeped me out. He'd already touched my tits. And I'd sent those doctored porn images, which weren't me, just to keep him close.

I might have been ambitious at any cost, but I'd promised myself never to suck a dick or fuck an old man.

Just in case my grandmother discovered all the bad things I got up to, I had to keep stringing Rey along by making myself valuable to him. Recruiting young, but not too young, girls had proven easier than I'd imagined. Girls were very willing to lose their cherries for money.

I couldn't sell mine. That ship had sailed.

Crisp thought I'd never fucked.

He had that wrong because I started illegally young.

No one forced me. It all came down to desire.

Not for sex or for the man in question, but for nice things like expensive clothes, makeup, and lingerie.

In short, my mother sold me to an older man when I was fifteen. He was kind of hot, in that at least he was in his twenties.

He also taught me to like sex.

I liked Peyton. He treated me well. I would have married him, but I got too old for him, and by the time I was eighteen, he'd found a girl whom I'm sure wasn't quite sixteen.

I never cried—I was tough. Maybe I was frozen just like my mother. The only reason she wept when Will got locked up was that the cops, dragging her away, had screwed with her carefully crafted sophisticated woman-of-the-world look.

Savanah was another woman I looked up to. She hated me, but I didn't hate her. I respected her effortless style. And it was fun having someone close to an older sister to poke fun at.

The biggest highlight of her wedding reception for me was seeing Drake filling his suit so well, I nearly fainted. He looked seriously hot, like a carbon copy of Harry Styles but with more muscles and tats.

He kept looking at me. Only there were all these older women circling. One, in particular, seemed very fucking familiar—a beautiful blonde with big tits and wearing one of those dresses with a long slit. I'm sure she didn't wear knickers. She laughed at everything he said, and he seemed chatty too.

He hardly said a word to me. All he gave me was a grunt or a nod.

It was at the wedding reception that my grandmother hugged me for the first time. Whether it was for show, I couldn't say. But it took me by surprise because my mother never ever hugged me.

"Manon, you look lovely," my grandmother had said. She had softened a lot. She used to frighten me a bit. All tough and take-no-shit approach, another quality I liked in her, but now that she'd fallen in love, she was all smiles.

I never thought I'd like being part of an extended family, but they were all growing on me. Despite all the shit I'd given them, they still seemed to tolerate me.

My mum put it down to guilt on Grandmother's part. Whatever. I just loved being at that fairy-tale mansion with my own ensuite, a balcony, and a walk-in wardrobe. And I was about to get a car. Yay. Which meant trips to London, where I planned to buy a ritzy apartment somewhere posh.

"How lovely to see you in that gorgeous dress," my grandmother had gushed. Instead of going for showing off my body, something I'd been doing since puberty, I'd decided on copying Savanah by adopting a more modest, stylish approach.

Taking my lead from her, as always, I'd visited some of Savanah's favorite designer stores, where I picked up a red Dolce and Gabbana knee-length dress. This time, I even paid. They had too many security cameras, so I couldn't feed my habit of freebies that started at the age of five. First, it was candy and toys, and then, as a teenager, having become an expert, I stole makeup, lingerie, and anything I could get my hands on. I'd become a little addicted to the thrill. A credit card with an eye-watering limit couldn't even stop me because pinching stuff had become second nature.

I liked this new modest look, as my grandmother put it. I guess it was her nice way of saying I wasn't dressing like a streetwalker.

The wedding was the highlight of my month if it weren't for Rey hanging around. Then his friend, the just as cringey Lord Pike, crashed the party and caused all kinds of issues.

"You killed my boy," he yelled, pointing his finger at my grandmother, and then he turned to Carson, who at the time had his arm around Savanah like it was glued to her waist. He hadn't shifted from her all day.

When the red-nosed creep yelled abuse at Carson, Drake removed his jacket, which made me almost melt on the spot, and I swear I heard a chorus of "aahs."

He grabbed the drunken lord like he would a child and dragged the ranting and raving old man off.

Everyone knew about his drug-addict son, Bram. I couldn't believe that someone as cool and sophisticated as my aunt would go for that piece of shit.

I'd met druggies like him before. All kind of arty and full of crap.

So he'd overdosed. It wasn't a big deal or surprise.

I hated drugs. I didn't get the appeal. And I hated needles. At least my skin was smooth enough to not need Botox injections. And my lips were fine just as they were. During my stint as a beautician, I'd learned to inject collagen fillers to give girls those "cock-sucking" lips everyone favoured. That was the beauty of being rebellious. I didn't feel the urge to get around with duck lips to attract anyone.

After he'd kicked out Bram's father, Drake returned, combed back his thick dark hair that always hung with a sexy lick over his forehead, and gave my grandmother a nod of confidence.

That's when I decided to change my life, for the better.

Corrupted by a billionaire, I'd done things I wasn't proud of.

But that was about to change.

DRAKE

Sheree bent down in front of me to pick up the weights. Dressed in a low-cut top, her tits ballooned out.

Carson was away on his honeymoon for a month and had me running Reboot. I'd even had to employ more instructors. I filled most of my day training. All were mainly older women who wore skimpy fitness wear, expensive gold trinkets, and were drenched in perfume.

For now, this was me: personal trainer to mainly rich, hot-to-trot women and performing security duties for the Lovechildes. I'd soon pay off my apartment and then I'd try something else.

Just before Declan found me, I was about to join the army when a punch-up got me into trouble. It wasn't my first offence. As a teenager, I had a thing for breaking into cars. It was my way of dealing with my sick mother. That's what I told the counsellor, which wasn't bullshit. I'm sure that kept me out of the lockup. And then Declan Lovechilde became my hero, and my life changed overnight. I became a gym junkie and a personal trainer.

Manon arrived wearing joggers and a tiny top, and my heart raced again. She was so beautiful I couldn't think straight. I knew she was up to something with Crisp. I couldn't stand him, and if she was screwing him, I couldn't exactly ask her out. Besides, I didn't share.

Up to now, I hadn't had to.

But I'd met no one like Manon. Nor had a girl made me so fucking hot just from a glance. She had the sort of attitude like the world owed her something, that made me want to kiss that pout off her face.

"I'll be there in a minute," I said.

Her big dark, almost-black eyes tranced me out again, and I almost forgot what I was doing.

When she'd asked if I could take her through the boot camp course, I was tempted to pass her over to someone else, but she fascinated me. It was like I couldn't refuse her anything.

She reminded me of a lazy cat. One of those seriously attractive pussies that lounged about while everyone stroked her. She didn't strike me as the type who'd take easily to orders, which is something we did as personal trainers—make people sweat.

I decided to take her for a run through the forest. I hadn't had a run for a couple of days, and I needed one, badly. Especially with her around.

Being by the sea and surrounded by the forest was as good as it got for someone who'd grown up in a suburb surrounded by concrete. I fell in love with the forest from the minute I set foot in it. I never admitted that at first.

Whenever I could, which was almost daily, I'd run to the cliffs and back, which was an eight-kilometer trip. That beat any drug out there, and I'd tried a few. Nothing compared to the high of exercising in nature, surrounded by the type of views that I'd only ever seen on TV.

"Where are you taking me?" she asked, as though I was about to lure her somewhere for hot sex.

I wish.

"We're going to run through the forest. There's a great path there."

She gave me one of her lingering brain-picking looks. "I thought it would be all about weights and machines."

I crooked my finger. "Come on. It's a nice day."

We jogged slowly for about ten minutes, and then she stopped.

"I need a break. I'm not used to this." Bent over, Manon rested her hands on her thighs.

I pointed to the path ahead. "Let's walk then. Keep the blood flowing. Yes?"

She nodded with her signature pout.

After a few steps, she asked, "Are you still going out with that older model?"

"No."

She stopped walking. "Do you prefer older women?"

"I thought this was about training. Not my personal life."

She shrugged. "That too. But you always run away every time I try talking to you. And at the wedding, you had all these older babes hanging off your arm."

I laughed at that exaggeration. "That was preferable to dealing with that drunken old geezer."

"Yeah. I saw that. You were nearly bursting through your nice white designer shirt." She chuckled. "What happened there?"

"He thinks that either Mrs. Lovechilde or Carson killed his son."

"But didn't he OD?"

"That's the official story."

Her pretty eyes stretched slightly. "Oh, really? You know something?"

All I knew was that I had to make a statement about Carson's whereabouts around the time of Bram's death. But no one, not even this gorgeous, troublemaking girl, was going to know that.

"Nothing. Let's keep going."

"Are you always this bossy?" She placed her hands on her hips.

"When I'm working, I am."

She stared into my eyes for a little longer, and I nearly forgot who I was. How would I get past the hour without kissing her?

"How about if we walk to the cliffs?"

"I've got a better idea." Intent on teasing as always, Manon's playful eyes sparkled as she took my hand and led me to a large oak.

Corrupted by a Billionaire is book 4 of Lovechilde Saga

ALSO BY J. J. SOREL

jjsorel.com

Printed in Great Britain
by Amazon

27924222R00149